THE MURALIST
OF MATTER DEEP AND DANGEROUS

CARRIE HAGEN

LUMINARE PRESS
WWW.LUMINAREPRESS.COM

Printed in the United States of America

Cover design by Elliott Woolworth

Luminare Press
442 Charnelton St.
Eugene, OR 97401
www.luminarepress.com

LCCN: 2022908535
ISBN: 978-1-64388-925-2

For Peggy Hageman
editor, champion, friend

SUNDAY

6:30 p.m.

ERIC ROSS RESET HIS WATCH BEFORE SPRINTING INTO PENN Treaty Park. On a good night, even with hindrances, he could finish his two-mile warm-up on Delaware Avenue in sixteen minutes. This evening, he clocked 17:23. The interruptions to his pace—red lights in front of the old Yards Brewing Company, taxicabs blocking crosswalks at SugarHouse Casino, tourists inching around the Penn's Landing seaport—had seemed endless.

The footpath circling Penn Treaty measured 353 meters by GPS: not quite a track's length, but close enough for half-mile repeats. Pavement turned to dirt past the east end of the park, which bordered the banks of the Delaware River just north of the Ben Franklin Bridge. Flattened cardboard boxes and food wrappings marked homeless campsites in the brush, on both sides of an abandoned row of townhouses branded a year ago as "The Future in Luxury Living" before the developer ran out of money.

By Ross's second lap, he had identified potential obstacles to his speed work. A pit mix sat under overgrown bushes along the river's rocky bank. On Ross's first go-round, the dog had raised its head and caught the runner's eye. Its collar and leash were poorly secured under a man's sleeping body. Just before he reached the pit bull, Ross dodged a Frisbee tossed by flirting teenagers, and just past the dog, where gnarled tree roots threatened his footing,

1

he noted almost invisible fishing lines stretching into the river. Under a cluster of elm trees close to a playground, old fishermen eyed the lines from wooden benches.

Ross marked his laps by a statue of William Penn holding a scroll at the park's entrance. It commemorated the settler's peace treaty with Tamanend, a Lenni Lenape tribal chief, in the seventeenth century. At the time, the land had held a village that the Lenape called Shackamaxon. On the same grounds, over three hundred years later, abandoned factories and a cluttered waterfront bordered Penn Treaty Park. The park's appearance softened at dusk, when the lights of the bridge reflected off the river, drawing attention away from the polluted riverbank.

Passing the statue a fourth time, Ross noticed the dog was no longer perched by the sleeping man. He scanned the brush for it, then hit the ground hard on his left side.

"Watch out!" a woman yelled.

Ross lifted his left hand. A piece of green glass hung from his palm.

"All right, man?" a male Frisbee thrower asked.

"What'd I hit?" Blood came quickly as Ross pulled out the glass.

"That guy over there." The teenager nodded toward a frail young man limping away. "You slammed into him pretty hard."

Ross took off his gray T-shirt and pressed it onto his cut. The man he had hurt shuffled out of the park with some urgency and held his right side with both hands.

"Was he limping like that before?"

"Mmm…" the kid said, wavering. "Don't know. You really nailed him."

Ross's left knee stung and stiffened as he traced the ailing man across Delaware Avenue, a boulevard running parallel

2

to I-95 along the riverfront and through a small residential neighborhood. The man's stride was painful to watch: hunched over, he seemed to push his right side forward to meet his left.

Ross turned his bloodied shirt into a tourniquet and paused to check the bottom of his sneakers. Something had smelled like shit for a block or so.

About fifteen minutes after the accident, Ross caught up with the man at a crosswalk on the other side of the neighborhood.

"Excuse me," Ross said.

The man breathed heavily and whispered to himself. Ross registered his profile. *Twentyish, Latino. Nervous. Emaciated. Thick stubble.*

"Hey, I'm the guy who slammed into you."

No response. Ross couldn't tell if he was being ignored or hadn't been heard. He tried to identify words in the man's whispers amidst the noise on the street. They stood at Girard Avenue, about two blocks from a public transit hub. Around them, young hipsters followed laughter and music in and out of brew pubs, gastro pubs, dive bars. The crowds on spring Sunday evenings were half the size of those on Saturday nights.

He thought he detected the name "Pedro."

"Pedro. Can I contact a Pedro for you?"

The man grunted as the light changed; he limped forward. Ross realized the source of the stench—diarrhea oozed from the stranger's right pant leg. Ross watched the man disappear into the streetscape.

Regardless of the crash in the park, the man clearly had a stomach bug and didn't want to be bothered. Ross turned back toward the river. He had to hobble quickly to make it to work on time.

3

7:10 p.m.

"Vamos," Pedro Martinez repeated to himself as he struggled off Girard onto Frankford Avenue. "Vamos."

Construction gates blocked the sidewalks between Fishtown's street cafes and outdoor bar patios. It had started drizzling again. Pedro could breathe better in the cooler air. Moving forward with tortured gasps, he pushed himself into another neighborhood of rowhomes. Two blocks later, he checked his watch. Thirty minutes had passed since he had left Penn Treaty. Right on time.

Pedro reached the cemetery gates and rested his forehead on the cool, wet iron bars.

"Please, Dios."

The gate was unlocked. Holding the door as a crutch, he pushed it open, shuffled in, and closed it gently behind him. Pedro clenched his stomach with both hands, hobbled to the brick wall, and fell to his knees.

It was there. He grabbed the feathery torso and threw up. Then he wiped the tears from his eyes, crawled behind the grave of one Marjorie Hunter, and unfolded the white sheet.

9:30 p.m.

RUBY'S CHEST HURT. IT HAD EVER SINCE SHE SAW THE figure in white from her bedroom window. She shouldn't have left her room but had to make sure Junie was okay.

Normally, Ruby liked sneaking into the graveyard on rainy nights. Brick walls and iron gates separated the cemetery from rowhouses on each side of its square. Inside, a walkway meandered around a couple of hundred markers dating to 1681. Tree cover kept streetlights from reaching Ruby's favorite corner, so when it rained at night, she could talk to June without worrying about anyone seeing *or* hearing her. Weather hadn't kept people away tonight though. Ruby glanced toward June's headstone about one hundred yards away. She had left her umbrella there when the police arrived.

Ruby tried to take deep breaths like her gym teacher had taught but teetered in her squat. Her thighs ached. So did her knees. The wind picked up and rustled the branches of sycamore trees, sending little pools of water onto her head. She shivered in her thin jacket and toppled into the gravestone in front of her.

"S—sorry, Martin," she whispered, pushing snot from her face with one hand and patting the back of the gravestone with the other. Ruby resumed her squat behind a Martin Anderson's headstone and peered through the holes of a cement Gothic cross. Her gaze shifted back and forth. To Ruby's right, lights illuminated a crime scene. To her left, two police officers stood next to one of the iron gates that connected the cemetery's brick walls. Any approaching onlooker was turned away.

Ruby's eyes flashed back to the lights. Photographers moved inside the boundaries marked by yellow tape. One, a woman with short red hair, lifted the tape for a man in a beige trench coat. A female police officer followed him. She looked back at the two male officers near the other gate. Ruby knew she had been lucky before, but she wouldn't have enough time to climb the tree if they came back with their flashlights.

The wind blew again through the trees. A small branch fell near her, sending a cracking sound through the cemetery. Flashlights moved in Ruby's direction. She ducked, squeezing her eyes. Then she looked again through the openings in the cross. The man in the coat was looking right at her. She fell backward onto her hands and scampered behind another grave marker.

9:35 p.m.

"What?" mumbled Detective Jessie Wren, a forensics investigator. She held a camera in one hand, a notebook under an armpit, and a pencil between her teeth.

Detective Eric Ross stared into the darkness at the far end of Palmer Cemetery.

"You flinched," Wren said, grabbing the pencil from her mouth. "And what the hell happened?" She nodded toward the Ace bandage on Ross's left hand. He held a clipboard with his right.

"Hey!" Ross called to the officers at the side gate. He pointed toward the noise. "Nothing at all back there?"

"Nothing and nobody," one said, approaching the group. "Went through a second time about a half hour ago. Just branches and squirrels." He smirked. "And ghosts."

"Such an ass," Wren whispered. The female police officer standing behind Ross shot her a look. Wren turned to a second forensics investigator, a younger woman studying shots on her camera.

"Get what we need, Mae?"

The woman stepped toward Wren and held up her camera. Her hand shook slightly. "Think so." Her voice cracked, then steadied. She blushed and looked at Ross. "This...this is my first killing."

"Homicide," Wren and Ross said simultaneously.

The woman blushed more deeply.

Wren turned to Ross. "Intern."

"It's okay," the male officer said with a smirk. He nodded toward his female counterpart, who still stood

7

behind Ross. "She's new too."

"What does that mean?" Wren asked.

"Officer Lopez here becomes *Detective* Lina Lopez tomorrow."

"Shut up, Rivera." Lopez rolled her eyes as Wren's shot toward her. The forensics tech grabbed her intern's camera and flipped through the photo roll.

"Looks good to me," Wren said. "Go ahead and start loading."

The younger woman obeyed.

Ross stepped back from the corpse and started taking notes. Amid headstones and the twisted roots of a beech tree, a man's body lay face up, eyes open, his head turned toward a beautifully preserved tropical bird on his right side. A thin white nightgown covered his upper and middle sections, leaving his legs and bare feet exposed. White theatrical makeup and thick circles of pink blush decorated his face. Eagle-sized eggshells were scattered around the body.

Slowly, Ross squatted. He winced in pain. "Who called it in?"

"Anonymous female," said Lopez. "Said she was walking her dog when it went crazy at what looked like a dead ghost inside the gate."

"As opposed to a living ghost," Officer Terrence Rivera said, sneering. "But yeah, said there was a dead body in white at the children's cemetery. Then hung up."

Ross looked up. "Children's cemetery?"

"What the locals call it," Rivera said. "Section in the corner over there is for kids. Has been forever."

Ross lifted the nightgown and let it fall.

"Medical examiner says poisoned then positioned," Wren added. "Left just before you got here. Judging from

8

the shit and the smell of garlic, he thinks arsenic."

"Arsenic," Ross mumbled. He moved toward the man's head, dropped to his knees, and leaned over the face. The makeup barely covered thick stubble on the victim's face.

"I know," Wren said. "Poison explains no sign of assault though."

Ross tried to stand and stumbled.

"You all right?" Wren asked.

He ignored her. "Let's see if anyone's going to miss him once we learn his name."

Wren nodded. "Should have it by tomor—,"

"And, Lopez," interrupted Ross, "see if anyone around here knows any bird lovers." He paused. "Or collectors. This is an impressive piece of taxidermy here. Maybe try the pet stores."

"Got it."

"You think the bird came from around here?" Rivera asked. "There a petting zoo nearby?"

"Yep, because you pet stuffed birds in petting zoos," Wren said.

"Okay." Rivera raised both hands. "Need anything else, Detective?" He smiled at Jessie Wren. "Detective Ross, that is?"

Ross shook his head no.

"Smart girls make you nervous?" Wren asked.

"Rude ones piss me off." Rivera walked toward the front gate. "Hey, Lopez," he called over his shoulder, "still my lowly partner for a few more hours."

Lopez looked at her watch. "Two and a half."

"Two and a half left to admire me then."

"I'll meet you at Homicide first thing?" Lopez asked Ross quietly.

He nodded.

Jessie Wren took off her gloves and watched the police officers leave. She turned to Ross. "I'll send over tonight's shots from the lab and text if we get a name."

"Thanks." Ross started to squat, then thought better of it.

"You okay?"

"Fell on a run. Body took a hit." He added to his notes. "Your eye catch anything off when you got here?"

"Vomit by his feet," Wren answered without a beat. "Was also over there by the wall, but no trace on his face."

"Think he threw up before he was in costume? Someone else clean him up?"

"Yes and yes. But timing is a problem." She dropped her notebook and stretched her upper back. "I poison you. You throw up. Then you die, and I stage your body." She paused. "Awful period between arsenic and death. Could take hours. Did take hours. Am I just sitting around watching you? In a public place?"

"You poisoned me somewhere else."

"Or somebody did."

"But am I in costume before I'm poisoned?"

"It would save time for the killer out in the open." She thought for a second. "But I don't think we'll find vomit on the white sheet here."

"So you put me in costume after I die. Must be pretty damn strong to stage me."

"Or there's more than one of me."

Ross stared straight ahead.

"Doc's right. Probably no struggle," Wren continued. "Otherwise more neighbors might have said something."

"Unless they were scared."

"A lot of old timers here with loud voices. They hate what this neighborhood's become. They fight anything new." She looked up at the rowhomes closest to where she stood. "I'm surprised there was only one call."

Ross followed her gaze for a minute.

"But why not his feet?" he asked. "Why clean up everything but his feet?"

"No time?" She shrugged.

They stood in silence together.

"New coat you've got there," Wren said.

Ross closed his notebook and caught her eye. "Came back a week ago, Jessie. Nothing much else to say."

"It's been a little longer than that."

"What do you mean?"

She stiffened. "I mean—we work in the same building. Word gets around."

He narrowed his eyes and turned back to the body. "Yeah."

"And you missed my birthday."

"Happy forty-fifth."

"Forty-first, jerk."

———•———

Ross sat on a bench across from the children's section. With his right hand, he scribbled notes on the clipboard propped on his lap.

An early April nor'easter had swept through the city a week before, giving way to unseasonably low temperatures. Snow trapped leaves in dirt-stained drifts against gravestones. Ross lifted his jacket collar and stretched his cramped, stiff left knee. The walk back to his apartment after the fall had exhausted him. Then, an hour out of the shower, he had gotten the call to get back to Fishtown.

While the forensics team wrapped at Palmer Cemetery, the detective had spent half an hour circling the graveyard on a sidewalk outside the gates. Without gaping, he tried to notice any activity or faces behind the windowpanes of the surrounding brownstones. He didn't have any luck. Blinds, drapes, or darkness protected the privacy of neighbors who supposedly had no idea a murder had occurred right before their front doors. Someone had to have seen something suspicious: a stranger breaking into the gates, the uncovering of a large dead bird, the placing of eggshells.

The coroner suspected the body had been poisoned hours before discovery. Ross knew he was right. The victim must have come directly here after Ross parted with him on Girard Avenue hours before. The detective had recognized the corpse as soon as he took in its stench. The victim's stubble confirmed his suspicion. Judging from the diarrhea Ross had noticed earlier that night, the man had been poisoned before the detective collided with him in the park. Why, though, had the victim walked all the way here in pain? To die in a cemetery? And why the costume? Why would someone put him in a costume after he died? What perverted reason would be worth the close contact with that smell? Perhaps the murderer had followed the man after poisoning him to make sure that he died. If that were true, then he would have been following Ross for a time as well.

Jessie Wren was right. Had any eyewitnesses watched the costuming of the dying man, they would probably have said something. This was an older section of Fishtown, not as gentrified as the blocks farther south. Historically Irish and Polish, it still held a centuries-old reputation for conservative politics. The sight of an outsider desecrating hallowed grounds would have led to more than 911 calls—but then again, maybe not. The neighbors were older, and who knows what they may have witnessed. What may have terrified them.

Ross winced as he tried to stretch his back on the bench. The throbbing in his hand had stopped, but his left hip killed. He circled his neck to the right, to the left.

He froze.

From the shadows of two very large headstones, a figure had emerged. It sprinted directly toward a brick wall across from him. The detective jumped and pulled his gun.

"Freeze!"

The image, about five feet high, flew over the wall. Ross ran to it. Pulling himself up, he felt his left palm split open. The detective jumped to the ground and heard footsteps running away. He eyed an alley across the street. The wind had picked up again. It sounded like a gate was tapping loudly against a latch. Gun raised, Ross moved into the alley.

On either side of the narrow street, a series of wooden and metal fences separated the back lots of the houses from the pavement. Ross heard the tapping, more like clapping, sound again, but it wasn't coming from a gate. Sidestepping slowly, he studied the fence tops for movement and listened for footsteps. A cat meowed and rubbed against his leg.

"Shit!" He stumbled over it.

A child giggled. A girl. Ross focused on a decrepit gray fence with loose planks. The clapping sound became louder. Ross stepped back—it was on the property's rooftop. A shingle must have loosened, sending a panel swinging into a chimney. Using the rooftop as a guide, he walked from the alley to the front of the house and stepped up to a red door. It opened before he could knock.

"What?" mumbled a short white woman from behind a chain lock.

White hair. Wrinkles. Plastic black eyeglass frames. Sixtyish.

"Sorry about the time. My name is Detective Eric Ross."

He pulled out his badge. She shrugged and looked away.

"Others came by," she said in a low, warbled tone.

"I'm just following up. Your name, ma'am?"

"Dorothy Thompson."

She avoided eye contact.

"Did you see or hear anything unusual earlier tonight, Ms. Thompson?"

"No," she mumbled.

"Does anybody else live here, ma'am?"

She shrugged again. "My granddaughter. She's asleep."

Ross identified the reason for the quavers in her voice. Ill-fitting bottom dentures.

"I don't think so, ma'am. I just saw her running outside."

Thompson stepped away from the small opening in the door. "She's asleep."

"A figure moved between the cemetery and this house a few minutes ago."

"No."

Ross spoke quietly. "If someone in your house saw something tonight, even if she says she didn't, she might be in some trouble, Ms. Thompson."

The door closed.

"I'm putting my card through the door here," Ross said. "Call me if you or your granddaughter remember anything."

"All right," she said loudly, catching Ross off guard. He stared at the door, at the peephole. His phone buzzed as he slowly walked back across the street. As promised, Jessie Wren had forwarded several of the night's crime scene photos.

Ross hoisted himself back over the wall. Blood seeped through the bandage around his left hand. The detective

14

wondered how the figure, short and stocky by his estimation, could have scaled the wall so quickly. Not finding any props or even a gravestone to aid a hasty climb, Ross took a closer look at a couple of trees a few feet away from the gate. He figured an athletic type, with practice, could push her body weight against a large trunk with one foot and spring from it to the wall. With some upper body strength, she could propel herself over. Ross peered up the larger of the two tree trunks. If its higher branches were just a little lower, a young climber could easily scamper up. Or she could start climbing from a position on top of the wall. He pulled himself back up, gritting his teeth against the pain in his left hand.

Balancing on the ledge, about a foot wide, the detective leaned into a tree limb and gazed upward. As he had thought, the network of limbs and branches offered an easy climb. He jumped back down and noted a small hollow facing the brick wall. Feeling around inside, he touched a spade and a handheld rake. Nothing more. Ross left the tree and strolled the children's corner of the cemetery. An opened umbrella covered part of one headstone. Ross lifted it and felt a tug. Someone had tied a large loop of string around the umbrella's handle and placed the loop around the grave marker. He dropped the umbrella and noted the marker's inscription.

"June."

No last name for a baby who had lived only one day— June 1, 2015.

Ross moved away from the tree canopy and into the open. Finding the chimney with the unsettled shingle, he looked to the windows of Thompson's house. A streetlight caught part of a girl's face staring at him from the second floor. *Black. Glasses. Ten?*

15

11:00 p.m.

"No way. He did not!" Officer Terrence Rivera laughed from behind the wheel of his squad car.

"Yep," said his soon-to-be former partner Lina Lopez. "Seriously acted like I was going to follow him into the bathroom."

"How do you know?"

"Come on, Rivera." She pointed to the clock in the squad car. "You have exactly one hour to tell me anything that I will forget."

He snickered. "Maybe he was testing you. See what you would do."

"He was mocking me. Because what *would* I do? Complain two days before I'm gone?" She tried to suppress her growing frustration on this, their final ride. Rivera and she were good partners, and both knew how much Lopez, a decade younger, had learned from Rivera's ability to identify motive and fault in most any altercation. But the redhead from Forensics was right. He was an ass. Rivera had the respect needed to challenge the meatheads in their precinct, but he wouldn't. He didn't like engaging in any topic that he had no direct power over. "Can't do anything about it," he would say.

"Fucking boys club," she said, directed to the window. "Leaves me alone for ten years, shows his true colors when I'm this close to the door."

"He's jealous," Rivera said. "We all are." He glanced at her. "You know that."

"Not for making detective."

"Sure we are. But proud of—"

"Bullshit. Any of you could have tried." She smirked. "Then when you failed, you could have tried again and again."

Rivera laughed.

"You're jealous I'm going somewhere else," Lopez said. "That I get."

Rivera sighed. "Don't I know it." His phone buzzed. He moved his eyes between it and the road as he texted. "Aughhhh. I'm. So. Bored."

"I hate it when you do this."

"I'm in deep shit with Lenore."

"You're going to kill somebody."

"I'll make sure it's someone headed into the 17th." He laughed.

"Not funny."

Rivera groaned and stopped the car in the middle of Lehigh Avenue so he could finish his message. "Such a pain in my ass."

Lehigh divided the Kensington section of Philadelphia into the 26th and 17th Districts. South of Lehigh, major crimes in the 26th District had decreased over the past ten years, one result of the revitalization spreading through the Fishtown and South Kensington neighborhoods. But that was changing.

For over thirty years, an abandoned line of train tracks that ran through the 17th District had served as the city's unofficial heroin hub. Users from around the country had migrated here, to an area of north Philadelphia called the Badlands. Across three acres of the old tracks, a thick line of trees sheltered activities and the decades-long encampment along Frankford Avenue. The police had their hands full in the Badlands, and on the fringes of "the Tracks," but they largely ignored the camp itself. Traffickers and users knew that if they maintained peace behind the tree line, the cops would stick to steady drive-bys and the occasional missing person search.

This agreement had lasted for decades—until the opioid epidemic brought hordes of young white men from the suburbs and beyond to the Tracks. When this population stayed, and their mothers reported them missing, police and reporters started asking more questions. The Tracks became a sensational subject for newspaper articles, damning editorials, and documentaries on cable news channels. New stories emerged of assaults in the woods on addicts who were too afraid of the police and forced recovery to make reports.

Three months before, officers from the 17th District showed up at the Tracks with prison-grade fencing and a crew ready to eject the tent city. Escorted through the shanties and then left to the streets, clusters of homeless junkies walked into Center City, where they camped in grassy squares or under the entryways of empty storefronts and abandoned churches. The majority headed south along Frankford Avenue, into the 26th District and its network of buses, trolleys, and elevated trains. Along that route, they constructed smaller, tighter tent towns under the out-of-use bridges that had serviced freight trains in Philadelphia's industrial heydays.

Two young white women wearing bandanas and carrying backpacks crossed Lehigh in front of the officers. Each wore jeans and boots and filthy T-shirts that billowed over their thin frames.

"Who let those two out of the house?" Rivera asked. He tossed his phone in the console and started driving again. "They'll be dead in a month."

Lopez watched the pair disappear down an alley. "Guess I'll be spending a lot of time back up here."

Rivera snorted. "As if Homicide's going to start investigating junkie deaths."

Lopez tapped the monitor on the dashboard. "Accident call coming."

"Come on!" He pounded the steering wheel. "With forty minutes to go!"

"I'm not going to miss this."

"Traffic calls?"

"No. Your whining."

Rivera glanced at his phone. "By the way, Lopez," he paused and started laughing, "Big Verdez is scheduled to ride with me next week."

Lopez punched him in the right shoulder. "Don't call her that!"

"Guess I'll be getting a bigger car—"

"Don't do that!" snapped Lopez. "How'd everyone find out?"

"That she was being detailed to the Academy to work out?" He stopped the car again for dramatic effect. "Come on. Tough to keep that one under wraps."

"Sergeant."

Rivera laughed. "Ramone wanted to know whether she was sick or on vacation, and Serg said neither."

"Then he told you."

"Come on. She has to fit in a uniform. They were helping her out."

"Will you drive already? Sarge needs to get his own ass to the gym. So do you."

"Hey! I'm in pretty good shape for forty-three."

Lopez sighed. "I'm upgrading. Did you see that head of hair on Ross?"

"Stop it," Rivera said, stroking his receding hairline. "Lenore thinks it's sexy."

A voice came over the radios on their shoulders. "729, Accident at Frankford and Thompson."

Rivera groaned. "I'm going to be stuck here all night."

"Serves you right." Lopez looked out the window. "Sergeant drinks, you hit the Ambien, Verdez eats. And nobody sends him or you for help."

Rivera drove in silence for a minute. "Heard Sarge talking about you on the phone today."

"When?"

"Guess about four." His cell phone buzzed again. Eyeing a red light in front of him, he texted a response and mumbled under his breath. A car honked behind him.

"Who the hell honks at a cop?" he yelled.

"Someone who sees one breaking the law."

"Kiss-ass." He eyed the driver of the car as it passed by. "Anyway, Sarge was surprised you'd be shadowing the great and powerful Ross."

"The great and powerful Ross?"

"His words."

"Would he have said that three months ago?"

Rivera shook his head. "I don't know."

"Sarge doesn't like him?"

"I don't know, Lopez. Just something you say."

She rolled down her window.

"He's supposed to be good." Rivera shrugged. "People like him. Sarge is just jealous you got matched with a rock star while he's stuck here."

"Not really a rock star," Lopez said slowly. "Took six weeks leave after the Strangler. Obviously pretty human."

"What do you mean?"

20

"What?"

"You think he was on psych leave?"

"What else?"

"Come onnnn," Rivera groaned. "Why else. Why else would he go on leave?"

She shrugged.

"729, you all there?" asked a voice over the radio.

"In traffic. Hold your horses, radio," Rivera said.

"Not seeing anything on the traffic screen," the voice responded.

"Aughh!" Rivera moaned to Lopez. "Lenore's going to leave me if I'm home late."

"So get a job closer to home. Be a cop in Jersey."

"You shut your mouth about Jersey."

Lopez smiled.

"You know what?" Rivera said. "I hope every dick in Homicide hates you."

"I'll make sure every dick in Homicide hates *you*," she quipped.

He chuckled. "Okay. Thirty-five minutes left in the Rivera-Lopez show."

She pretended to wipe tears from her eyes. As they approached the accident scene, Lopez saw a teenager sitting on the curb, his parents on either side of him. The other driver sat in the passenger seat of his car, door opened.

"So I have one thing left to tell you," Rivera said.

"You serious?"

"Yeah. Listen and be educated."

She rolled her eyes. She hated how his tone changed on a dime to suit his purposes. He could be a puppy dog one second, an angry teacher another, and a frat boy the next.

It worked on the street when they needed to pump people for information, but she resented it when they were alone.

"Soooo serious," she said.

"Watch yourself up there. You're savvy but still a little naïve. Ask questions as soon as you get there. Better to be a pain in the ass than a pushover."

"Huh? Rivera! Naïve?"

"Yeah. With authority. You accept what you're told too easily."

"After everything we've been—"

"*Because* of everything. I'm not going to be there to—"

"To what? Tell me what to do?"

"Stop it." He turned and looked her in the eye. "You came here, you knew what to do. Keep your mouth shut and follow my lead. That was smart. But you can't have the same approach there. You don't go in there owning your shit, your approach, your instincts…you become a pawn."

"Pawn?"

The family on the curb stood and started walking toward the police car. Lopez opened her door and motioned them back.

"Why are they putting you with Ross?" Rivera asked. "Six weeks is odd leave time. Standard's eight. He comes back, and you're assigned to him. There's a reason for that." He paused. "They think you'll do whatever they tell you. You're better than that."

"You're jealous."

"You're not ready!"

Both were taken aback at his loudness. The party on the street seemed to hear him. Lopez opened her door.

"Does it really make sense that he's your first partner up there?" Rivera asked.

22

Lopez turned sharply. "So you're saying I'm going in as a tool? A spy? Some kind of punishment for him?"

"Think about it."

"Why did you have to do this? Now?"

Rivera tossed his phone on the dashboard and opened his door. "I'll be here when you realize something doesn't add up. And you don't know whose direction to take—Ross's or the captain's."

"I'll take my own."

"I hope so."

Lopez slammed her door and headed to take the family's statement.

MONDAY

6 a.m.

DETECTIVE ERIC ROSS STRETCHED HIS LEFT FINGERS FROM under the tightly wound bandage. Across the street from his condo building, two toddlers and a dog ran around a small pocket park in front of a tired father watching from a bench.

Ross tied and retied his sneakers before jogging down the middle of 9th Street. For blocks, vendors on either side of the street readied for the day's Italian Market business. Scents of cheese, chocolate, doughnuts, and coffee beans overwhelmed the odors from butcher and fishmonger shops. Ross dodged the water runoff as power hoses sprayed the sidewalks in between fruit and vegetable stalls. His side ached and his hand felt ripped in half, but he needed to make up the mileage he had lost the previous night. To block out the pain, he counted as he ran: first his inhalations and exhalations, then the soft extended steps of his feet, then the number of people he passed who wore navy blue.

Ross cut through the Theater District on Broad Street, made a left at City Hall, and cut across the multiple lanes of the Ben Franklin Parkway to reach the Art Museum. He ran around the museum toward the banks of the Schuylkill River, then walked for a bit along Boathouse Row, where the air was thick with pollen and the sickeningly sweet smell of azaleas. Ross doubled back along the river and sprinted up an incline leading past Lemon Hill Park into Brewerytown.

There, he turned onto Girard and headed the three miles back into Fishtown.

The city was waking up, although it never exactly slept at the foot of Temple University's campus at Broad and Girard. Night and day, horns honked and brakes slammed in a constant jam of pedestrians, cars, police, and trolleys moving between the intersection's four corners of public transit stops. The 15 trolley inched along tracks that ran down the middle of Girard. Each time its doors closed, someone with a backpack, a briefcase, or stumbling from a storefront would bang on its side and start yelling to have the doors opened again.

Past Broad Street, Girard Avenue was decorated with strip malls, an abandoned community center, cracked tennis courts, and two methadone clinics. Here, north of Independence Hall and the Liberty Bell, the River Wards communities stretched along and from the Delaware River. Pockmarked by abandoned warehouses and factories, neighborhoods featured luxury condos and tax-abated townhouses built in industrial ruins.

Ross turned left on Frankford Avenue and ran a few blocks north toward Palmer Cemetery. The gates were open. A few people with leashed dogs meandered around grave markers. The only evidence of the previous night's crime scene was a long strand of yellow tape crinkled and clinging to a tree trunk. Rakes and shovels rested on a pile of mulch in the center of the property. Inside the entrance, next to a community posting board, a small shed held caretaker tools and trash cans.

Ross noted an elderly white man staring at him from behind the screen door of a rowhouse directly across from the entrance. The man's shoulders moved back and forth as if summoning the detective. As Ross approached, the smell of cat urine hit him.

"You the cop here last night," the old man said, wheezing. Ross noticed his right hand on an oxygen tank.

"Yes. Lieutenant Eric Ross."

Eighty. White. One-hundred-twenty pounds. Hepatitis? Skin cancer? Dermatitis.

"Good cop name," he said, cackling.

"Can I help you?" Ross asked. He wondered how many other neighbors would recognize him during daylight. Ross could feel their stares the night before, gazes coming from dark perches behind curtains and windows. The crime scene lights had shone brightly on him. Astute observers would recognize the Ace bandage still on his hand.

"I heard you were talking to that Thompson woman," the man said, gasping. He moved his neck forward as a way of pointing.

Ross waited for more. The man wanted to be asked.

"Did you see anything suspicious last night, sir?"

The man closed his eyes and shook his head no.

"Did you witness the death that occurred here?"

Again, no.

"What is your name, sir?"

"Robert." The man coughed. He closed his eyes and shook his head no again. "Cop cars. Dead body. These things," he said, wheezing, "don't happen here. Didn't used to." His yellowed eyes narrowed. Ross wondered how much cat hair layered his throat. "Goddamn shit from the Avenue coming here," Robert said, increasingly agitated. "All different kinds. Now the addicts." He paused. "They piss everywhere."

"Robert, did you see anybody unusual around here last night? Or lately?"

"Are you listening?!" He stomped his foot. "All the time. Goddamn people need to go back."

"Who exactly?"

"Goddamn junkies." He lifted a gnarled finger. "Obama people, all of them."

"You know he's no longer the—"

"All of 'em!" Robert wheezed again. He coughed without covering his mouth.

"Did you see anybody here around the time of the killing?"

Robert shook his head no and leaned into the screen door. Ross noted four, five, six cats in the room behind him.

"All these fuckin' people," Robert said. "Any of 'em did it. It don't matter."

"I'm going to be back later," Ross said, "and I'll leave a card here in your mail slot. Call me if you remember something, or someone, okay?"

The old man lowered his eyes. He stood as if asleep.

Slowly, Ross backed away toward the cemetery. He circled it a few times from inside the gates, attempting to peer into as many windows as possible across the street. Nobody except Robert was looking in his direction. He sat down on the bench where he had stationed himself the night before and stared at the area where the shadow had jumped over the wall. Neighbors had seen something or they hadn't. The girl had either seen something or she hadn't. He had already decided to focus on her and leave it to the others to find any witnesses among the neighbors. His pursuit of both could create animosity between the girl, her grandmother, and the people they had to live among. He had seen it happen too often before.

8:05 a.m.

RUBY WAITED FOR A MINUTE AFTER SHE SAW THE DETEC-tive leave the cemetery. She was tired. It had been a long night for her—and for June. She worried her little sister was still afraid the police would come back and take her away. Holding on to a tree limb, she jumped onto the wall and slipped on the wet bricks, slamming into the tree trunk before hitting the ground. Bark skinned the length of her forearm.

"Aughhh!" she cried, then jumped up and ran to June's gravestone.

"It's okay, Junie," she said softly. "I'll be back later. Everything is okay."

She leaned closer to the headstone. Gently, she closed the umbrella and lifted the loop of string that connected it to the grave marker.

"I'll put this back. No, nobody saw me. They were all still sleeping." She paused and furrowed her brow. "Yes, even her. But who cares if she did see? She wouldn't say nothin' anyway."

Ruby blew on her stinging arm.

"No, I'm okay. Just banged up." She smoothed her blue uniform jumper and stood. "I left my bag back at home. I'll see you after school, Junie!"

Ruby started toward the wall, changed her mind, and ran to the front entrance. The old man across the street leaned against his screen door. Ruby shot him a dirty look as she raced back home.

10:20 a.m.

AT THE INTERSECTION OF FRANKFORD AND GIRARD AVE-
nues, abandoned storefronts sat next to longtime corner
bars, transient pizza shops, and well-reviewed Mexican
restaurants. Trolleys and buses crisscrossed paths underneath an elevated subway stop positioned between the historic district and north Philadelphia. Ross paused in front
of a falafel shop. He surveyed the addicts gathered in the
corners of the intersection. Most would know Michaela's
whereabouts.

Ross had hated coming back to Fishtown. Until the
night before, he hadn't heard from his brother in a couple
of months. He saw Liam's shadow now in every one of the
dirty white junkies wearing baseball caps.

It was hard to separate users from those in treatment at
the methadone clinics. Both groups staggered down Girard,
nodded off mid-stride, and spoke with slurred speech.
Commuters and locals were conditioned to avoid the erratic
behaviors. Ross watched one woman push a jogging stroller
past another struggling to focus on a spoon of food she was
trying to feed a screaming toddler.

Ross walked toward a small group sitting on the steps
of the "24-Hour Fantasies" strip club directly underneath
the El. In an adjacent alley, a tired dancer in fishnets and a
too-tight hot-pink jacket took a smoke break.

Ross nodded at the dancer.

*Twenty-five. White. One-hundred-sixty pounds. Lip
pierced.*

A few minutes later, a gaunt figure in a filthy T-shirt

made his way up the alley. He pushed a shopping cart full of scrap metal.

"Evening, sweetheart," he said to the woman.

Conor Mathew. Ross had known him for about a year. His team had paid him as an occasional informant for a little longer than that. A former user who had made a life on the streets of Kensington, Conor Mathew hadn't wanted—or known how—to change his scavenger lifestyle once he got clean. Conor's recovery included occasional twelve-step meetings, a lot of meditation, and an adherence to a strict schedule. When Ross had needed Conor's help, he knew he could find him somewhere under the El tracks between the Spring Garden and Girard stations between 10 a.m. and 11 a.m. Whether Conor Mathew felt like helping was a different story.

If he wanted money, the thirty-year-old passed along observations that had helped break cases. If he was in a bad mood, he blended yesterday's stories with anecdotes a drunk uncle had told him years before.

The man looked even thinner than Ross remembered, but he still wore the same untied red Converse sneakers. Conor scavenged but didn't beg. The cardboard signs affixed to his cart held jokes, not pleas. Today's read, "Have you sponsored a homeless diabetic lately?"

Conor pretended to ignore Ross. The back gate of a house bordering the alley opened and an older woman hauled a trash can outside. She glared at the junkie loo-kalike who made a beeline for it, then slammed the gate behind her.

"What ya bring me today, honey?" Conor yelled. He started emptying the can. "Money, honey? Honey, honey? Honey fried chicken, honey?" He laughed.

"Conor Mathew," Ross said.

"Mr. Detective," Conor said without making eye contact. "You scared Victor's going to come kill your ass? Need my help? No, no. Not with that fucker. You are on your OWN big man."

Ross rolled his neck and caught his breath. So Conor knew. There was only one person who would have told him. The dancer flicked away her cigarette butt and lit another. Conor foraged the carcass of a rotisserie chicken and started shamelessly sucking the marrow from its bones.

"Not so good for a homeless diabetic you know," Ross said.

"FUCK you know about my health?!" Conor yelled.

"Seen Michaela today?" Ross asked.

"Nope." Conor lifted a box of Cheerios over his mouth and let the crumbs fall into his face. "Seen your brother though."

Ross winced. Ever the bullshitter, Conor Mathew had the right to mention Liam. Not too long before, Ross had asked for his help with him.

"Down the park," Conor continued. "Not so good for recovery when your support system disappears after you get all nice and clean!" He poured more cereal down his face.

"You're disgusting," the dancer said.

Conor laughed and shook the box. "Want to have breakfast with me, baby?"

She gave him the finger.

"Ooh. We can do that too!"

"Anything on the cemetery death, Conor?" Ross asked.

"Nope."

"Did you know the victim?"

"Maybe."

Ross waited.

"Maybe some other bad man is in the BAD-LANDS. HA! A poet. And ya didn't even know it. Ha ha." He faced the girl again. "Don't worry, princess. This big brave officer will protect you."

"Okay, Conor." Ross turned to walk away. He could feel the man's shift in tone.

"Had a job at the library."

"Who?"

"Guy who died," he said quietly.

"Which library?"

"Down by the clinic."

"Was it a job program?"

"Don't know."

"What's his name?"

"Don't know."

"Was it Pedro?"

"Don't. Know." He looked at the stripper. "Detective here just went deaf, Tinkerbell! You give him syphilis from over there? Damn!" Conor laughed.

"How do you know he worked at the library?" Ross pressed.

"I don't!" Conor yelled. "Sheesh," he whined. "Fuck off."

The dancer stared at Ross. Reaching into his coat, the detective walked toward Conor, who was elbows-deep in a plastic bag of chicken wing bones. Ross flicked a twenty-dollar bill into the trash can.

"You know where to find me."

"Just fucking with you by the way."

"With what?"

"Your brother. Haven't seen him anywhere."

"Conor, how do you know about the victim's job?"

"What victim?" Conor lost interest in the pile of garbage and pushed his cart back down the street. Ross stared after him.

"She's at the GYM," the dancer said.

Ross's head jerked toward her. "What?"

"Pastor Michaela," she said impatiently. "Already brought breakfast sandwiches by. Says I eat too much shit here." The woman flicked her cigarette butt.

"You probably do," Ross said.

"FUCK you know about my health?" she shouted.

It took him a second to realize she was making fun of Conor Mathew.

"Thanks." Ross grinned.

The dancer grinned and turned toward the addicts clustered at the door.

"Move it!" she snapped.

They did.

11:00 a.m.

THE GOTHIC REVIVAL EDIFICE OF ALL SAINTS LUTHERAN
Church had loomed over Girard Avenue since 1880. Ross
kicked aside dirty napkins and broken bottles on his way up
the steps to large wooden doors. Over a marbleized, arched
entrance, the words "St. Paul the Apostle" were carved into
granite.

Inside, rows of chairs filled a surprisingly small and
simple sanctuary. As St. Paul the Apostle, the building had
welcomed thousands of immigrants in its first decade. Most
congregants then were Irish or Polish, and priests offered
mass five times a day to suit their working parishioners.

Time dwindled congregation numbers. In the 1960s, the
Archdiocese sold the building, and the following decade
it became the home of "All Saints," an activist church that
grew out of a social justice movement on Temple's campus.

Detective Ross saw Pastor Todd Orner, an overweight
middle-aged rector, as soon as he entered. Pastor Todd was
in the foyer, organizing products from the church's latest
donation drive. Tables overflowed with formula, diapers,
wipes, and jarred food. The men nodded at one another.

Short and squat, Pastor Todd was burdened with the
responsibility of paying bills with a congregation of aged hippies. He handled the challenge well, renting rooms and even
the sanctuary to theater companies needing rehearsal space.
He had also recruited grandmothers to operate a half-day
preschool. On paper, the rental income covered the building's
bills. But its largest need for funding was greater than drafty
hallways and leaking pipes: it was "the GYM," a combination

34

shelter, food closet, and health center that operated off the books in a gymnasium at the back of the building. A woman named Michaela Alvarez had unofficially served as its figurehead for as long as anyone could remember.

Everybody on the Kensington streets knew "Pastor" Michaela. Nobody knew exactly whom she worked for. People assumed the church, the denomination, or one the many city agencies that had been affiliated with All Saints Church over the years.

In the sanctuary, dull light reflected through dirty stained-glass windows. Rows of chairs stood where pews had once lined a grand interior. On a staircase next to the pulpit, Michaela sat in front of a couple huddled in the shadows of the front row. She spoke quietly. From behind one of the doors leading into hallways and meeting rooms, three children burst in, laughing and chasing each other in a game of tag. Ross traced an index finger along the back of a chair. He breathed in deeply and exhaled.

"That's right," said a quiet voice beside him. "Just keep on breathing."

He flinched. She laughed.

"Your disappearing act gets better and better," he said.

"Yet slower and slower," she said, smiling. A look of concern passed over her face. She patted him on the back. "Let's sit." She pulled two chairs from the back row.

The man in the front pew snapped at the laughing children in another language. Their play ended.

Michaela Alvarez and Ross sat in silence.

"Let me guess. You just got back."

Ross's eyes followed the children, who tiptoed from behind the man and woman and started running up and down the center aisle.

"I know you know how long I've been back."

"You on this killing last night?" Michaela asked.

"Yeah," Ross answered. The victim's name had been released to the press early that morning: Pedro Martinez, a twenty-eight-year-old with a couple of burglary arrests but no history of violence.

"I didn't know him." She leaned forward. "Used to know all of them. Not now. Too many coming through."

"But you would have if he came often."

"I asked the boys this morning if anyone came in talking about it last night." She popped a mint into her mouth. "Want one?"

"No."

"They didn't. Said it was quiet."

"When did you hear about it?"

"Last night." She crunched on the candy and popped another. "Officer Rivera called Pastor Todd. Wanted to know if we knew anything. He's intense, that Rivera. Good looking too." She laughed.

Ross stretched his neck and waited a minute. "Seen Liam?"

"Yes. Every other week or so. Comes for group and stays to talk. He's at the Germantown Gospel Mission now. Been good for him."

Ross tapped his right fingers on the chair in front of him.

"He taps his fingers like you do." She nodded at Ross's hands. "Always waits for me to say something first."

"He working?"

"Somewhere."

"Is he—"

"Eric," she interrupted. "He's your brother. Not mine."

"Okay."

"But you're here for another reason too."

He leaned forward.

"Where'd you go?" she asked.

"Around."

"Sounds nice."

"Yeah."

She put a hand on his shoulder. "You made the right choice."

Ross recoiled.

"You know that." She spoke quietly. "Otherwise, you wouldn't have come back."

Ross bowed his head. "It was the right choice for you, Michaela." His voice became quieter. "But that's not why I made it." He stood and turned too quickly, catching a chair with his right foot.

"What happened to your hand?" Michaela asked. Ross left without answering.

She waited for a moment in her seat. Pastor Todd sat next to her.

"Not to worry," she said.

"I'm always worried."

"He's still a friend. But let's clear out the second floor."

"There's no more room—"

"There will have to be," she insisted. "Or they can go somewhere else." She closed her eyes. "I can't take care of the whole damn city."

The children at play jumped back and forth from the stage to the ground. One fell and started to cry, leading the father into another round of reprimands. He grabbed another child by the arm and flipped him around for a spanking. Screams echoed through the sanctuary.

Michaela walked toward the family with open arms and a smile.

Noon

ERIC ROSS ENTERED THE MARLBOROUGH DINER ON Girard at Front Street. He chose a corner booth diagonal from a table where elderly men chatted in front of coffee cups and chipped plates. A few crooked pictures of Greek islands decorated the white walls.

"Coffee?" asked a tired waitress holding a pot in each hand.

"Sure. Two mugs."

A thin man in his early thirties opened the door a minute later.

"Trademark," thought Ross.

No socks. Black sneakers, black sweatpants, black short-sleeve shirt, backward-facing Phillies hat.

The waitress eyed the man skeptically.

"Oh, turn that frown upside down," the man said to her. "I'm legit, Miss," he leaned in to read her nametag, "Fran. Got a detective here to vouch for me." He pointed and Ross nodded.

"He with you?" she asked incredulously.

Ross stood and the two men embraced.

"Where's your—" Ross tapped his left ear.

"Lost it."

"You mean you sold it."

"What kind of dealer wants a hearing aid? Didn't have diamonds on it." He collapsed into the booth. "Been gone a year now, bro! You just didn't notice last time."

The waitress came back around with two mugs she dropped onto the table. Coffee sloshed out of each.

"He'll take pancakes. And eggs," Ross said.

"No. My stomach can't handle it."

"You sick?"

"No, training."

"For what?"

"Coast Guard."

"What?"

"It's true, Eric baby." He extended his arms across the table like a small child. "Following in my big brother's military footsteps."

"How'd you swing that?"

The waitress interrupted. "All right with the reunion. Pancakes and eggs for you both." She walked away.

"Haven't seen you in three months," Liam said. "Don't look so surprised. You know how it goes. Enrollment's down, ex-cons can get in."

"But—"

"Six months sober."

"How'd you think of this?"

Liam shrugged. "Workin' at that mission in Germantown. Co-worker gives me a ride to the Salvation Army rec center nearby. Met a Coastie recruiter there. He talked it up, and I'm leaving for basic at Cape May in June."

"And they don't—"

"They don't need to know about rehab. The mission vouched for me. Said I was a wayward, traveling soul on a journey that led me to Jesus and the ocean." He smiled and laughed. "Kind of true."

"Cape May."

"That where you went just now?"

Ross nodded yes. "Got back last week." He paused. "But Michaela already let you know that."

39

Ignoring the Michaela comment, Liam took off his hat and ran a hand over a fresh crew cut.

"You cut your hair."

"Now you believe me."

"I do. I do." Ross nodded. "And I'm glad for you."

The waitress dropped two platters of food and a check in front of them.

"Michaela says you keep in touch," Ross said.

"Little bit. You seen her yet? Since you've been back?"

"Yeah."

"Were you getting therapy down there at the beach?"

"Ocean's therapy."

"Worried that Victor asshole's watching you?"

"How'd you know about that?"

"News."

Ross braced himself. He wasn't in the news though.

Liam leaned closer. "Victor Rafaella. Come on. Had to have rattled you."

"What did Michaela say to you?"

Liam looked confused and shrugged again. "Said what happened. That you refused to identify Victor at a crime scene."

Ross tensed. She must have said something to Conor Mathew as well.

"She shouldn't have told you that. And I didn't refuse to do anything."

Liam's face whitened.

"You seen Conor Mathew recently?" the detective asked after a pause.

"He's stayed away from the GYM for a long time now."

"Why?"

"Don't know. Asked Michaela. She didn't know."

40

Ross glimpsed over at the old-timers across the restaurant. "Don't guess you've heard from Dad?"

"Yeah, about a month ago. Probably in Florida now."

"Why?"

"Following some chick. He'll be back. Hey"—Liam tapped a dirty fingernail on the table—"Eddie's birthday last week. Been almost thirty years."

The waitress circled.

"Can you make that to go?" Ross asked her.

His brother slumped back in the booth.

"You serious?" she snapped.

Liam shifted and recoiled quickly. "This is a big deal detective," he snapped back. "He's got places to go and people to nail."

She swore under her breath. Liam slapped his hands on the table.

"So we done here?" Liam said. "See you at Christmas?"

"Liam." Ross leaned in. "I wanted to see you. That's why I texted you last night."

"See me after Michaela told you I was okay."

Close, Ross thought to himself. He had invited Liam to lunch so his brother would know he was going to be in Fishtown. Had Liam fallen back in the habit, he'd steer clear from where Ross might wander while he was in the neighborhood.

"I wanted to see you," Ross repeated.

"It's okay. I'd probably do the same." Liam caught his brother's eye. "And here I thought you wanted to see if I ever shot up with that dead guy. Or maybe apologize for thinking I raped those women."

The old men were now watching the brothers.

Ross looked into his coffee. "Did you know Pedro Martinez?"

41

"Nope."

The waitress dumped a bag of food on the table and slapped the check she had already laid down. Liam put a ten-dollar bill on the table.

"No," Ross said.

"Yep," his brother said. "Next time, I'll have enough to cover the whole tab."

Liam shot out of the booth. "Gotta go. Love ya, bro." He walked away quickly.

Ross put down another $10 and took the bag with him.

1:00 p.m.

Ross tried to match his strides to his breath as he walked the few blocks from the Marlborough Diner to Penn Treaty Park. So he had seen Liam. He should feel calmer, not more worked up. His brother, for the first time in a long time, had a goal. A path. He had clothes, shelter, friends, a job—all the things Ross had wanted for him.

It was easier, he could admit, when Liam was on the street, and there was nowhere for him to move but up. Now he was in the hands of the Coast Guard. If he showed up for basic training and survived it. Michaela was clearly coaching him through the decision. He was irritated that she had told Liam about his brother's role in Victor Rafaella's release, but it made sense. The more agitated Liam was, the more Michaela would have needed to calm him down with a story of his beloved brother's own struggles.

Ross walked around the park circle. Slowing his inhalations, he breathed deeply and tried to channel any sense memories from yesterday evening's run. He conjured the figure of the ailing young man who had limped away from him, surely suppressing cries of pain before he ended up decorated and dead in a cemetery a mile away.

Pedro Martinez. Pedro on Girard. Pedro whom he had tried to speak with just before his bizarre end. Ross had considered why the man had been stating his own name under his breath. Had the dying man been thinking of another Pedro? Or just talking to himself?

Ross thought again of the man's profile, and of the incredible abdominal pain he would have suffered as he

43

walked. Pedro couldn't have costumed and staged himself. Had the killer followed Ross as he followed Pedro the night before? Had one killer poisoned him at or near Penn Treaty Park and a second staged his body?

As he walked and thought, the detective noted an increase in real estate signs on abandoned lots adjacent to the park. New York developers had arrived on the scene about five years before when SugarHouse Casino opened on the Delaware River. Its advent further polarized River Wards communities already at odds over gentrification. Again and again, at public meetings hosted by civic associations, churches, and rec centers, the old guard argued with young progressives. The casino would foster lecherous behavior and attract unwanted people, said the old. It would provide jobs and economic incentives, countered the young.

SugarHouse had indeed become a key economic driver, offering hundreds of jobs and awarding an admirable number of grants to nonprofits engaged in revitalization efforts. The fight over it, however, had weakened the social fabric, exhausting reformers and distracting attention from the much uglier and rapidly encroaching opioid epidemic.

A little online research had revealed that Penn Treaty was community-run. Ross hadn't been able to find names of a director, board members, or a caretaker. Key information would only come from regular visitors. Ross approached two middle-aged dog walkers speaking to one another in the center of the park as their dogs ran free around them.

Caucasian females. Retired? Out of shape. Smokers.

"Good morning, I'm Detective Eric Ross with the—"

"Oh my God," one of the women cried. "Benji, Benji, get the hell over here!" A beagle about one hundred yards away stared at her. "Get your ass back on this leash."

"No, no, I'm not here about that," Ross said, grinning. "Although, yes, leash the dog's ass." Neither woman laughed.

"I'm looking for a person of interest in a series of burglaries. Kid in his twenties. Latino, black hair, skinny. Might have a limp. Name's Pedro."

He took out his phone and showed the women a photo of Martinez, a mugshot that ran underneath the morning's *Philly.com* headline "Gruesome Death in Palmer Cemetery." Neither woman recognized him.

"What'd he steal?" asked the first.

"Series of residential break-ins nearby," Ross lied. "Do you know of any security cameras that might have picked him up?"

"No," the second woman said. She appeared more thoughtful than the first. Ross waited over a long pause for her to say something more. "A bunch of car windows were bashed in a couple of weeks ago. Right over there." She pointed toward a residential neighborhood that Ross had followed Pedro through. "People asked the same question on Facebook."

"Was this on a certain page?" Ross asked.

"Penn Treaty Neighbors."

"Cameras anywhere around here?"

"Newer townhomes a couple blocks up. Nobody saw anything. Or didn't say if they did."

"Anybody you know spend a lot of time here at different times of day?"

"Lot of people," the first woman said. "Fishermen."

Ross looked down toward the riverbank. No fishermen there now.

"Thanks."

Ross walked back through the parking lot and again conjured the ailing Pedro. He kept a vision of the man in front of him as he traced the route he had tracked Pedro Martinez through. Crossing Delaware Avenue, Ross scanned homes and businesses for security cameras and/or signs threatening potential burglars or vandals with cameras. He wrote down the names of places likely to have working ones—auto body shops, newer bars, SEPTA transit. When he reached Girard, Ross followed the most direct path Pedro Martinez would have taken to Palmer Cemetery, adding likely locations with security cameras to his list until he reached the cemetery gates. Ross pictured Pedro Martinez at the entrance. Who had left the gate open for him? Somebody had to have been waiting inside, eager to stage the dying man's body and exit the scene without attracting attention.

He knew of one person who could slip in and out unnoticed. A child sensitive enough to keep raindrops off a gravestone.

7:15 p.m.

BY THE TIME ROSS RETURNED TO THE CEMETERY, IT WAS nearly dusk. He passed a couple of dog walkers, but the grounds were empty save for the young black girl playing not too far from the murder scene. She glanced at him and away more than once as he approached. Ross sat on a bench near where she played.

"Hello." He took out his badge. "My name is Eric Ross. I'm a police detective."

She concentrated on the earth around the "June" gravestone, dusting it and the surrounding ground with the petals of a yellow flower.

Ross leaned in. "That your cat I tripped over last night?"

She grinned. He sat back against the bench.

"Whose grave is this?"

"Did you read it?" she asked.

"Yes."

"Then you know."

"I know it's for a June, but I don't know who she is."

The girl touched the letters on the grave marker.

"Was she your sister?" Ross asked.

"She IS my sister."

Ross nodded. "Of course." He paused for a moment. "Did you get your umbrella back then?"

She pretended to ignore him.

"You live in the house with the red door?"

She shrugged.

"Was that—your grandmother I talked to last night?"

"Yep. My white grandmother."

47

Ross grinned. "What's your name?"

"Ruby," she said proudly.

"Ruby."

"I don't talk to cops."

"Okay." Ross sat for a minute. "I'm trying to figure out what happened here last night. My job is to help keep your neighborhood safe."

Her eyes met his. "Well you aren't doing a very good job then."

Ross smiled. He waited a minute for Ruby to speak again.

"I come to sit with my sister," she said.

"That's good of you."

"She's in heaven. I'll see her again."

"Yes."

"She was only a couple hours old when she died."

"People in heaven are smarter than we are," Ross said.

Ruby smiled.

"Ruby," Ross said, leaning forward. "Were you sitting here with June when someone was killed here last night?"

"I'm glad you call her June."

"What do others call her?"

"It. Or her. My mom acts like she never lived."

Ross looked at the ground. "Does your mom live with you?"

"No, just my grandma. She's standing behind you, you know."

Ross swung around and stood up. Several feet behind him stood Dorothy Thompson, Ruby's grandmother.

"Wow, you're a really good detective," Ruby said.

Thompson hunched her shoulders and leaned slightly forward.

48

"Time to go inside," she said in her muddled voice. Ross again noticed her bottom teeth. Ruby obeyed.

"Leave her be," Thompson said.

"Ma'am, I need to know what she saw."

"She saw nothing."

Ross's phone rang. "I don't believe that. Ruby knows more than you think."

"How do you know?"

"I just do. And so might someone else. Someone you don't want knocking on the door one night."

"Didn't want you knocking on the door last night."

Ross caught her eye for a second.

"You bein' here don't attract attention?" Thompson mumbled, turning away.

Ross's phone rang again.

"Yep," he answered. "Where?"

8:00 p.m.

Ross met Lopez in the parking lot of Central High School. One of the city's highest achieving schools, Central attracted thousands of applications from Philadelphia's eighth graders every year. Well-funded by alumni, Central had more extracurricular activities and sports programs than most city schools, as well as state-of-the-art facilities and well-known coaching staffs. No degree of stellar reputation, however, could disguise the school's home in Olney, a section of north Philadelphia.

A block off Broad, pedestrians walking to and from the Olney Transportation Center could watch any of the school's track meets and football games through a chain-link fence that divided the property from the sidewalk. Trees along the fence offered some coverage for the school grounds, and it was against a tree trunk in one of these patches that Lopez and Ross saw a costumed corpse, the second within twenty-four hours. Pockets of people gathered along the gate. Nobody was surprised at police activity near Broad and Olney, but rarely did any take place on the grounds of Central High School, a point of community pride.

Spotlights on the all-purpose track shined brightly on the body, the tree border, and a small set of wooden bleachers to one side of the track. Jessie Wren and her intern spoke with a medical examiner inside the crime scene tape.

"Responding officer found a wallet on the vic," said now-Detective Lina Lopez. "Name's LeAnn DeVille. Foster care worker. Lives in the suburbs. Husband thought she was on a home visit. Said she was a guidance counselor here a few years ago."

Ross jotted notes on his clipboard as they approached the crime scene.

"Canvassed Fishtown this afternoon by the way," Lopez said. "Two pet stores—nobody there knew about exotic bird collectors. Neighbors around the square didn't know either. Made some calls. No pet shops reported stuffed birds missing, none missing from the Philadelphia, Cape May, Delaware zoo gift shops. Zoos didn't have leads on any tropical bird collectors or taxidermists around here."

An officer approached.

"Officer Lukens, Detective Eric Ross," Lopez said. "He was the responding."

"That man over there called 911," Lukens said, pointing to the bleachers to an older black man in a black sweat suit. "Night watchman. Came out here on his rounds and ran into this."

Jessie Wren called to Ross from her crouched position next to the body. "Stabbed in the throat. Fucker went right through her voice box."

"Any other punctures?"

"None."

"Medical examiner coming?" Ross asked.

"Too clear-cut. Haven't heard but probably not—busy night already."

Inside the crime scene tape, a woman in her sixties was propped against a tree trunk. Her head leaned forward, and her legs sprawled in front of her. A purple flower costume encircled her neck, and drapes of fabric fell over her upper torso. A gold spray-painted surgeon's mask covered her mouth.

51

"Propped and positioned again," Wren said. "Different COD. Signature. Doesn't feel the same." She stood and stepped back. "Although sure does look it."

Ross walked toward the night watchman. Lopez followed. The man sat in the middle of the bleachers with his arms propped on a bench behind him and his legs spread in front of him. He stared at the track.

"Hello," Ross said, offering his hand.

African American, seventy, balding, arthritis. Cool blue eyes. Former runner.

"I'm Detective Eric Ross. This is Detective Lina Lopez." The watchman nodded at Lopez and shook Ross's hand.

"Fred Jacobs," the watchman said. "Don't have too much to tell you. Been night security—day security too, sometimes, for thirty-four years now."

"You said you found the body on your rounds?" Lopez asked.

"Yep."

"Can you describe your rounds?"

Fred Jacobs shifted his gaze from the track to her. "Sit in the office, get up, walk around the building, circle the track, go back to the office. Repeat."

"Video surveillance in that office?" Lopez asked.

He grunted. "Been broken for years. Can't afford a new one, they tell me. Kids have no idea."

"No booster club for video cameras?" Ross asked. Jacobs grunted again.

"Bring it up during football season," Jacobs said, chuckling.

"Just you on night duty?" Lopez asked.

"Yep."

"Where were you when you spotted the woman?" Ross asked.

"Entered the gates where you came in just now, noticed something off right away. Saw the setup." He paused. "Thought maybe a kid was drunk or a homeless guy had climbed over...got closer, saw whatever that is. Called 911."

"And you waited here for the police?" Lopez asked.

"Yep."

"Call anybody else?" Ross asked.

"Nope."

"Have you seen this woman before?" Lopez pressed.

"No."

"Apparently, she worked here as a counselor a few years ago."

"Heard that."

Lopez looked at Ross. He scribbled on his clipboard.

"Nothing familiar about her, Mr. Jacobs?" she asked.

The man stared at her. "Familiar? About this?" He pointed toward DeVille's body. "Masked woman dressed like a purple flower with her throat cut open?" He shook his head. "Sure as hell hope not."

Twenty minutes later, Lopez leaned against the metal fence and watched people come and go from the Olney stop on the other side of Broad Street. Ross was circling the track with his clipboard, absorbed in his notes.

"We're done," a voice said behind her. "Tell Ross I'll text."

"Yep," Lopez said. She could sense the redhead lingering behind her.

"First official day?"

"Yep." Lopez inhaled deeply and pivoted.

"Let me know if you have any questions on our end." Jessie Wren smiled. Lopez didn't think it suited her. The woman hadn't been warm at all the night before—only efficient and rude. Lopez could respect that.

"Or about Ross," Wren said. "I've worked with him for awhile now."

"What kind of questions?" Her response sounded harsher than she meant, but Lopez was in no mood for coyness. The watchman bothered her. Wren was bothering her now. She didn't like the attitude the forensics detective had taken with Rivera the night before, and she didn't like the way she had dismissed her intern. Even now, the poor young woman stood awkwardly by the track, pretending her camera was more interesting than it was.

"Come on." Wren shot Lopez a knowing look. "I don't need to spell it out. Happy to share what I can."

Lopez narrowed her eyes. The woman was either trying too hard or marking her territory. Maybe Ross had nailed her. Or was the other woman trying to warn her about something? Lopez couldn't forget what Rivera had said the night before. Was she some form of punishment? Or some sort of test?

"If you need to warn me about something, just do it."

Wren's smile faded fast. "Forget it."

Lopez turned back to the fence. She hated feeling out of her element. The anticipation of a promotion had been so exciting that she hadn't thought through what it would be like to start all over among a group of people who didn't know anything about her. No longer would anyone expect her to do the same rotation, on the same beat, with the same people. Her time was hers, and she had to figure out how to use it. Eric Ross obviously wouldn't be much help.

For a moment the night before, it had seemed like he would take her along with him, dole out assignments and advise her as a mentor would. The two hadn't met before. That their first case together had occurred in District 26 was a coincidence. She had assumed she would start her first day as a detective by meeting Ross at Homicide, as he had said, and shadowing him. Instead he hadn't shown up.

After introducing herself to an ornery receptionist, Lopez had found her way to a shared desk. She spent a little time getting to know another detective, an Oscar Marino, but he was obviously as busy as she wished she were. At least she had one time-consuming task: figuring out the origin of the large preserved tropical bird from the night before. After two hours of phone calls to zoos, pet stores, and any collectors she could sniff out, she had gone to the Philadelphia Zoo and then back to Fishtown to follow up on her phone conversations. The only reason she'd known to go to Olney was that the Captain had called her looking for Ross. He wasn't pleased they weren't together.

Lopez herself had been surprised when the Captain told her that Eric Ross would be her training partner. She had heard his name quite a bit two months before, when his capture and arrest of a serial rapist called the Strangler confirmed what many had considered an urban legend: that one man had raped and murdered over fifty female prostitutes in a ten-year period. For at least a week, the arrest had elevated the force in the press. It was a lucky break in more than one way. News of the Strangler's identification and arrest detracted attention momentarily from a *Philadelphia Inquirer* report on police brutality in north Philadelphia.

A scream from the Olney transit station brought her back to attention. Two SEPTA transit police officers had someone pinned to the ground.

Lopez strolled toward Ross as he finished another lap. Thinking again on Rivera's comments, she tried to remember if Ross had himself been lionized in the press, or if it was Homicide and the larger department that got the credit. She didn't know.

"Screw you, Rivera," she said quietly.

"Want a ride back?" Ross called. He scribbled something else on the clipboard that he held in the crook of his left arm. As it had the night before, his posture seemed stiff. She wondered how he had hurt his left hand.

"How did you get here?" he asked.

"Grabbed the El. And the redhead from Forensics says she'll text you."

"Detective Wren."

"Detective Wren," Lopez repeated. She followed him toward his car.

"She also said if I have any questions about you, I can ask her."

The comment caught him off guard. She had hoped it would. He stopped and made a bit of a show, Lopez thought, in searching his deep jacket pockets for his keys.

"Do you?"

"Have questions about you?" she asked.

"Yeah."

"Sure. Weren't we supposed to meet at Homicide this morning?"

Ross unlocked the car and opened the door.

"Right. That didn't happen."

"No."

He paused. "Can I ask you a question?"

"Sure."

"How do you take notes?"

Lopez pulled a small memo pad from an inner pocket of her jacket.

"Notes. All the time. Talk less, note more. Note every detail."

Had she talked that much at all? Fine. She'd keep the damn thing out every second.

"Right," she said. Lopez felt uncomfortable agreeing, agreeing, agreeing.

"You getting in?" he asked.

"No, I'll take the El. I'll meet you at Homicide."

"Okay."

9:45 p.m.

A BULLDOZER BLOCKED THE CENTER TWO LANES AND THE trolley tracks on Broad Street. Horns blared. In the northbound lanes, work crews had staged bright lights where they were drilling into the street. Ross squinted at the brightness and groaned. Flashing lights at night increasingly gave him headaches. Traffic moved slowly as two lanes dwindled into one.

"Come on! Enough!" a stuck trolley driver yelled at a construction worker waving traffic through with a measly orange flag.

Traffic stopped completely as the bulldozer turned around.

"Shit," Ross mumbled. He closed his eyes and pushed his right thumb and middle finger into his eyelids. A group of teenagers got off the trolley and cut in front of Ross.

"Turn down the fucking lights!" one yelled.

The trolley driver yelled at workers on a smoke break.

"Where's your foreman?!" he yelled. "Neither department cleared this with SEPTA. No detour notice!"

A burly man in a yellow baseball cap appeared from behind the bulldozer.

"Your trolley would be in a sinkhole if we didn't fix this pipe, jackass."

"Fine. But where's the warning?"

"Here's your warning: get the hell out of my face."

A ragged looking mom holding a screaming baby stepped from a front door.

"Isn't there a noise curfew? Aren't you supposed to stop at eight?"

The same man turned toward her. "Ma'am, we've got to fix a pipe. If we don't, that baby won't have any water tomorrow."

"You've been saying that for an hour," she said in a choked-up voice.

"Here it comes," Ross thought. He opened his eyes and saw her looking right at him. The mother started walking toward the police car.

"Shiiiit," Ross murmured. He pulled over to the side of the road and stepped out, wincing at the lights in front of him. He blocked their glare with his hands and turned his head to the left. A mural spanned the brick wall of an industrial building on the other side of Broad Street. Ross did a double take.

"Officer!" the mother cried. "This is illegal! They aren't listening!"

Shading his eyes with his arm, Ross shuffled through the work zone and stepped in front of a car moving slowly from the opposite direction. The driver hit his brakes, but the car tapped against Ross.

"Want to die?" the driver yelled.

Ross stumbled onto the curb. The breadth of the picture made him dizzy. He took a step backward, then forward again, processing the enormity of the scene. Painted along the brick wall, a figure dressed in white spanned the length of the mural. One hand stretched toward a colorful bird. Broken eggshells were painted under the body.

"Officer!" the mother cried.

Ross was oblivious to the crying baby, screaming mother, furious drivers, and frustrated construction workers. For the second time in six months, he had a serial killer on his hands.

59

11:45 p.m.

THE HOMICIDE DIVISION OF THE PHILADELPHIA POLICE
Department sat across North 6th Street from Independence
Mall, three acres of grass that separated Independence Hall
at its north end from the National Constitution Center at
its south. Directly opposite the small brick building that
held the Liberty Bell, Homicide occupied the first three
floors of the department's newest building: a fifteen-story,
state-of-the-art structure that also housed Forensics and
two floors of holding cells.

Every day, school buses lined the east side of 6th Street
as thousands of tourists milled Independence Mall. And
every day on the west side, vans carrying violent criminals
entered and exited through an underground garage. At
night, National Park Service guards patrolled the grounds,
making sure they stayed quiet and closed to activity.

Ross parked on the street and went to the office of
Captain Antony Mikovich on the second floor. Mikovich
had worked with Ross the detective's entire career, and as
his direct supervisor for the past five years. One of four
Homicide captains, Mikovich ran his team with few words
and a long leash. At six feet five, his figure commanded the
respect given to fit men in positions of authority. He worked
hard, kept up with paperwork, and in his twenty years with
the Philadelphia Police Department, had not shared one
thing about his past—no simple feat for someone with an
Eastern European accent. Mikovich owed his professional
trajectory to three things: his drive, his work ethic, and his
ability to intimidate violent criminals without raising his

voice. Six weeks ago, he had been on the fast track to another promotion. And then he had been marked as incompetent by Mayor Glynda Green. Four years before, Glynda Green had been a committeewoman who ran a cleaning business; now she ran the city, and with one phone call to the commissioner, could ruin Mikovich's career. For all he knew, she might have already made the call thanks to Eric Ross.

For two years, Homicide and Narcotics had worked together to nail now twenty-nine-year-old Victor Rafaella, a Penn dropout who managed his cousin's pharmacy. Victor—he insisted on only using his first name—had left school for Vegas after winning a fortune playing online poker. He reappeared in Philadelphia a year later after the FBI arrested his cousin as part of a sting targeting dealers who sold opioids on the darknet.

Within months, authorities suspected Victor of operating a heroin ring connected to a series of near-deadly assaults, but they had no evidence. That changed on an October night the year before, when Detectives Eric Ross and Oscar Marino showed up at a warehouse looking for information on its owner, a New York-based real estate developer whose waterlogged corpse had surfaced on the banks of the Delaware River. Inside the warehouse, they found a severely beaten heavy equipment operator and two figures rushing out two separate back doors. The detectives gave chase but failed to nab the suspects. Ross, however, saw the reflection of one of the men in a store window. The face resembled Victor Rafaella's. The operator died without identifying his attacker. Ross asked Marino if he had seen the reflection. He hadn't but was willing to say he had.

Back at Homicide, Marino reported to Mikovich that they had their man. Ross didn't say anything. Mikovich called the district attorney, and City Hall celebrated. The detectives' testimonies would finally give them something to charge Victor with. But three hours after Victor entered custody, he walked away, gleefully grinning at photographers.

Detective Eric Ross, Mikovich had told the district attorney in a second phone call, would not be willing to say definitively that he had seen Victor at the murder scene. Marino would testify that he witnessed Victor's reflection, but if asked, Ross would say he couldn't be sure. The captain apologized for his department's earlier fervor. Yes, he could see the embarrassment. But better to release him now and look for more pressing evidence than keep Victor on a charge that wouldn't hold up, allowing his defense attorneys to forever say the police had falsely accused him.

Newly elected Mayor Glynda Green had been particularly excited about the arrest, a symbol of her administration's early efforts at curbing crime. Homicide's retraction felt like a slap in the face, a ploy to make her—Philadelphia's first female mayor, and a Black one at that—look weak. Captain Antony Mikovich took the brunt of her anger.

And then, most ironically, one night later, the Philadelphia Police Department announced the capture of the Strangler, a serial, almost mythologized rapist who had evaded the police for a decade. The culprit was a man named James Rosen, a middle-aged grocery clerk who had worked at a bodega under the Kensington El since high school. The arrest buried the story of Victor Rafaella's walk.

It was Detective Eric Ross who had made the arrest, but when he declined all interviews, Captain Antony Mikovich became the go-to source for quotes, a role that positioned him publicly as responsible for the Strangler's demise. Had

Ross taken his due for the Strangler's arrest, Mikovich would surely have become the fall guy for the Victor ordeal. Instead, the captain became the hero of a much larger narrative. For this, Mikovich knew, Eric Ross had redeemed himself to Homicide. But not to Glynda Green. The mayor knew—as did the entire force and most journalists—that the Strangler's arrest came too soon after Victor's release to be a coincidence. Somebody was treating them like puppets. And while Mikovich didn't know who was pulling the strings, he was pretty sure that Eric Ross did.

When Eric Ross entered the captain's office, Mikovich sat behind his desk with his hands folded. Lopez was visibly uncomfortable as she stood by the door.

"Good break with the mural ID," Mikovich said. "Lopez tells me that Forensics identified Pedro Martinez as a former employee of SugarHouse Casino."

Ross was taken aback with the employment detail.

"Just got off the phone with Wren," Lopez said quickly. "She tried you first."

Ross pulled out his phone. Two missed phone calls but no message.

"And that's why you should be together every second." Mikovich stared at Ross. "But a lot has happened tonight." He turned toward Lopez. "Anything we know about this Martinez?"

"No sir," she said.

"He might have been a regular at a Northern Liberties library," Ross contradicted. "I'm on it."

Mikovich noted Lopez's surprise. "No, you're BOTH on it." He paused. "And the victim at Central?"

"LeAnn DeVille," Lopez said. "Social worker, late fifties, husband thought she was on an emergency call."

"Why would he assume that?" Mikovich asked.

"Part of her job, sir," she said.

"Who do we have trying to source the Central murder mural?"

"Marino and McGee are making calls," Ross said.

"Good. So two bodies staged, different parts of town," Mikovich reviewed. "Camera at the high school out, and we haven't been able to find one on the cemetery. Eyewitnesses?"

"None," Lopez said.

"None that I'm sure of," Ross said after a moment.

"Sure of?" Mikovich unclasped his hands and sat back in his chair.

"Fishtown kid." Ross put pressure on his brow with his right thumb and middle finger. "A girl might have been playing in the cemetery around the time of the killing. I doubt she saw anything. Just mentioning it."

"Why mention it?" Mikovich asked.

"Just keeping you up to date."

Mikovich pressed his hands into his desk and rose. "You tell me twenty-four hours after realizing a minor could be in danger?" He stepped from behind his desk and leaned against a window. "That's not up to date." He looked at Lopez. "You agree?"

She didn't answer.

"Introduce Lopez to the girl."

"Lopez, could you wait outside?" Ross asked. She left the room quickly. "Give her to Marino," Ross said, lowering his voice. "We're all on this now. I can't do my job and have to explain every move I make to a rookie. He thinks out loud. Better for her."

"No."

They stared at each other.

"You're spying on—" started Ross.

"Not a spy. A partner."

"Come on, Mikovich."

"Enough. You took this team down. We had your back. This is your way of saying 'thank you.'"

Ross's body tensed. He stepped backward and focused on the window behind Mikovich. Three blocks away, the lit steeple of Christ Church stretched into the sky. He willed his body to relax, his mind to concentrate on something other than Mikovich. The captain sat back in his chair.

"The mayor wants your ass," Mikovich stated slowly. "She doesn't know who you are, but she wants you out."

Ross inhaled deeply. "I'll take her for a week. Maybe two. Then it's someone else's turn. I'll go back and check on the girl tomorrow."

"With Lopez."

"With Lopez."

Ross scanned the room for Lopez as he walked out of the captain's office. She wasn't at anyone's desk or any of the shared workstations. He walked toward a stairwell in the front hallway and saw her waiting by the elevator.

"Meet me in the Fishtown cemetery at eight" he said, almost pushing his way past her to the stairs.

"Maybe," she wanted to say. But she couldn't, because it was only her first day on the damn job, and nobody really cared what the hell she thought. Lopez closed her eyes as Ross's footsteps echoed on the stairs. She hated that she missed Rivera.

———•———

JESSIE WREN RESTED HER HEAD ON HER DESK IN HER shared office on the sixth floor of Forensics. The night's work was done—as much as it could be—and she was exhausted. She had been waiting several weeks to hash it out with Eric Ross though, and after what she had pulled on the phone an hour earlier, figured he might show up soon.

Two degrees hung on the wall behind her desk: a Master of Forensic Science from a satellite campus of Penn State, and a Bachelor of Education from Temple University.

For ten years, she and Ross had pursued the Strangler together, analyzing evidence, plugging away on theories, and ignoring other cases that demanded their attention. She needed to know why he had made an arrest without telling her, without even calling to debrief afterward. It was she who had convinced him they were looking for one man, not multiple lowlifes who targeted vulnerable sex workers in Kensington. It was she who had argued that they weren't looking for an occasional resident of the Tracks, but someone more established. James Rosen was a name she had suggested years before: a full-time employee of a corner bodega that sold everything from one-dollar soft pretzels to headbands and packaged belts that hung from the ceiling. During a three-year lull between attacks, his name had disappeared from their suspect list. Both considered that a killer attached to the neighborhood wouldn't have had the self-discipline to pause for such a long period. But much that happened in the woods surrounding the Tracks went unnoticed, Wren had argued. Ross thought maybe the killer had either died or fled.

And then, out of seemingly nowhere, Ross had arrested James Rosen and Rosen confessed to it all. Just like that. Ross alone received credit within the department, and Captain Antony Mikovich alone took credit for the department in the press. Her work, as usual, went unnoticed.

Most of the time, Wren didn't care about public acknowledgment. She couldn't. Things didn't work that way. To function successfully, her team built on one another's discoveries and observations. Conclusions validated their collective contributions. The pursuit of the Strangler had been her—and Ross's—pet project, and Ross's silence stung. He had nabbed Rosen without a word after acting on a lead he had not shared. And then he had disappeared for six weeks.

Wren's desk phone rang. Reception.

"Yep," she answered. "Thanks for the heads up."

She was almost glad when Ross hadn't answered her call earlier. It gave her a reason to talk to his new female partner, a move that she now found incredibly desperate as Ross appeared in her doorway.

"Seriously, Jessie?" he said with weariness.

She grabbed a rubber band to fidget with. "You're going to have to talk to me sooner or later."

"So you compromise a case by—"

"Compromise?"

"Come on, Jessie." He sighed.

"She's your partner, Ross."

"She's not my partner. And we both know it."

"Sorry you didn't pick up your phone."

"Not doing this now."

"You're the one who came here."

He turned to leave. Without thinking, she shot the rubber band at his butt. He spun around. Each stared at the other and smirked.

"You're right. We can do this later," she said. "Go—"

"Just shut up for a second." He rested his forearm against her doorframe and pressed his hand against his temple. "The victims—they were both staged in mural scenes."

"What?"

"I passed it tonight—a mural on North Broad called *Dreams in Flight*. Exact scene from the cemetery murder is painted on a brick building in the middle of a construction zone."

"And the—"

"Don't know about tonight's. Still waiting for a call."

He stretched his upper body and yawned.

"Ross, why didn't you tell me—"

"Just unfolded like it did. No time to think of anything but getting that asshole away from women forever. That's it."

"That's not it."

"Well that's it for me."

TUESDAY

6:30 a.m.

ROSS STOOD IN THE MIDDLE OF A GAS STATION PARKING lot on South Broad Street, directly south of City Hall in the theater district. He wore the same clothes he had worn the night before.

In front of the detective, against the brick wall of a homeless shelter, the mural *Ode to Life* spread across the wall. The work positioned different types of performing artists inside of a dollhouse, which was in turn painted inside of a music box. Above the dollhouse, a white female figure wore a gold facemask and purple frilly costume. Eyes turned to the sky, her expression begged to speak. Next to her, a ghostly face hid behind broken glass, mannequins, and masks.

A middle-aged officer approached Ross from behind.

"Morning, boss!"

"Bobby. Good to see you."

Officer Bob Alexander tapped an iPad and enlarged a headline on *Philly.com* that read "Murders Linked to Murals." He opened the picture of *Dreams in Flight*, the Olney mural, and held it in front of *Ode to Life*. The two men compared the paintings silently for a few minutes.

"Thought you might swing by," Alexander said. "Couldn't believe it when I heard the call. Been patrolling this neighborhood for years, and I've never really stopped to look at this one." He nodded at the mural.

69

"Any spectators since the news broke?" Ross asked.

"No, but it's early. Tourists are the only ones that pay real attention. Walking tours will start in a few hours."

"Pictures of the vics on there?"

Alexander pulled up another photo from the article that juxtaposed the victims' faces and stepped closer to the detective. Ross flinched. He remembered the guy was a leaner.

"What's the closest high school to here?" Ross asked. "Creative and Performing Arts?"

"Yeah, think so."

"They have a track?"

"No." Alexander thought for a second. "Southern High down on Snyder—that doesn't either."

"Other direction—Franklin?"

"Nope." Alexander stared at the ground. "Guess Central is the closest one with a track. But why stage it there? On a track? No track in this picture. Could have staged that body anywhere." He laughed. "Disgruntled pole vaulter maybe."

"A cemetery," Ross said, "and a track."

Alexander shrugged. "Not necessarily connected. Killer might be screwing with us." He gestured toward the newspaper. "Three thousand murals in this city. And this freak isn't done."

7:50 a.m.

DETECTIVE LINA LOPEZ WAS ALREADY AT THE CEMETERY gates when Ross arrived. A notebook bulged from the pocket of her jacket, but he didn't care to mention it. He knew he had been an ass the night before. He found himself wary of Lopez. He didn't know if he could trust the reason Mikovich gave for pairing them. If the captain was using her as some type of spy, Ross doubted the rookie realized it. The first thing he had noticed about Lopez was that she wanted his approval far too much.

"Listen," Ross said, "starting at noon today, we ride together."

She shrugged. "Okay."

"After this, I'll meet you back here."

"Fine. Your hand's better."

Ross nodded. He had replaced the Ace bandage with a small wrapping covered in athletic tape that circled his thumb and wrist.

Together, they approached an elderly man with thick white hair who was sweeping the sidewalk just inside of the closed cemetery gates. He had several bags overflowing with branches and debris gathered to one side.

"Excuse me," Ross said.

"Yep?"

Eighty? Caucasian. Five feet seven. Skinny. Hair like a wig. Flattened nose. Former boxer?

"Detective Eric Ross, Philadelphia Police. This is Detective Lina Lopez."

"Ted Morris," the man said as he unlocked the gates. "Here about the murder?"

71

"Yes, sir," Lopez said.

"Come on in."

Ross gazed past Morris. Ruby played in the far corner of the cemetery.

"Don't know anything." Morris spoke quickly. "Locked this place like I do, around dusk, went to McGrady's Pub around the corner. Someone told me later a bunch of cops had shown up. Junkie had died."

"You locked up at dusk," Lopez said. "Did you see the body?"

"No. Pretty sure I would have, but you know how routine goes."

"See anyone unusual since then? Suspicious?" she asked.

"Nope. Usual visitor types. It's pretty empty. Just me and Henry most mornings."

"Henry?" Lopez asked.

"Eh, Henry's a hawk." He chuckled. "Lives in that tree over there."

"Hawks are good luck, right?" she asked. Morris smiled at her.

"Are you a paid employee of the cemetery?" Ross asked.

"Sorta. Started as a volunteer—now a little money comes from the neighborhood association."

"Work anywhere else?" Lopez asked.

"Garrison's Garage—a few blocks over."

"Nice place," Lopez said. "Good people."

"The best." Morris smiled at her again.

"Why do tourists come here?" Ross asked.

"This place is historic," Morris answered. "Anthony Palmer was a founding father. Founded Fishtown too." He paused and spoke directly to Lopez. "In the eighteenth century, his daughter died and he realized kids needed a special burial place. Still known as Palmer's Children's Cemetery."

"But the children are only in that far corner over there," Lopez said, pointing.

"Not necessarily. Just historically."

"Ever notice any kids hanging around here?" Ross asked.

Ted hesitated. "You mean Ruby."

"Unaccompanied girl?"

"Sort of, yes."

"What made you think of her?" Lopez asked.

"Ruby's always here," he said. "She's over there now. You see her. Junior volunteer of sorts. Comes to see her little sister almost every day."

"How did her sister die?" Ross asked. Lopez shot him a look. She wondered how much investigating he had done the day before, and what he hadn't told the captain the night before.

"Ahhhh," Morris shook his head. "Premature childbirth. Her mother's no good. Dorothy—the grandmother—hadn't seen her daughter in years when she showed up pregnant with Ruby. Left Dorothy with the baby and didn't show up again until she was ready to deliver the second one."

The keeper pointed toward Ruby. He grinned. "Can't keep the girl out of here. She hops over the wall most mornings before school."

"What led you here, Mr. Morris?" Lopez asked.

"Ted, please." He ran a dirty hand through his hair.

"Ted then."

"Grandparents buried here, raised in the neighborhood. Just find it peaceful."

"Thanks," Ross said.

"Nice to meet you, officers." He smiled at Lopez. "Have something to write on?"

Amused, Ross handed over his clipboard and a pen.

Morris wrote his name and number. "In case anything else pops up…or you need to get inside. We're usually open 8 a.m. to dusk, but things come up."

"Thanks," Lopez said. "By the way, who else has a key?"

"Few people over the years," he mused. "Dorothy, for one, could let you in."

"Dorothy?"

"Dorothy Thompson, Ruby's grandmother."

"Why does she have one?" Ross asked.

"She used to be in charge of the Old Fishtown Civic Association. They helped pay for the landscaping—head of those groups usually end up with one. Never asked for it back, especially with Ruby's using it all the time." He chuckled. "Not that I've ever seen the girl enter through a door."

"Are you a member of that group?" Ross asked.

"No. Collapsed a few years ago. Too many fights over construction, development. Young versus old…always fighting."

"Any money left in the association when it folded?" Lopez asked.

"Sure, a few hundred. Maybe a grand. That's about it."

"Where did it go?"

"I get paid a little bit from it. And, in theory, preservation. These grave markers don't tend themselves."

"Well, you do good work here, Ted," Lopez said. "Thanks for your time."

"Don't be a stranger."

The detectives walked toward the children's corner of the cemetery.

"Where did she go?" Lopez asked.

"Jumped on over while the grave digger was hitting on you."

Lopez shrugged. "Mansplaining, more like it." She stopped near the brick wall. "Pretty athletic kid to get over this."

"She uses the tree," Ross said.

"How do you know?"

"Saw her."

Ross pointed out June's gravestone and Dorothy Thompson's house to Lopez. Reviewing his steps from Sunday night, he showed her the tree, its hollow, and the branches that could easily conceal an athletic child. Lopez used the tree to scramble on top of the brick wall. She peeked inside the hollow.

"Gardening tools. And…Ross…" She pulled back.

"What?"

"Eggshells."

"Weren't there on Sunday."

He walked over to June's gravesite. Broken eggshells lined the bottom of the headstone. Ross knew they would match what they found next to Pedro Martinez's body.

"Here, too, next to the grave," he said. "You don't happen to have—"

Lopez pulled two small clear evidence bags from her pocket. She offered them to Ross. "I keep them next to that notebook I use all the time."

He smirked and used one bag as a glove to carefully put the eggshells in the other.

Lopez crouched on the wall. "How many times have you talked to this kid?"

"Once."

"And grandma?"

"Twice. She's not a talker."

"Maybe I just talk to her first?"

"Go for it. I'll come knocking in ten."

75

8:15 a.m.

Dorothy Thompson opened the door fully when Detective Lopez knocked, once again anticipating an arrival. She stepped back into the house.

"School starts at 8:30. She'll be late I guess…" Thompson's words warbled together in clear frustration. She shut the door behind Lopez and walked into the living room.

The detective noted the thin carpet, sparse furniture, and an old television. The edges of the chairs were frayed. On the walls, a few pictures of Ruby and a couple of paintings hung from old frames. Lopez sat on a well-worn couch, opposite a chair that Thompson now rocked in. A small table outside of the kitchen held a stack of mail and an open package of printer paper half full.

"Are you okay, ma'am?" Lopez asked.

The woman shrugged. "Tired of the neighbors seeing police here." Lopez tried to figure out what was off-putting about her voice. It was deeper than expected, and the woman slurred her words. Was she drunk? Thompson rocked more slowly. Head tilted to one side, she grasped the arms of the rocking chair with gnarled fingers.

"Anyone come knocking since Detective Ross came over, ma'am?"

"No. But he's been here since. I see him staring at our house."

"Well, that's going to keep happening. Until we know what your granddaughter witnessed."

Thompson played with her fingernails.

"We need to know this for her safety. And yours." Lopez

heard a stair creak. "A young man died outside your door in a circumstance we don't understand."

"Nothing to do with us."

"We don't know of anybody but Ruby outside during the time of the murder."

Thompson stared at her nails. Ross knocked at the door. "Oh, Lord," she murmured and shuffled to the peephole.

Ruby came downstairs and sat on the sofa. She smiled at Lopez.

"Might as well..." Thompson said, opening the door and leaving Ross to let himself in.

"Thank you." He sat on the other side of Ruby.

"Girl's got to be at school," Thompson said.

"I can write her a note," Ross said.

"No," the grandmother whined. "I'll do it." She shuffled to the small table next to the kitchen and took a sheet from the package of printer paper.

"Ruby," Lopez said, "I'm Detective Lina Lopez. I want to help you and your grandmother with what happened. But we need to know a few more things. Did you see anything different than normal on Sunday night? Or day?"

"A dead body was different," Ruby said in a bold tone.

"Manners, girl!" snapped Thompson. Lopez smiled.

"Did you see the man killed, Ruby?"

Ruby shook her head no.

"Did you see him enter the cemetery?"

"No."

"Were you there earlier in the day?"

"Yes."

"When did you come inside?"

"Dinner."

"What time was that?"

"Six," Thompson answered.

"What did you eat?"

"Macaroni and cheese," Ruby answered. "Same thing I eat every night."

"Ah, you know," Thompson mumbled, sounding embarrassed.

"And then?" Lopez asked.

Ruby sighed. "Then homework, then I read." She glanced at Thompson. "Lights out at 8:30!" the girl practically yelled. Lopez's eyes widened.

Thompson muttered something unintelligible.

"Did you go right to bed?" Lopez asked.

"No."

"Why?"

Ruby shrugged and glanced at her grandmother.

"Sometimes my mom calls…"

"No, she don't," Thompson said. "She don't call, she don't visit."

Ruby folded her arms across her chest.

"No crying now," Thompson said, her voice warbling.

Lopez kept up her momentum. "What did you read that night?"

"*Bobbsey Twins.*"

"*Bobbsey Twins?*" Lopez asked.

"My mom's books."

"Your mother didn't read. They were my books," Thompson mumbled.

Lopez paused. "So 8:30. Lights out. Do you go right to bed?" she asked gently. "Or maybe look out the window to say goodnight to your sister?"

Ruby nodded yes.

"And what did you see?"

"Someone in a white dress. Looked like an angel on the ground."

"Nobody else?"

Ruby shook her head no.

"When did you go outside?" Lopez asked.

"Then. I wanted to protect June." She picked at her fingernails.

"How did you get past your grandmother?" Lopez asked.

"She was sleeping in her chair. I snuck through the back door."

"And then what?"

"I ran to the grave." Ruby's voice dropped to almost a whisper.

"Through the entrance?"

Ruby shook her head no.

"She climbs up the wall," Thompson said.

"What did you do then? Did you go to the body?"

"No, I went to June. Then the police came, and I got scared."

Lopez looked at Ross, who had an eye on Thompson.

"And you came back when Detective Ross saw you jump back over the wall?"

Ruby nodded.

"What did you do for all that time in the cemetery?"

"Hid from him!" She gestured toward Ross. "He didn't go away like the others."

"What made you come back?"

"I got tired!" the girl said impatiently. "Thought he'd be there all night."

"Did you hear her come back in, Ms. Thompson?"

"Yes."

"And nobody has been back since Detective Ross knocked later that night?"

Thompson shook her head no.

Lopez turned to Ruby and moved a little closer to her. "Ruby, has anybody tried to talk to you about the crime?"

"No."

"Have you talked to anybody at school, or on the computer, or on a phone, about it?"

"Just him," Ruby said, turning to Ross.

"She don't talk to anybody not buried," Thompson answered.

"Ruby," Ross said quietly. "Do you ever talk to anyone in the cemetery who isn't buried?"

She flashed a glance at her grandmother.

"Just people I know."

Ross pulled the evidence bag from an inside jacket pocket. "Ruby, we found eggshells in the tree's hollow and by June's grave today. They weren't in either spot on Sunday night. They look like the ones we pulled from the crime scene."

Thompson moaned and moved back to the rocking chair.

"Ruby, I need to know when you got these," Ross said.

"That night," she whispered.

"Did you walk right up to the dead body, Ruby?"

"Close to it, but then I got scared." Her voice wavered. Lopez moved closer to her on the couch.

"Is that when you took the shells?" Ross asked.

"Yes."

"Why did you take them, sweetie?" Lopez asked gently.

"Never seen such big shells before. I just...I just took a small piece that had broken off a big one. And then cracked it into tinier ones.

"Why did you bring them back here?"

80

"I put them in my pocket when the police came and then I forgot."

"When did you put them back in the cemetery?" Ross asked.

"Last night."

"Why?"

"I thought they belonged there."

Lopez leaned in. "Ruby, is there anything else you took? No matter how small?"

Ruby shook her head no. Tears welled. Lopez turned to Thompson.

"We need to stay in touch." She pulled a card from her wallet. "My number. You have Ross's." Thompson nodded.

"We're going to make sure there is an unmarked car nearby," Lopez continued. Thompson slouched further into herself.

"Ruby," Lopez said. "You or your grandmother needs to call if you see anybody different around, especially if they try to talk to you. About anything. Promise?"

"Promise."

Lopez hesitated. "Ruby," she said slowly, "does June ever communicate with you?"

"No! She's dead!" Tears spilled onto her cheeks.

"She ever see things she tells you about somehow? People visiting?"

"Nooo!" Ruby tried not to wail.

"Okay."

Ruby trembled. Without warning, she threw herself into Lopez. The young detective embraced her and glanced at Thompson. The grandmother made a guttural sound as she rocked.

"THINK SHE'S ABUSIVE?" LOPEZ ASKED AS THEY LEFT DOROthy Thompson's house.

"No..." Ross sighed. "Something's off...might just be that the woman's awkward and doesn't know what to do with her."

"A child that she raised."

"What do you think?"

Lopez lowered her head. "My tolerance for child abuse is pretty high."

Ross waited for her to correct herself. Lopez's face registered no emotion.

"Why?" he asked.

"Come on. Most anything's better than protective services."

They walked a block to Frankford Avenue. Across the street, middle school kids in blue uniforms screamed with laughter at a crowded bus stop. Boys teased a few of the girls, who charged at them with pretend anger. Two older kids threw a football back and forth across the busy street as others ate potato chips and scrolled through smart phones on stoops.

"So how do you call it?" Lopez asked. "Wait as long as you can?"

"Instinct. Every time is different."

A breeze blew the smell of cut grass up Frankford.

"What?" Ross asked.

"Huh?"

"You flinched."

"Déjà vu."

One of the kids tossing the football missed a catch and crashed into the side of an SUV. Kids at the bus stop burst into raucous laughter. The driver, a woman with kids strapped into the backseat, had seen him and stopped just before he collided. She rolled down a window.

"You all right?" the lady asked.

The kid grabbed the ball and ran off.

Lopez smirked. "Serves him right."

"There's something I need to do," Ross said. "Should take about an hour, maybe more."

"Noon then. I'll meet you here?" She started walking away from him. "I'll follow up on any security camera leads. Maybe check in with the 26th."

"That's right," Ross said. He stopped and focused on the ground. Lopez didn't know if he wanted her to walk away or wait. She waited.

"You deal much with Michaela Alvarez there?" Ross asked.

"Michaela Alvarez." Lopez tightened her lips. "Known *of* her a long time. But beyond following leads, not much contact."

"She ever give you leads?"

"No."

"Ever hear of her trading information for a favor?"

"Not specifically," Lopez hesitated. "But she needs us to recognize her as the Mother Theresa of Kensington."

Ross smirked. "How did you see her doing that?"

"She knows how to talk to cops. Acts like she's helping more than she is."

"That the opinion of most?"

"She didn't come up that much."

"Go to her now," Ross said, checking his watch. "She might be on rounds, but she'll be back at All Saints soon if so. Tell her you're following up on my conversation yesterday. See what she says. Sniff around."

"Got it. By the way, made an appointment with the head of City Murals. Woman named Reverend Donna Raymond. At 2:30 at their office in Fairmount."

Ross cocked his head.

"That okay?" she asked.

"Yeah. Good."

9:25 a.m.

LOPEZ USED THE WALK TO ALL SAINTS TO CONSIDER ROSS'S attitude shift toward her. Had it really changed though? He didn't seem to be interested in games. Perhaps Mikovich had ripped him a new one after she left the night before. But that would probably give him cause to dislike her more, not less. She knew it didn't matter. She had already decided that Rivera was right. She was a type of punishment that Ross had to accept.

He had surprised her with the name Michaela Alvarez. Lopez was a little surprised Ross had gone to her about Pedro Martinez—if that was the topic of their conversation the day before. In her several years as a cop, Lopez and her colleagues had never considered Alvarez anything but a pain in the ass. Hers had been a figure on the streets for years. Lopez had known several women like Alvarez while bouncing around foster homes in northwest Philadelphia, neighborhoods full of liberal churches and small nonprofits that competed for the same funds to do the same type of work with the same people. Middle-aged and assuming pastoral roles, women like Alvarez were focused in the moment and forgetful otherwise. The good ones made sure their vulnerable populations had at least their basic needs met. The others went to meetings, shuffled papers, and delegated their responsibilities to volunteers. LeAnn DeVille, Lopez assumed, was one of the latter.

The police, she knew, had engaged most with Michaela Alvarez, Pastor Todd, and their congregation of hippies when All Saints had led local protests against the closing of the Tracks. In the six months leading up to the eviction of homeless addicts from their decades-old home, Alvarez had spoken at community meetings, civic associations, churches—wherever she could find an audience to rally behind her message: that displacing a community of outsiders, no matter how controversial their behavior, would have social ramifications beyond what anyone might anticipate.

Lopez had seen her in action at a meeting of the Frankford Development Corporation, where Lopez had served as the precinct's liaison to address neighborhood concerns. Alvarez had clearly articulated her opinion during a question-and-answer session that turned into an impromptu call for action to block police efforts. Her cry had been so successful that, by the end of the meeting, nearly everyone in the room had plied Lopez with the same questions that Alvarez kept repeating.

Where will these people go? Are the police ready to protect us and our children? What will you do when sales, users, dealers increase on the streets?

Lopez had texted Rivera to get her out of there. The next day, she reported Alvarez's vision at roll call. The woman was clearly leveraging her reputation to enroll neighborhoods in far more than letter-writing campaigns, Lopez said. She was implying they riot. Her fellow officers shrugged. Michaela Alvarez was right, Rivera said. Closing the Tracks would exacerbate the problem. Addicts would shoot up on street corners, under closed storefronts, in neighborhood pocket parks. Begging would increase, and so would overdoses on street corners. Only parts of urban America realized the scope and sadness of opioid addiction. Most of the progressive do-gooders who lived elsewhere had no idea how shitty it was to live near its wastelands.

But the police had very public orders. They would close the Tracks and deal with the fallout when it happened. By then, said the sergeant, Michaela Alvarez would be back to handing out peanut butter sandwiches as junkies migrated to new homes on the street.

Lopez entered the GYM the way most of its visitors did: from a back door in an alley behind All Saints Church. In one corner, several children played with toys under the supervision of a kind-looking elderly Hispanic woman. Across the gymnasium, two bouncer types were in the middle of transitioning the space, breaking down tables from the morning's hot meal and placing chairs in circles for the mid-morning Narcotics Anonymous group. They piled the folded tables onto a roller cart that they then pushed into a hallway that led to the sanctuary, storage rooms, Sunday School rooms, and a small kitchen that could crank out an impressive amount of food.

The GYM operated on food donations and the charity of church volunteers. It did employ security guards. This all-male team of bouncers kept the peace by maintaining and enforcing a simple code of conduct: if anyone stole, stalked, fought, or behaved indecently, that person's name and photo were added to lists on the back of the entrance door. Once a name or photo appeared on a list, that individual could never enter the GYM again. There were no second chances. The lists were short.

Opposite Lopez, heavy curtains framed the front of a stage. She knew it blocked cots from the view of passing cops like her. For decades, the GYM had offered temporary shelter for people in need, an off-the-record setup that authorities knew about. Because the GYM fell under the auspice of All Saints, it assumed a type of amnesty afforded to religious institutions. Rarely did the police bring it into investigations. If the 26th had a question about a missing person or a person of interest, it communicated with the small security team or Pastor Todd. Lopez had come by a few times on such calls. Nobody connected to the place ever said much of anything.

Michaela Alvarez had trained her staff to say only what was absolutely necessary. That was why the police largely left her and her operation—if it was, indeed, her operation—alone. Between the sanctuary provided by the church and the basic needs it met for people shut out of overcrowded shelters and thirty-day rehabilitation programs, the GYM made Michaela Alvarez and Pastor Todd off-limits to the police. The authorities needed them to be as productive as possible, especially with the sharp increase in young addicts roaming the streets.

A large African American security guard approached Lopez. He wore a Temple Football black T-shirt and black sweatpants. Each scanned the other and realized they had spoken before. The guard motioned for Lopez to approach as he walked past her and sat on a high-top stool near the back door. She bristled but forced a small smile.

"Off duty?" he asked.

"Just different clothes. It's *Detective* Lopez now."

He smirked.

"I'm looking for Michaela Alvarez," she said.

"Okay." He sat still for several seconds, making no attempt to look for anyone else to help her. Lopez had expected some resistance but not so soon. She pushed back.

"And I also want to know how often a Pedro Martinez came in here?"

"Never heard of him."

"Really? With all the traffic you get?"

"He might have been here, but I don't know the name."

"You know his picture though—he's been in the news."

"Sorry."

"What about your colleagues?"

"You'll have to ask each of them."

They stared at one another.

"You know how many cats come in here," he finally said. "If his name isn't on the list, and his photo isn't on the list, and he only shows up once in a while…we don't know. Wasn't a regular. That's all I know."

"So where's Michaela?"

"Don't know. Probably on her rounds or in the sanctuary. Helping people. Because that's what we do here." He spoke slowly. Too slowly. Lopez shot a look around the room. Nobody was in it except for the old lady and the kids.

"Security cameras here?"

"No."

"That's odd."

"Don't need them."

Lopez and the guard locked eyes. She pulled out her notebook.

"What's your name?

"Jake Ward."

"I'll take myself to the sanctuary then, Jake Ward," she said, writing down his name. Lopez took her time walking across the floor toward the hallway. Every few steps, she paused to jot down a few things for dramatic effect.

Entering the corridor, she was surprised that it was also empty. Surprised and relieved—she needed a moment to collect her mind. Jake Ward reminded Lopez of each of her older brothers: dismissive know-it-alls. Rivera hadn't liked the way she handled the type, said she got too defensive too quickly, evidence of three older brothers ordering her around. Lopez disagreed. She had only lived with her brothers until she was seven. Observing them had prepared her for foster care.

Lopez had survived eight years in the system. She didn't have stories of abuse, neglect, and abandonment like other former foster kids had. The one thing her shitty family had taught her was how to focus on one specific goal at the expense of all else. Her father had focused on teaching his sons how to make money before he left them. Her mother had focused on getting pills. Her brothers had focused on their father's lessons, and she, overlooked by them all, had chosen physical safety. That meant that she slept with a knife under her body, and when one of her mother's dealers showed up in her bedroom, she cut him. Then she told a teacher, and she never saw anyone in her family again.

Her focus now was being the one to uncover Pedro Martinez's story. She knew the neighborhood better than anyone on her Homicide team. The story was hers to break, hers to prove herself with.

Lopez looked in the window of each closed door that she passed in the hallway, and in the open kitchen. The guards who had cleared the room with Jake Ward had to have gone somewhere. From what she could tell, most of the empty rooms she passed served as storage areas; each had the lights off and the door locked. At the end of the hall, Lopez climbed two flights of stairs and entered the sanctuary from behind the pulpit. Michaela Alvarez wasn't there. Neither was anyone else. The silent room held only rows of perfectly aligned chairs.

A heavy thud in the balcony startled her. Lopez put a hand on her gun holster and crouched behind the pulpit. A minute later, she crossed the sanctuary and entered the foyer behind the church entrance. An empty chair sat next to a long table filled with stacks of flyers and church bulletins. In front of the chair on the table, a Bible was opened to the first page of Psalms, and a spiral notebook to a blank page. Lopez flipped through the notebook. Longhand cursive filled other pages with what looked like sermon notes and scripture references. She scanned the foyer for security cameras. None that she could see.

Back outside, Lopez made a call far sooner than she had planned.

"Rivera. A favor. Can you get to All Saints and try to nail down exactly what's going on behind that red curtain at the GYM?"

She grinned.

"Yeah, besides the Wizard of Oz, jackass."

11:45 a.m.

Ross walked around the dirt path surrounding Penn Treaty Park three times before approaching the fishermen. Two elderly white men stood with fishing lines on the river's edge, below a rocky ledge and a row of bushes. In the afternoons and evenings, the same types sat on park benches under elm trees across from the ledge, behind fishing lines that arched over Ross's running course.

The old men, both in baseball caps, studied the water, which occasionally yielded small catfish and trout. Their shoes had sunk slightly into a narrow stretch of mud otherwise littered with Cheetos and Tastykake wrappings, beer bottles and crushed cans of Red Bull. Blocks away, bells from a Catholic church rang a noontime hymn fifteen minutes too early.

The only other person fishing was a teenager playing hooky. He stood behind the ledge, about ten yards from the detective, next to a bike he had stashed between the bushes and a metal fence crowned with barbed wire. Reaching about forty feet in the air, the fence ran the length of the park's north end. It separated Penn Treaty from run-down factory grounds.

Ross walked to the ledge, far enough from the kid so as not to startle him. With Pedro's picture extended in front, he called toward the old men.

"Excuse me, gentlemen." They didn't turn around. "Excuse me," he said in a sterner, louder voice. One of the men startled and jabbed his companion with an elbow.

"What?" the other yelled.

Eighties. Caucasian. Leathery skin, red faces. Hearing loss.
"I'm looking for a missing person. Can I show you a photo, please?" He beckoned for the men to come up.

"What's he sayin'?" the second man yelled again. The friends scraped their muddy shoes on a rock and helped one another through the brush and up the bank. Ross wondered how long it had taken them to descend.

He extended the picture of Pedro Martinez.

"Have you seen this man?"

Both looked closely and shook their heads no.

"We have reason to believe he was here at the park on Sunday night, and perhaps for good amounts of time before that. He's slight, about five feet five, and very skinny."

"Nope."

"Are you sure?" Ross asked.

The hard-of-hearing man looked at the other, who spoke for both of them.

"We don't much talk to kids that come and go."

"But you would recognize regulars?"

"No, I wouldn't say that. We focus on fishing."

"But you would say you are regulars."

"Sure."

Ross noticed the teenager paying attention to the conversation.

"Anybody ever bother anyone while you're here?"

"Music too loud sometimes."

"Okay," Ross said. "Here's my card if you remember something, or see something strange worth noting."

The men turned and gingerly began to help one another back to the water.

Ross moved toward the teenager.

"I don't know, man," the kid called out.

Seventeen? Bad acne. Loner.

"At least look at the picture." He approached with Pedro's photo extended. The teenager's eyes didn't flinch.

"That's the dead guy. From the mural killing."

Ross nodded.

"Why you acting like he's still alive?"

"His name was Pedro Martinez. Did you see him here alive?"

"Looks familiar."

"Need a truancy officer to help you remember?"

The kid sighed, rested his pole on the fence, and took out a cigarette.

"Those old dudes seen him, too, they just don't know it. He'd hang around down on those rocks down there."

"How long did you notice him here?"

"Don't know. Couple of months off and on."

"Alone?"

"Yeah. With a big black dude sometimes. Huge. Others too I guess."

"Would you recognize the black guy?"

"No. Only really saw from behind."

"Ever talk to him?"

"Nope."

"Ever talk to Pedro?"

"Nope."

"Ever see Pedro anywhere else?"

The kid nodded yes and looked toward the entrance of the park. "He'd stand by that old statue up there."

"Of William Penn?"

"Guess so. Would just stand there and stare. Walk around it and stare."

"At what?"

"I don't know. Statue, I guess."

Ross paused to think about the statue. It stood on top of an obelisk positioned on a circular cement platform.

"That's what I thought when I saw he had died."

"What?"

"That's the weird kid by the statue."

"Why did he stand out?"

He shrugged. "Happened enough."

"Do you think he was homeless?"

"Maybe. Didn't live here though."

"How do you know?"

"Just could tell."

Ross handed him a card. "Let me know if anything else comes to mind."

The kid pocketed it and grabbed his fishing pole. As Ross walked away, he turned to see the teenager absorbed into the same stance and scene as the old timers below him.

———————————•———————————

THE STATUE OF WILLIAM PENN WAS ONLY ABOUT THREE feet high, yet it served as the crown of a tribute at the front entrance to Penn Treaty. It stood atop a cement platform with the circumference of a large tree trunk. Several plaques decorated the tribute: each reviewed the history of the site, believed to be the location of William Penn's ceremonial peace treaty with Shackamaxon, a Delaware Indian chief, in a tribal village north of Penn's Landing. One related the history of "The Great Elm at Shackamaxon," a centuries-old tree under which the ceremony may have taken place. After a storm toppled the tree, local historians memorialized it with a pillar.

Ross again traced Pedro's route to the cemetery: through the parking lot, across Delaware Avenue, through a neigh-

95

borhood, across Girard, left on Frankford, right on Berks.

As far as he knew, the 26th District had no luck in finding footage of Pedro Martinez entering the cemetery, and without an eyewitness, the police still didn't know if he was alone or accompanied. He would ask Lopez to push them more.

Shit, he thought. *Lopez.*

"Ross! Hey!"

She was yelling from across the street.

"What—? Ross, it's 1:30. You walked right past me. We were supposed to meet at the intersection back there an hour ago."

"Sorry. Got sidetracked." He paused. "Why didn't you call?"

"I don't have your number, Ross. And I didn't want to call Homicide and ask for my partner's number." She paused, irritated. "And the car is locked."

"Okay, let's go." He stepped past Lopez on the way to his squad car. She followed.

2:15 p.m.

DETECTIVE LINA LOPEZ RODE SILENTLY IN THE PASSENGER
seat during the two-mile drive from Fishtown to Fairmount.
The car was cleaner than any she had shared with the 26th.
Rides with Rivera had always smelled of the Wawa coffee
that sloshed from his cup onto the wheel, the dashboard,
the computer keyboard…she had hated the sticky residue
that never lost its smell.

Already, though, her old partner had come through for
her. Rivera had called during the hour she had to kill waiting for Ross. He and a few other officers could confirm her
understanding of the stage: it held about a dozen cots and
served as a temporary shelter at any given time for about a
dozen people. Rivera had stopped by the GYM with some
fake story but couldn't get a peek without putting up a fight,
and he wasn't sure it was time for that. She agreed.

"Went by All Saints. No Alvarez," she said as Ross
searched for parking.

"Talk to anyone?"

"Security guard gave me the runaround."

Ross's seeming absentmindedness that morning had
put the previous night's activities into the perspective she
needed: he wasn't testing her, and he wasn't pissed that she
was tagging along. He was just preoccupied, and he damn
well wasn't going to change his habits for her. And why
should he? They were after a killer who was going to strike
again. There was a job to do, and if she wanted in on it, she
would have to prove herself enough to make him remember
to include her. This next visit was a start.

Once Lopez had learned of the connection between murals and the homicides, she had thought to contact City Murals. The nonprofit was well known to the city's social service agencies: it had partnered with many of them to complete paintings in public spaces throughout Philadelphia for nearly two decades. Lopez had worked on a couple of murals herself for service credits in high school, and as a cop, she knew City Murals participated in restorative justice and rehabilitation programs citywide.

City Murals shared its headquarters with a church tucked into a wealthy block in the Art Museum neighborhood. In the late 1980s, a forward-thinking minister had saved the grand Romanesque Revival building, home of an aging congregation, from growing maintenance bills and hungry developers by renting unused spaces as artist studios. City Murals had found a home in an old gymnasium on the church's second floor, and the visionary minister, Reverend Donna Raymond, retired from the pulpit and became the program's director.

Donna Raymond greeted Detectives Ross and Lopez at a side door to the church.

"You take lead," Ross murmured to Lopez just before the door opened.

She had planned on it.

"Detectives, hello," said Raymond, a woman in her sixties with silver hair. She wore baggy black workout clothes and seemed pleasant enough, but Lopez could sense irritation.

"Follow me," she directed.

Ross and Lopez trailed Raymond up two narrow staircases and onto a decrepit balcony that overlooked the gymnasium workshop. On one side of the building, an adult instructed a group of teenagers holding paintbrushes. They huddled around two tables, one full of photographs and another covered with a thin tapestry.

"I've been thinking over your questions, and certainly the situation," Raymond said. "No names stand out. You do know that thousands have assisted us over the years." She gestured below. "This is an advanced art class from Benjamin Franklin High School. They're working with parachute cloth."

"Parachute cloth?" Ross asked.

"We haven't just painted on walls for years now," Reverend Raymond answered.

"So what is it?"

"A thin tapestry. Those students near the photos will pick one as the mural's illustration. We'll then hang the tapestry on a wall, project the photo onto it, trace the projected image onto the cloth, put the tapestry back on the table, and then the kids will do a type of paint by numbers job."

"Then you'll hang the tapestry on a building?" Lopez asked.

"It's a synthetic. We'll attach it with acrylics."

"Is this how most murals are made then?" Ross asked.

"Yes," Raymond said, smiling. "We can control the elements better that way."

"And this is how convicts participate in prison?" Lopez asked.

Raymond flinched. "We have weekly art clinics and a prison workshop at Graterford Prison, yes."

"How many work on the average mural?" Ross asked.

"No average. Usually a head artist or two, assistants, and countless volunteers—sports teams, elementary schools, neighbors, and yes, prisoners."

Lopez and Ross gazed down on the scene in the gym. A few of the students noticed they were being watched and waved up at Raymond.

"Come to our office." Raymond turned back down a hallway.

Bookshelves, printing equipment, and corkboards filled with photographs of people, monuments, parks and houses framed the inside of the City Murals office. The floor-to-ceiling shelves—full of art publications, manuals, and leaflets—looked unsteady. Donna Raymond gestured toward chairs and turned off a loud printer. She pulled a material resembling wallpaper from the printer and sat in a chair across from the detectives.

"Have you all contacted your artists?" Lopez asked.

"Some," she said, grimacing. "They're thinking."

"Some more than others?" pressed Lopez.

"What do you mean?"

"How long has City Murals worked with the court system?" Lopez asked.

"From the beginning."

"There must be a running list of volunteers on probation or formerly incarcerated," Ross said.

"Perhaps several very, very long ones," Raymond said, "and compiled in different databases and emails and spreadsheets. We don't keep fastidious records, I'll admit." She paused. "The best we can do is try to think of those who didn't want to cooperate, but of course it's easier to remember faces than names, and—"

Lopez interrupted. "Excuse me…"

Raymond stared at her.

"This is a double homicide investigation," Lopez said, "and one in which your murals play a prominent role. We're asking you to review every name on every list, email, and piece of paper that you have—"

"No," Raymond said coolly. She paused for dramatic effect. "You are investigating two illustrative murders perhaps patterned after our murals."

Lopez glanced at Ross, who stared at Raymond.

"Your killer, detectives, could have any number of interests, and any number of connections to the victims. Correct?"

"Yes," Ross said.

Raymond lifted her hands and shrugged her shoulders. "So I'm not so quick to judge any Tom, Dick, or Harry who wasn't so enthusiastic about painting."

Ross cleared his throat and spoke up. "The two murals 'perhaps patterned' in crime scenes so far, can their artists recall any problems surrounding construction?"

"No."

"Any artist who worked on both?" he asked.

"The lead artists did not overlap. As for volunteers… again, nearly impossible to know."

"Can you think of a time in recent memory when a mural upset people?" Ross asked.

Raymond answered without hesitating. "Not necessarily. On occasion, community members criticize a mural's theme. But, in general, neighborhoods welcome our work. The list of requests to beautify spaces is quite long. Once a spot is selected, we convene community meetings, and themes come from these conversations."

"Can you give us examples of controversial themes?"

Raymond sighed. "Restorative justice. Suicide prevention. Environmental abuse. Pet abuse. Domestic abuse. LGBTQIA+ rights. Veterans' rights. Addiction…more?"

"The murals in question?" Lopez asked.

"*Dreams in Flight* is about transcending brokenness, and *Theater of Life* is about the arts. Neither was controversial in the least." Raymond stood up. "Tomorrow evening, we have a community unveiling in Mantua. Come if you like. See the process at work." She cocked her head to the side. "It's quite joyful," she added without a smile.

———————•———————

THE DETECTIVES DROVE FOR SEVERAL BLOCKS WITHOUT talking. Lopez knew that she had gotten too defensive. She wasn't sure what bothered her more: Donna Raymond's dismissive tone or her seeming indifference to the murders.

Trolleys and road crews slowed the busy intersection at Broad and Girard. Through Ross's driver's side window, Lopez stared past a Kentucky Fried Chicken to a mural it partially covered.

"I've passed this intersection most of my life," she said. "And I've only ever paid attention to the KFC sign." Ross followed her gaze. The busy fast-food joint covered a sweeping mural of black activists leading into and during the civil rights movement: Octavius Catto, Bayard Rustin, Cecil B. Moore, A. Philip Randolph, Carolyn D. Moore, Jessie Fauset. Their faces, names and history loomed larger than life over one of the busiest intersections in the city, but the average passerby was focused on getting from corner to corner, stop to stop, meal to meal.

"Someone needs to hit that meeting tomorrow," Lopez told Ross. "*Philly.com* already interviewed former clients of DeVille's—former foster kids who said she ignored them in abusive situations."

Ross stared straight ahead.

"I'll track them down," Lopez said.

"Good."

Another light cycle and they hadn't moved more than a yard.

"Can I ask you something?" Lopez asked.

"Yep."

"Were you pissed I was assigned to you?"

"Part of the job."

"Just thinking through the warm welcome and all."

Ross smirked.

"What did you think I was going to ask?"

He shrugged. "Can't guess what someone's thinking."

"Isn't that what we do? Figure out what people are thinking? Why they do what they do?"

He paused for so long that she thought he was ignoring her.

"Two different things much of the time," he finally said. "People don't always think before they act. Motive, we look for. Purpose. Drive. But you can get too caught up trying to understand *a* thought in *a* moment. Distracts from larger plan and purpose." He glanced at her. "You know what I mean."

"Give me an example."

"You back there with Raymond. Who knows why she was acting like that. Maybe she's pissed we're there. She's certainly pissed about murals being targeted in this way— the PR of it all. Or maybe she's getting a divorce or having a hard time with a few of those kids or worried about funding. Then we show up."

They drove a couple of blocks in silence.

"Or," he continued, "maybe she is the mastermind behind both killings and wants to get us the hell out of there. Probably not, but maybe. We just take what she gives us, keep all the options open, and think on it. No point in getting heated with one interaction. You need to do that on the beat, I get that." He paused. "But now you have to be more patient."

"Hang on." Lopez pulled out her notebook. "I need to write that down."

Ross grinned.

"What's next?"

"I need to track down a few leads on security cameras," he said. "I learned earlier that Pedro Martinez spent time at this local library coming up on the right. That he worked there in some capacity. Why don't you go in and ask around?"

"You learned this earlier today?"

"I learned it earlier."

He pulled up at the corner of 6th and Girard. Across the street, clusters of adults hung out in front of a laundromat connected to a rundown doughnut shop. Lopez recognized several of them. People constantly passed between the parking lot in front of the doughnut shop and a methadone clinic operated by Temple University Hospital a block away.

"I'll stay in the car and make some calls," he said.

"Can I see that clipboard of yours?" Lopez asked.

He grabbed it from the dashboard and handed it to her. She wrote down a phone number.

"This is mine. Text me yours."

"Will do."

4:30 p.m.

THE RAMONITA DE RODRIGUEZ BRANCH OF THE PHILA-
delphia Free Library was located at 6th and Girard on the
western edge of Northern Liberties. Abandoned renova-
tions and check cashing joints dotted the blocks east and
west of the small building, but a mosaic along its brick
walls brightened the otherwise bleak urban landscape.
Encircling the library were tiles that paid homage to book
topics and their corresponding numbers on the Dewey
decimal system. Like most branches of the Free Library of
Philadelphia, Rodriguez was a haven for the homeless, and
like most of the city's librarians, its employees had come to
accept their primary audience of downbeat patrons. A small
branch, the library devoted half of its space to a children's
literacy center. As soon as she entered, Lopez realized her
visit coincided with the library's most popular event: after-
school programs for middle-school kids.

A kind-looking female librarian with masculine features
greeted her from behind the checkout counter. On the left
side of the library, homeless men read newspapers at tables
in the adult section. On the right, preteens talked loudly,
closely watched by a security guard who monitored their
activity from a video camera feed.

Lopez approached the guard, stationed across from the
checkout desk.

"Hello, I'm Detective Lina Lopez."

The guard's posture immediately straightened.

"How can I help you?" she said, smiling. Red lipstick
covered part of her two front teeth.

"I'm here inquiring about a former employee. A man named Pedro Martinez."

"Mm-mmm, Pedro didn't work here."

"He didn't?"

"Nope," the guard said. "He was in and out of here all the time though." She gestured toward the adult section. "Just like most of those birds over there." She shook her head. "Horrible what happened. What kind of shit was he mixed up in?"

"Didn't work here at all?" Lopez asked. "Mop the floors, clean the bathroom, even as a volunteer?"

"No, no. Ask Ms. Jerry if you want." She pointed to the librarian and leaned toward Lopez, mumbling something.

"I'm sorry, I didn't quite get that," the detective said.

Laughter erupted from one of the kids' tables. The guard leaned toward the monitor and squinted.

"Knock it off, Kamiah!" she yelled.

"Didn't do nothin', Ms. Marie!" a short seventh-grade boy with a mischievous grin yelled back.

She spun around in her chair. "Didn't do nothin' to get kicked out of here in a minute!" The kids laughed harder.

"I said"—the guard turned back to Lopez—"She's *in transition!*"

Lopez took a step back. The kids quieted but soon returned to their normal volume. Lopez tried to redirect her. "Anything make Pedro stand out?"

"No," Ms. Jerry said from behind the desk. She continued stamping books as if she hadn't been spoken of like a character in one of their stories. "He just read. Newspapers mostly."

"Anything else?"

"Mmmmm…you know, he was interested in history."

"What kind?"

"Philadelphia—this neighborhood, the River Wards. He asked if I could help him find a book on Penn Treaty Park once."

"Did you?"

"Yes, but he didn't like it."

"Why?"

"Too academic. The history of the park is a smaller story in larger ones about Philadelphia's history. They bored him."

"Why was he interested in the park?"

"I don't know." The librarian sighed thoughtfully. "He liked spending time there. He knew about its historic importance—that it was where William Penn supposedly made friends with the Indians." She smiled. "He didn't like the word *Indians. Native Americans,* he'd tell me to say. And he didn't like the word *supposedly.*"

"What do you mean?"

Ms. Jerry shrugged. "He liked the idea of it being in a real setting, not just a rumored spot. He told me to prove it. So I found him a book and he flipped through it, gave it back."

"Could he read?"

"Sure he could read."

The librarian motioned for Lopez to approach the desk and then leaned forward. "See those men over there?" she whispered, gesturing toward homeless-looking men sitting around a table with newspapers. "You'd be surprised how many read the papers—every word."

"Thank you," Lopez said.

"And one thing," Ms. Jerry said. "Papers got it wrong. Pedro might have been homeless, but I don't think so. And they seem to think he used." She shook her head no. "Always alert. Never saw him on anything."

"That's right," the guard said.

Lopez walked to the adult side and browsed the stacks. She paused in front of the Local History section and skimmed the titles, pulling out a book on the city's murals. Flipping through it, she circled the small tables occupied by several men. Each held a newspaper from the front desk. Lopez sat in an open seat and leaned toward three of the men.

"Excuse me," she said, putting a picture of Pedro Martinez on the table. "Could you gentlemen tell me if you've seen this man?"

One shook his head and went back to reading. Another leaned forward.

"Who's that? Can't see that."

"It's Pedro!" the third man said loudly.

"I don't have trouble hearing!" said the farsighted man.

"You must, cause they was just talking about him!"

"Sure," said the farsighted guy. "We knew Pedro. Dead now. Sad."

Lopez smiled. "What do you remember about him?"

"You know," the third man said, "he was real nice. Always looking for a job here, over there, between them two doors."

Lopez turned toward the exit.

"There, by the exit?"

"Yep."

"Ever ask him why?"

"Didn't need to. Assumed he was looking for work."

"Why?"

"Because," he said impatiently, "that's where they post the jobs!"

"Ah," Lopez said. "Thank you."

She went into the foyer between the two exit doors. Sure enough, flyers, advertisements, and index cards covered the community board. Pulling out her phone, she snapped pictures of them all.

———————•———————

Ross was on the phone when she got back in the car. He hung up.

"Anything?"

"Not yet. Kid was a reader—librarians liked him, homeless birds hanging out there liked him."

"Say anything about his death?"

"No."

"Job?"

"No." Lopez had decided not to tell Ross about the job postings. He wanted to pursue his leads, fine. She would pursue hers. If nothing else, she wouldn't feel left out from the investigation. Something on that job board felt pertinent.

"What'd he read?"

"The papers. And history books."

"What?"

"Librarian said he was interested in the history of Penn Treaty."

"The park?"

"Yep. Asked for a book on it. Hung out there. Didn't like her telling him the story of William Penn signing a treaty with Native Americans was more or less a rumor, not a fact."

Ross fell into another silence and pulled back onto Girard. Lopez flipped through the photos on her phone. The jobs board had layers of the typical postings one would expect to see: handwritten or typed descriptions of apartments with rooms to rent, handymen looking for work, bands looking for guitarists. Spanish, Math, and SAT tutors seeking clients had phone numbers written on flaps ready to rip from the bottoms of pages. The owners of a missing cat named Betsy offered a reward for her return. Lopez found the bulletin board reassuring. Offline communications in a public space served certain types of people: those without or unwilling to use the internet. Drifters, recent ex-cons, stubborn retirees. People worried about others tracking their behavior—paranoid high schoolers, wandering spouses. People living off the grid.

Ross made a left onto Frankford and got stuck in a bottleneck caused by jaywalking pedestrians and yet another street closure. This time, one lane of the two-lane road was shut down. A utilities worker halfheartedly directed traffic with an orange flag as a jackhammer plowed through pavement.

"Water and Streets Departments might as well set up a site around here," Lopez mumbled. "Every damn day a pipe bursts or sinkhole appears." She stared. "Where we going?"

"To meet Michaela Alvarez," Ross answered.

5:20 p.m.

FOR DECADES, THE CORRIDOR UNDER ELEVATED TRAIN tracks crossing Frankford north of Lehigh was a dodgy but well-lit passage for pedestrians and cars. Several blocks north of Fishtown, the underpass connected blocks of vacant lots and sagging rowhomes. It was a preview of the deeper poverty that lay farther north.

The Frankford Development Corporation aimed to attract settlers to this fringe of Fishtown by helping business owners secure city grants for seed money. Their first two projects had instant draws. South of the Lehigh Avenue Bridge, the Columbus Brewing Company had attracted customers with an outdoor patio, a toddler play area, and sharp landscaping full of indigenous plants. A block north of the bridge, a popular gymnastics program had rented an old abandoned school and outfitted it as a tumbling studio. The civic association had planned to follow early development success with a produce co-op, a daycare center, a few more bars, and luxury townhomes. It was a tall order for a zip code that had one of the highest levels of poverty in the country.

Parents and caregivers did grumble a bit about the location of the tumbling studio. Those with cars could park in a gravel lot behind the old school building. Those needing public transportation had to take the 5 bus to Lehigh Avenue, walk little ones through the trash-laden, spray-painted bridge tunnel that stunk of urine, then pass an abandoned lot full of bony cats. At one end of the lot, piles of rocks stood against a single decrepit house, the only remnant of a former block of rowhomes. Thin young addicts entered and exited the house through a broken window on its first floor.

Over the past three months, public transportation parents had stayed away from the tumbling studio for a different reason: the sidewalks of the bridge tunnel had become impassable, now home to dozens ejected from the Tracks. Tent encampments on either side of the underpass overflowed with huts made from cardboard, sheets, rags, and trash. Between the makeshift shelters, people lay on backpacks or blankets, rolled up in sweaters and sleeping bags.

The Lehigh Avenue Bridge tent city was one of four that had sprung up under defunct industrial bridges in this particular neighborhood. Editorials now centered on rumors that the mayor's office would evict these transplanted residents of the Tracks.

Neighbors certainly hoped so. With real estate prices skyrocketing and development at an all-time high, young families had left condos in established neighborhoods for new construction and ten-year tax-abatement plans on sketchy blocks. Now there was a surplus of addicts walking past their front doors and dealers openly selling on the corners. Try as it did, the Frankford Development Corporation was having a harder time coaxing businesses to take grant monies.

———•———

MICHAELA ALVAREZ MOVED SLOWLY BETWEEN THE people under the bridge and the gravel parking lot behind the school-turned-tumbling-studio. She was tired. Her hip hurt. She felt old. She was old. And yet again, she had been proven right by the ignorance of powerful people.

Closing the Tracks had made life worse in Kensington. Caving to negative press, the city had closed the site only to receive increased attention for its now-labeled opioid crisis. Michaela had wasted her own breath warning City Hall this would happen. Like so many of the liberals who Michaela had supported over the decades, City Council didn't have a consistent agenda. Philadelphia's political leaders ran on platforms that valued people but acted only on things: cleaner parks, more festivals, construction permits, paving and repaving the damn streets. And all the while, children went hungry.

Michaela refused to even think about the mayor. Glynda Green. Even Michaela had been shocked at how quickly Green's grassroots campaign galvanized women and executed an unprecedented voter turnout. Less than two years in, Green's office had become so damn liberal that it served nothing but progressive ideals. The mayor's latest publicity stunt had hit too close to home for Michaela. She still wasn't sure how she would punish that one.

Just two months before, Green's office had announced a proposal to cut city funds for all religious foster services that refused to work with potential LGBTQIA+ foster parents. The act was noble in appearance but deadly in practice. By cutting funds to religious agencies, critics cried, the city wasn't punishing anybody but vulnerable children and overworked caseworkers. Before the announcement, the need for foster care was growing exponentially every month; doctors from local university hospitals were featured in a public relations campaign that begged people to consider becoming caregivers. At a time when authorities were removing more neglected and abused kids than ever, their leader had chosen a political statement over babies' lives.

As Michaela made her rounds with food for the parents of these babies, Glynda Green made her rounds with hot air on cable news.

Michaela bit her tongue though. She knew public opinion would force Glynda Green into a one-term act. The larger the opioid camps became in Center City, the hotter the heat on the mayor to solve a problem that would never go away.

Michaela rubbed her hip and entered the gravel lot where, each week, All Saints and a team of outside volunteers gathered to sort the week's donations. Tonight, several members of a co-ed social fraternity at Rowan University stood around two shopping carts filled with bagged meals, clothing, and toiletries.

"Phones off and away," Michaela said softly in lieu of a greeting. "I mean it. I see a phone, and you aren't welcome back. Who's in charge?"

A clean-cut kid in a hoodie raised his hand.

"You're in charge of that for me."

He nodded, and the nervous smiles on the others' faces started to fade. Michaela turned around and headed back down the hill.

"Well, come on now," she called behind her shoulder. "Those things aren't going to hand out themselves." Footsteps scurried. Michaela could feel the tension escalating among the students. She couldn't stand any of them.

Years before, when her work began, Michaela had seen the bright, educated young people who showed up for meal distributions a little bit differently. With open arms and effusive gratitude, she would prepare them with pep talks to encourage returning investments in her work. No more. Only a small percentage of volunteers came back twice, and after a decade of trying to build empathy in the haves for the have-nots, she just stopped. Actions spoke louder than words, and the street life spoke for itself. What these kids would see, even if they stuck together and talked only among themselves, would form an impression they wouldn't forget. After an uncomfortable forty-five minutes, they'd head back up to the parking lot, get in a white van, go back to wherever, and at some point down the road maybe contribute money and supplies for someone else's turn.

The homeless population here was different from those of the latest do-gooders' parents. Until about a decade before, those who came to feedings were largely middle-aged veterans or former prisoners suffering from mental illness, addiction, or apathy. They came for food and then they left. Now, the population was whiter and younger—so much younger. They hadn't served in a war or much if any time in jail. Pills and addiction had brought them and kept them lingering in filth and urine and hunger.

Michaela couldn't, and didn't want to, explain all of this several times a week to white guilt. It was up to those who sent the students to tell them what to expect, what to do, how to interact with a smile and eye contact, and where to direct any questions. She did have to maintain the appearance of gratitude because she needed the contributions provided by colleges, churches, sororities, and schools. These institutions and organizations could send their charity anywhere, but they chose Kensington because of her. She had cultivated their loyalty through years of showing up and getting mentioned in news reports every few months or so. Michaela had served the neighborhood longer than any other pastor or social worker, and she had worked with them all, nurturing their knowledge and their know-how.

Michaela paused before entering the tunnel with the latest group. She turned around with a soft smile. Already their faces were white and their hands fidgety.

"We will slowly walk down one sidewalk and back up the other handing things out," she said gently. "Everybody gets a meal and one other thing. Don't worry about whether clothes fit. They know how to multipurpose anything."

The group started following again, and she stopped abruptly.

"Don't just hand things out," she instructed. "Say hello. Talk to them. Ask their names, where they're from. At least smile and look them in the eye. They are people. Don't pass 'em by and make them feel even more like animals."

Michaela led them into the underpass. Her team at All Saints had been there for an hour with medical students. Young doctors in training distributed toiletries, wrapped small injuries, and listened to heartbeats as Michaela's people handed out clean sheets and chatted with those lucid enough to talk back. The presence of the medical team had sparked something under the bridge. Michaela smiled. Nothing lightened a load like feeling heard. Four or five young men made a beeline for the new supplies. The students pushed the carts forward and stepped back.

"Take your time," Michaela cooed. "There's enough for everyone."

She grabbed an armful of peanut butter sandwiches and gently tapped on the cardboard walls of the shelters.

"*Piss off!*" a muffled voice yelled.

"There's a sandwich here for you," Michaela said, putting it on the makeshift roof. A horn blasted next to her. Rush hour had backed traffic up behind the light by the bridge. Drivers uncomfortable looking out the window were stuck inching through the campsite as prime targets for panhandling. Most stared straight ahead, ignoring the weathered men and women with matted hair, red faces, and signs that begged for help with a GOD BLESS YOU. Some tossed out change, maybe a cigarette. Michaela glanced back at the college kids. A couple were glued to the carts. Two crouched next to a tearful woman eating a peanut butter sandwich. Another was summoning the courage to approach a couple sitting on the curb. Good for them. For their own sakes, she hoped they didn't promise to come back. She knew they never would.

Michaela was happy to see a man and a woman waiting for her at the opposite end of the tunnel. The undergrads could handle taking the carts up a sidewalk and back to the parking lot by themselves.

"Get me out of here," she said to Ross. "I need a drink."

———•———

MICHAELA ALVAREZ DRANK A GIN AND TONIC THROUGH a soda straw in one corner of the Cook and Shaker taproom. Ross sat between her and Lopez in the mostly empty bar, located a few blocks south of the Lehigh Avenue Bridge encampment. Michaela ordered buffalo-fried brussels sprouts.

"You like working with him?" Michaela asked Lopez.

"Sometimes."

Michaela chuckled.

Opposite from where they sat, an oversized flat screen showed a program on Asian street markets.

"How's your hand?" Michaela said, watching the television.

"Fine," Ross answered.

117

"Still running?"

"Yep."

"Ever try yoga like I told you?"

Ross didn't answer. He had figured Michaela would try rattling him by sharing pieces of his private life in front of Lopez. He had trusted her more than anyone not too long ago, when he clearly played a role in her agenda.

"I heard you saw Liam," she said.

And there it was. Small but mighty. Their conversation in the sanctuary had been a telling one. Perhaps he should have considered their first encounter after the Victor Rafaella/Strangler mess more deliberately. To Ross, their talk in All Saints was the first in a series of conversations. To Michaela, it was the moment to see whether Ross could accept that she knew best, that she held a separate authority from the authorities. His indirect answer had been no.

"Coast Guard, huh?" she asked.

"Could do worse," Ross said dismissively. No matter what happened between the two of them, they would always have Liam in common. Without Conor Mathew, and without Michaela Alvarez, Ross knew that his little brother would still be on the street. That meant something.

Michaela's hardened eyes were fixed on the television. Ross knew she didn't have much on him. Sure, she was informed about his actions in the Victor Rafaella case, but so were his captain and his Homicide team. She could embarrass him in the press, yet that took time—and he had, after all, played directly into her Strangler plan. All Michaela could do, Ross surmised, was threaten his precious privacy by disclosing the few details she knew to people he wouldn't want to know.

"Tell us about Pedro Martinez," Ross said.

118

"Officer Lopez learned what we know about Pedro this morn—"

"Detective," Ross interrupted. "Detective Lopez."

"I'm sorry." Michaela made eye contact with Lopez. "Detective, of course."

She signaled for another drink. "As you found out, Detective, Pedro Martinez was not on our radar."

"I was hoping to speak with you in person this morning," Lopez said.

"Yes." Michaela smiled. "I make it a point to keep to my own schedule on my own time."

"Seemed as if someone hid when they saw me coming."

"I don't hide."

"Can you speak for everyone you work with?"

"No." Michaela smiled.

"So the open Bible and notebook weren't yours?"

"Does it really matter?"

Behind them, a young man with a lame foot swept the floor. Ross had noticed him eyeing the trio from a table across the room where he had been rolling silverware when they arrived.

Bad haircut. White. Twenty-twoish. Nervous type. Disability?

"What did you find out about Pedro?" Ross asked. He had, just then, decided how he was going to handle Michaela Alvarez. Keep her on her feet. Make her worry a little. Ross's phone buzzed. It was Mikovich, probably following up on the kid. He turned it off.

"Pedro Martinez," Michaela said slowly, "didn't live on the street. Just looked like he did. Lived with a blond woman and another young man in a rundown house near Penn Treaty Park."

119

"Addicts knew him though?"

"He was kind. Gave away food when he had it. May have come to a meal or two at the GYM."

"His male roommate," Ross said, "was he a large black guy?"

"Yes," she answered.

"What'd he do for work?"

"Pedro? This and that. Like I said, he lived with others. Maybe he did nothing." She started devouring the brussels sprouts when they arrived. "I'm not the only one working on the street, you know. Ask someone else."

"We have. Seems he worked at SugarHouse as a janitor," Lopez said.

"Then there you go. Why you askin' me?"

The threesome fell quiet. Michaela licked her fingers. "As I've always said, I won't keep anything from you that I know, but I'm not supposed to do your jobs."

"I'm not sure about that one, Michaela," Ross said.

Lopez's phone buzzed. "It's Mikovich," she said.

"Leave it," Ross directed.

They sat in silence for a minute.

"You know," Michaela said to Ross, "When you first started coming around years ago, I knew what you were looking for. After just a couple of conversations with you. I knew then and I know now. It wasn't Jesus."

Lopez's phone started buzzing again. Relieved for an excuse to exit the conversation, she took the call outside.

"You just needed someone to say good job," Michaela said quietly. "To say, 'You're doing well. In a world of gray, you're doing just fine.'"

She pushed the plate away and downed her drink. Then she swiveled in her bar stool toward Ross. "You're waiting for me to make some kind of apology. It isn't going to happen."

"And you're waiting for me to say thank you."

"No, I'm not. I'm waiting for you to get the fuck over it." Her tone became sterner. "You nabbed the Strangler. You're a hero." She paused. "Could have been anyway. I gave you that—"

"In your time, you did," Ross interrupted. "Not a second sooner."

"What's that supposed to mean?"

"Coincided exactly with Victor's release."

"You want to say it, say it."

Ross threw a twenty-dollar bill on the table and stood up. "You knew James Rosen was the Strangler before you called that day, tipping me on how exactly to catch him in the act and take him in."

"Should I have called another?"

"It was a thank you."

"For what?"

"For refusing to lie about whether I had definitely seen Victor."

"Ohhhhh." Michaela shook her head no. "So this is where we are. You versus me."

"Just letting you know that I'm not your private detective. Victor didn't walk because I was doing you a favor."

"Bullshit, Eric." She stared at him. "Deep down, you knew it wasn't Victor's time. For the greater good. Why'd I call you, you ask?" She paused.

"Sure, Michaela."

"Because you feared your own brother was involved, and you needed to catch James Rosen yourself to prove he was the only one responsible."

"I never said—"

"You didn't have to. But you caught the real guy, which means you suspected him, which means Liam now knows you believed it wasn't him."

"Ross!" called Lopez.

"So let me be the one to say," Michaela said in a low voice, "Good job. You are doing a good job."

Ross started walking away.

"Or do you need daddy to say it," Michaela called after him.

Ross caught his foot on a sidewalk crack, tripped, and rebounded back to an upright position after hitting what felt like an iron in mid-air. It was the sweeper's forearm. The man's quick reflex and strength snapped Ross to attention. Too stunned to say thank you, the detective followed Lopez across the street to the car.

7:00 p.m.

JESSIE WREN ARRIVED ON THE SCENE BEFORE HER TEAM DID. The call came two miles in on what she hoped would be an hour-long run along the Delaware River waterfront. She hadn't slept well since Sunday night. She hadn't run since then either. Twice in a row, she had pulled near overnights at work to analyze the crime scene photos and push as many colleagues as possible to expedite forensic results. She was most interested in those from LeAnn DeVille's murder. Wren wondered what latent fingerprints might be pulled from the costume and props. As for the inquiry into Pedro Martinez's death, she didn't expect anything to surface outside of what photographs might provide. And thanks to her eager intern, they had a collection of more photographs than she had ever before studied from two crime scenes.

The thought of the younger woman made Jessie Wren run faster. It was a beautiful spring night with temperatures in the mid-fifties. Breezes blew through flags flying high above the harbor. Ripples in the water caught the sunlight and sent flickers of gold along the river.

Wren knew she was being hard on Mae Brunnell, and it wasn't because her intern was twenty years younger and cuter. The woman couldn't know how to do a good job with so little experience in the field, but neither could any other intern; regardless of background, each came from the same pool of idealism nurtured by *CSI* reruns. Necessary skills came only from long hours of observation of body after body, photo after photo, investigator after investigator. With only a few months to spare, interns could never be very effective. And that's what bothered Wren more about Mae Brunnell than her youth and good looks. She, in all of her twenty-something years, wanted approval too much. The intern shadowed her constantly, and it drove Wren nuts.

Jessie Wren had taken her phone on the run, as if willing a call from work to interrupt her regimen. All day, she had awaited a report of hit number three. The pace of the two mural homicides had everyone on edge, and Wren was sure something big would hit that day.

When the phone did ring, it summoned her once again to Fishtown—for two bodies this time. Both were staged in one scene just a few blocks away from where Pedro Martinez was found.

Jessie Wren ran straight to Palmer Park, a small pocket park on the Frankford business corridor. Two residential streets bordered the park square, as did Frankford Avenue on one side and a low-income retirement home on the other. Benches, tall elms, and a path lined with vibrant flowers sprawled through the center of Palmer Park. At its back end, right off a small street, three police officers, including Terrence Rivera, had secured the scene and were warding off onlookers gathering in the park and on sidewalks. Sirens and horns echoed up and down Frankford.

Stopping in the middle of the path, Wren hinged at the hips to catch her breath. She felt someone approach from behind and pivoted.

"I know, I know," said Officer Rivera, grinning. "I take women's breath away."

Shit, Wren thought to herself, noticing Rivera scanning her running outfit: shorts, tight top, baseball cap. She willed herself to ignore him by staring at the cars on Frankford.

"Before dusk. In front of rush hour," she said.

Traffic indeed lined Frankford Avenue's two lanes. In both directions, cars and buses stood at a standstill. South, closer to Frankford and Girard, a demolition crew blocked part of one lane, forcing cars in both directions to navigate the other lane without colliding.

"You the responding?" Wren asked.

"Yep."

"Who reported it?"

They headed to the crime scene.

"Anonymous caller again. Arrived and here they were, a young couple in love. Looked like they were sleeping."

Postures and props, but no costumes this time. Over a line of toy ladders positioned between their young adult bodies, the man's left arm and the woman's right arm reached above their heads, and their hands toward one another's. An ice cream cone, almost melted, seemed to have fallen from the male's hand. White flower petals were scattered around the bodies. Azalea blossoms.

"We talked to three different dogwalkers present in the park when we arrived," Rivera said. "They said they'd been here for a half hour and didn't realize two people had died in front of their eyes."

"Where are they now?"

"One's over there on the bench. The other two left. Douglas has their info. Had a hard time keeping their dogs away."

"From the bodies?"

"Yep. Get a little closer. Shit coming from both. Just like Martinez."

"Any other witnesses?"

Rivera cocked his head. "Shouldn't I be saving this for Boy Wonder?"

Wren rolled her eyes.

A VAN PULLED UP ON THE SIDEWALK A FEW MINUTES later. Two of Wren's colleagues and Mae Brunnell jumped out. The intern rushed toward her mentor with a jacket, gloves, a notebook, and two cameras. Ross and Lopez arrived at the same time as the van and went directly to the scene, standing outside of the taped-off scene until the tech team finished its investigation for evidence.

"Broad daylight this time," Lopez said. She slowly turned around in a circle, noting the surroundings. The retirement home in particular caught her eye. It had seven floors, each with several windows facing the park.

Jessie Wren took gloves and a camera from her intern.

"Rivera the responding again," she told Ross.

"Anonymous caller," Rivera said. "Secured the scene and talked to those here. That dogwalker over there remembers seeing them come in. Said they looked a little drunk and seemed to be helping each other. Noticed them sitting on the grass but stayed away. Thought they were junkies. Another said he noticed them lying down later. Thought they were taking a nap."

"Did they notice the ice cream cone?"

"Not sure. Douglas!" Rivera called.

A redheaded officer approached.

"Ask the dogwalker if he remembers an ice cream—"

"First," Ross interjected, "ask if he remembers the man holding one when they came in. Then if he had one when he saw them sitting down."

Officer Douglas obeyed. Rivera shot Lopez a look of contempt. Her former partner didn't handle interruptions very well.

"Rivera and I can canvas the neighborhood," Lopez said. "I'll take that block," she said directly to Rivera, "you that one, and we'll hit the retirement home together?"

He agreed.

Ross watched the forensics team make three passes of the scene before he entered the tape. On the first walkthrough, Mae Brunnell followed the investigators as they expanded the crime scene a few feet in each direction and only observed what lay before them. On the second, Wren and her two thirtysomething colleagues—Adam Vance, a skinny white guy, and Mike Lee, a larger Asian man, divided the scene into zones and combed through each one, instructing Brunnell on where to mark evidence by placing small orange flags into the ground. She designated the victims' clothing and hair, their hands, their shit, the ice cream cone, the ice cream, the petals, and trash on the scene—a torn Styrofoam cup, an empty packet of Doritos. Gently, Wren searched their clothing.

"No wallets, no ID," she called to Ross.

"So how did he pay for the ice cream?" Vance asked.

The three primary investigators played rock, paper, scissors. Vance emerged as the loser and groaned. Dividing up the zones, the team started extracting evidence by each orange flag, then packaging and logging the contents. Vance was responsible for the feces.

"How come I always get the shit?" he asked.

Mae Brunnell laughed. She had begun sketching the crime scene on an iPad.

"Stool," Lee said. "Watch your mouth. We have a minor present." He winked at Brunnell.

"I'll do it," she said.

"Huh?" Vance asked.

"No!" Wren said with more harshness than she intended.

"Come on, boss," Vance said. "Let the girl get a little dirty."

"She's sketching."

"I'll do it afterward," Brunnell said. "If you don't mind."

"Fine," Wren said. "Weird but fine. You walk her through it Vance."

He exchanged his tool bag for the iPad and watched Mae Brunnell select a sample from the man and package and log it.

"Anything I missed?" she quipped in a quiet voice.

He grinned. "That's about it."

She did the same for the woman's feces.

"Can you just replace him, Mae?" called out Lee. "I'm tired of his bitching and moaning every time he hits a bodily fluid."

Brunnell crouched back down near the woman. "Speaking of bodily fluids, there's a pool of black liquid getting bigger under her."

Wren walked over. "Vance, sample it," she said.

Mike Lee moved on to the ice cream cone and extracted a gob that hadn't yet melted. "This is eerie," he said. "The cone smells freshly baked."

"What kind of ice cream?" asked Brunnell and Wren simultaneously.

Lee bent closer to the ground. "Smells like lemon."

"Lemon?" Wren asked.

"Yeah."

"Fancy flavor." She turned to Ross, taking his own notes nearby. "Bet this is from some overly priced hipster place."

"Any wrapping on the cones?" Ross asked.

"No," Lee said.

"Detective," called the redheaded officer, back from interviewing the dog walker.

"What did he say?"

"No memory of ice cream. He thought about it and kept shaking his head no. Said they were both doing what they could to help each other walk a straight line."

"Okay. Is there an expensive ice cream shop nearby?"

"Yeah. Three."

"Go to the closest and ask if they sold a lemon flavor—or something that might smell like lemon—to a couple matching the description of these two. Or to anyone who might have bought it for someone else. If not, see if there's another nearby parlor that might have."

"Got it," Douglas said.

"Ross!" Lopez called. "No leads from those who answered their doors. We're heading to the retirement home. Might be there a while."

"Okay. Good. I'll text you."

Fifteen minutes later, news crews had arrived and set up on the perimeter of the park. Backup officers arrived to keep them far enough away from the scene.

Ross crouched next to the bodies and spent several minutes studying each.

"Faces getting yellow."

"I'll be surprised if it isn't arsenic," Wren said. "I suspected it with Pedro, and I'm fairly certain now."

"But not in the ice cream."

"It moves fast, but not that fast."

"So the same question then: was the prop in his hand before he died or put there after?"

"And why was DeVille stabbed and not poisoned?"

"That was either a copycat or someone who wants us to think so." He rested back on his heels. This scene was obviously more similar to Pedro's than LeAnn DeVille's. "I say it's the same killer for the third time," he said quietly to Jessie Wren.

"I don't know," Wren said. She stared at the bodies. "So all three of the Fishtown victims were poisoned off-site. Each ended up at the final destination in some kind of discomfort, as noted by Pedro's vomit and the account of the dogwalker."

A few minutes later Officer Douglas returned. "Closest place is called Cream Big. Place was packed. Girl at the counter says lemon is their newest flavor but everyone wants it. Can't remember anyone matching the vics' description."

"Security camera?" Ross asked.

"Yep, but not facing the counter. Positioned in the front corner of the store toward the front door. I said we'd be back to get the footage."

"Good. Can you follow up with that tomorrow?"

"Can do it now."

"Fine."

Douglas grabbed his radio from his right chest pocket and listened to dispatch. "Hey," he called to Wren, "where's the medical examiner?"

"No ETA. It's a busy night," Adam Vance answered.

"Ross!" Douglas called. "Radio says a few reports back on the mural. Matches a scene called *Summer Rendezvous* over a milkshake place in Rittenhouse."

Jessie Wren stared at the ground. "I agree with you," she said, ignoring Douglas and the latest mural connection. "If DeVille's killer were a copycat, he would have been operating on knowledge we didn't have until after the Olney scene, when you drove past the mural matching Pedro's death."

"Unless a potential second killer knew about the first one."

8:25 p.m.

LOPEZ AND RIVERA DIDN'T HAVE A PROBLEM GETTING AN
okay to question residents from the retirement director, a
middle-aged black man dressed in tennis whites.
"Sure," he had said. "One thing, though—you're going to
have a hard time getting away from some of these people."
"Why's that, sir?" Rivera asked.
"They haven't had visitors in quite some time."
Of the building's ten floors, seven were residential. The
lobby, offices, and a common area made up the three other
floors, with the library being on the side of the common
area that faced Palmer Park. It had closed at 6:00 p.m., as
had the office spaces. Each unit facing the park, Lopez and
Rivera learned, had two or three windows. The director
showed them a map of the building and identified twenty-
one units with a view directly into Palmer Park. Three
of those tenants, he said, were away, and another five in
the hospital. Lopez and Rivera divided up the remaining
thirteen apartments.
    Rivera finished fast and first. His low tolerance for small
talk aided his inquiries. He spoke to someone in six out of
the seven residences on his list. Several people said they had
looked out their windows at some point between 6:00 and
7:00 p.m., just after they got back from dinner, which was
served from 5:00 to 6:30 p.m. Nobody noticed the couple.
After one man cracked a joke about his weakening eyesight,
Rivera realized that the distance from the higher floors to
the crime scene was farther than he had realized, perhaps
too far for an elderly resident to see in much detail.

131

Lopez had six apartments, all of which had someone to answer the front door. By the time Rivera had found her, she was only at her second door. He waited for her to finish and led the way to the third.

"If the answer is 'No, I didn't see anything,' move the hell on!" he grumbled.

"You know everything, don't you, Rivera?"

Lopez followed his advice at the next two apartments but had a funny feeling when the door of the fifth apartment on her list opened. Something felt different about this unit. A smell of lavender emanated from it, and classical music played quietly in the background. A woman with straight, straggly hair and eyeglasses greeted them. She wore a light brown sweater, and her white walls were covered with minimalist artwork.

"Yes?" asked the woman.

"Detective Lina Lopez, ma'am. This is Officer Terrence Rivera."

The woman nodded.

"Ma'am, we are investigating a crime that took place at Palmer Park within the last two hours. Have you been home during that time?"

"Yes," she said and smiled.

"You didn't go to dinner?" Rivera asked.

"No. I cook for myself." Another smile.

"Did you happen to look out one of your windows during that time?"

"Oh, always."

"Did you happen to notice a young couple stumble into the park, sit on the ground, and then lie down?"

"Oh, that happens all the time."

"Did it happen tonight?"

"Well, it might have." She smiled again. Lopez found it irritating.

"Do you remember seeing such a couple tonight?"

"No."

"Do you need to think about it?" Rivera asked.

"No." She seemed comfortable with the silence. Lopez wondered if the woman aimed to unsettle them.

"I'm sorry I can't help you, officers," the lady said. "Anything else?"

"No, ma'am," Rivera said.

"Well, good night then." She closed the door.

"She's the white version of Michaela Alvarez," Lopez said to Rivera. "Keeps her mouth shut and damn you if you try to open it."

Rivera took the lead on the last door. They left the building five minutes later. Before they crossed the street, Rivera pulled Lopez's elbow back.

"You mentioned Michaela Alvarez back there," he said.

"Yeah?"

"Something is a little different over there."

"All Saints or just the GYM?"

"Both."

Lopez waited.

"Came up at roll call this morning. Remember Eddie Adams?"

"Yeah. Drug Enforcement."

"Someone noticed him sniffing around lately. Hit the strip club under the El. Ear there says he's asking about an increase in heroin addicts on nearby blocks."

Lopez snorted. "You kidding me? This a joke?"

"No."

"This that stripper with the black bob? That who saw him?"

"Yeah."

"Why would he ask such an obvious question? Looking for bullshit?"

"I don't think so. She said he was specific about the blocks between All Saints and the El."

"Which has been a drug corridor since 1958."

Lopez went to cross the street again.

"Wait a minute." Rivera pulled her elbow again.

"Stop doing that."

"Listen to me." He stepped closer to her. Lopez noticed an intensity in his eyes. "Like I said, it came up. And a few guys said they've noticed it."

"What?"

"More and more addicts hanging around All Saints."

"Maybe they've added more meetings."

"Maybe. But here's the thing—Sarge got quiet and dismissive. Something's off there. Be careful."

"Okay."

"Not okay. Something happens, Ross isn't the one taking the fall."

"Got it."

"Michaela Alvarez punishes people who go against her. You know that. Helped get the last mayor booted through bad press. She could ruin your career."

Lopez looked over at Ross. He was watching them.

"Okay," she said.

10:00 p.m.

"Yes, sir."

Detective Lina Lopez finished her call with Captain Antony Mikovich and felt blinded by her new "partner's" behavior once again. She sat on a park bench, boring eyes of frustration into him while Forensics wrapped the scene. Rivera joined Officer Douglas and his partner in loading the body bags into a police van and accompanying them to the medical examiner's office where the bodies would be autopsied.

On the phone, Mikovich had been pissed at both of them. Said he had called their team together for a meeting a half hour ago, and everyone was there except for her and Ross. Where the hell were they?

Investigating the most recent murder scene, she had answered.

But Ross had told him they were almost done. Said they would be there.

"We're on the scene, sir."

"Get here," Mikovich said as he hung up.

Lopez didn't like that he had reamed her out instead of Ross. He was the senior investigator. Was this how it was going to be? Ross ignored everyone, and she acted as an intermediary? He did what he wanted, and she got called out?

She started to charge toward him and someone stepped in her way. The Forensics intern.

"Yeah?" Lopez asked.

"Sorry, I…" the woman stammered. "I just…"

"What do you need?" Lopez asked impatiently.

The young woman seemed shaken. From afar, Lopez had seen her taking the shit samples. Now the intern's hands shook.

"I need to tell you something," Brunnell said quietly. "It's...not essential, but important. I think."

Ross walked toward them.

"So what is it?" Lopez asked.

Mae Brunnell followed her eyes. "I'm sorry. Not in front of him. Can I talk to you in private?" She spoke in a near whisper.

"Hang on." Lopez sighed. She was in no mood to deal with a frazzled newbie.

"I'm out of here, Ross," Jessie Wren called from across the park. "Will text the pics."

"I'll meet you at the car," Lopez said to Ross sharply.

She led Brunnell aside.

"Could...could I talk to you another time, privately?" the intern asked. "It's complicated."

"Not now."

"Tomorrow morning?"

"Has to be early. 7:30?"

"Great. Mugshot Diner?"

"Fine."

Lopez spun around and headed toward Ross's car. Yanking open the passenger's door, she sat and slammed the door. He watched her.

"Captain says we were due at Homicide an hour ago. He's pissed."

Ross nodded his head. "He often is."

"Why'd you tell him we could make it when we couldn't?"

"Thought we could."

She thought for a second and froze. It was her fault. The interviews at the retirement home had gone long. Wrapping up conversations with vulnerable people had always been her weak point. Ross could have been annoyed with her, and instead, she was acting like a child.

"Right. So we go now."

"Not yet."

Lopez felt her frustration returning. "Why?"

Ross turned on the car.

"Word isn't out yet that these two died. Not in the places we want to look."

"Will you tell him we aren't coming?"

"Nope. But you can, if you want to."

10:25 p.m.

PENN TREATY PARK WAS SLIGHTLY MORE CROWDED AFTER dark than it had been in the morning. Eric Ross pulled into the parking lot and turned the car's bright lights on the statue of William Penn. A group of teenagers scurried away. Curfew wasn't for another half hour, and it wasn't really enforced, but bright lights at night in the park indicated a search for someone or something.

"Who are we looking for?" Lopez asked.

"A guy named Conor Mathew."

"How do you know he's here?"

"Lives here often enough." He handed her a flashlight and frowned. "You know the name?"

"No, don't think so."

Ross kept the brights on and locked the door.

"Stay with me," he said.

They walked past the statue and through a playground. Several college-aged kids at a picnic table didn't try to hide bottles wrapped in paper bags. A young couple spoke intently while sitting on swings. Ross and Lopez stopped at the metal fence that framed the side of the park next to the abandoned factory. He turned on his flashlight.

"Let's keep the beams together and low to the ground."

Ross and Lopez moved along the fence and then the waterfront. Halfway around the park, they came to the area of overgrown brush where Ross had eyed the pit bull on Sunday night.

Darkness and the shrubbery camouflaged homeless sleepers well. The scene was a far cry from the overcrowded

138

camps lit with fluorescent streetlights underneath Kensington's bridges.

The detectives passed eight people sleeping in this area of the park. More were likely in the thicket that descended to the river. Even in the daytime, the dense growth was difficult to navigate. Overgrown indigenous and invasive plants tangled together in complicated knots that had gone ignored for decades. Scattered throughout the slope, shrubs of holly offered spotty yet thick coverage to sleepers who braved the prickly, yellowed leaves.

Two or three faces rolled toward the flashlight beams. Others lay huddled in small piles of clothes or dirty blankets. Two had sleeping bags. In her decade with the 26th, Lopez had never entered the park at night. Hearing only the gentle lapping of the water against the jagged shoreline, she found the search more and more disquieting.

Ross's phone buzzed, startling both of them. A dog's low growl followed. Ross reached for Lopez and shoved his body in front of hers. Both flashlights had missed a large pit bull lying in an open patch of grass near them. Lopez stifled a cry of surprise.

"Don't—don't worry about him," a voice said. "He's friendly." An elderly man in a worn green terrycloth bathrobe rose to his knees from behind the dog. Both he and the pit bull had been resting on cardboard. The man smiled a toothless smile.

"We're looking for Conor Mathew," Ross said.

"Yep, around here somewhere."

Lopez noticed the dog wasn't on a leash. She stepped backward as Ross stepped forward.

"Could you look at a photo for me, sir?"

"Yep. Come on over. He won't hurt you."

The dog growled as the detectives approached. Ross held out a picture on his phone of Pedro Martinez's mugshot. The man squinted, groaned, and ambled closer to Ross.

"Yep. He was here."

"Notice anything about him?"

"Would sit on a rock. Stare at the water. Reminded me of an Indian. Used to be Indians here. Long time ago."

"Ever talk to him?"

"Nope."

"See him with anybody?"

"Nope. Buster probably did."

"Who's Buster?"

The dog growled.

"Him."

Ross pulled up a stream of photos from the murder scene at Palmer Park. He showed the man a close-up of the couple's faces. They looked like they were asleep.

"Seen them before?"

The man raised a dirty finger into the air.

"Maybe. Both of 'em? Not sure. Got another one?"

Ross moved to a photo of the bodies on the ground.

"No!" the man yelled, realizing the couple was dead. The dog sprung to his feet and crouched. Ross froze. He heard Lopez cock her gun.

"No," the man mumbled, kneeling back onto his cardboard.

Both detectives stayed still for a minute then slowly inched backward. A soft laugh came through the darkness.

"Officer, officer. Looking for a swimming hole?"

About thirty yards away, someone lit a cigarette.

"We're coming closer to you, Conor," Ross said.

"Nah," a voice drawled. "I'm getting up."

Conor Mathew's figure walked toward them from a tree line that bordered the side of the park directly opposite the abandoned factory. On the other side of the trees, a new metal fence divided the park from a razed lot that had held an abandoned apartment building and before that an old tire factory.

Lopez did think Conor Mathew looked familiar. Thick brown hair stuck up from his head in a pompadour. Had he not laughed, she would have thought him just asleep. His red-streaked eyes held deep fatigue.

"Whatcha got for me coppers?" he asked quietly.

Ross put his phone in front of Conor's face. Pedro Martinez's mugshot filled the screen.

"Yeah, yeah, I already told you. Hung around here some. And at the library."

"The Rodriguez library. Tell me something else about it."

"Nothing else to tell. Just saw him there a few times."

"He didn't work there. Worked at SugarHouse," Ross said.

"Damn good detective work, officer!"

Ross moved the photo roll forward. The next shot was a close-up of LeAnn DeVille.

"Her?" the detective asked.

"Nope."

"Any murmurings on it?"

"Nope." He yawned.

Ross pulled up another photo and held it again in front of Conor Mathew's face. It was of the two bodies found hours before at Palmer Park. Ross then shifted to the next one, a close-up of a faint smile on the man's face.

"Come on!" Conor said loudly. He winced and put a hand over his eyes. "That's some…some Batman Joker shit."

"You know them."

"I've seen them."

"Where?"

"Here, there," he turned his back to Ross. "You can't hit me with that shit in the middle of the night, copper."

"Where did you see them, Conor? Was it together, or separately?"

Conor Mathew shook himself as if to wake up.

"Same killer?"

"We think so."

"Where'd you see them before?" Lopez asked.

Ross winced. Lopez realized too late that she had inserted herself as a distraction. Conor Mathew's eyes widened.

"My, my, my." He smiled. "A lovely woman."

"Shut up, Conor," Ross said. "Tell me where you saw these two. Focus."

After a moment, Ross lifted his flashlight into Conor's face.

"Fine!" he whined. "I'm telling you already. They've been here, there, around."

"Ever see them with Pedro Martinez?"

"I don't know. No. But they both hung out here, so maybe."

"What does hung out mean?"

"Means spent time here. Not for a while though, I don't think."

Ross turned his light out. Lopez did the same.

Conor Mathew started talking in a low voice. "Came around a couple of weeks ago."

"Why do you remember them?" pushed Ross.

"She was deaf."

"They used sign language?"

"No, I don't know, man. She could definitely yell. Showed up at the doughnut shop a week or so ago bitching about someone stealing her tired-ass bike. Kept going on about it, accusing everyone."

"And the man?"

"Dude'd just laugh. She jumped on him once and hit him with a rock."

"Know their names?"

"No. Don't know nothing!" Conor started stomping in place like a toddler. "Tired. Come on. Hand it over and get out of my house."

Ross gave him a twenty-dollar bill and started back to the car.

"Ross," Lopez said.

"What?" He didn't stop.

"Hang on. Hang on!"

"What?"

She caught up to him. "Ever ask this guy about All Saints? The GYM?"

"Not recently."

"Something's up there. Rivera said it's come up at roll call. Nobody knows what. But not enough to act on right now."

Ross stared at her. She blushed under the intensity of his gaze.

"This guy here—could he do an undercover job?"

"No." Ross almost chuckled. He exhaled loudly and then walked back toward the tree line, the shadows, the pit bull, and Conor Mathew.

WEDNESDAY

7:30 a.m.

MAE BRUNNELL WAITED FOR DETECTIVE LOPEZ IN A BOOTH at the front of Mugshot Diner. Facing away from the door, she gazed through the floor-to-ceiling window that framed one length of the diner. She wished they could have met somewhere more private, but part of her had been surprised the detective was willing to meet with her at all. She pulled the sleeves of her black hoodie sweatshirt up to her elbows and touched her sole piece of jewelry, a bracelet with a heart charm on her right wrist.

Lopez arrived dressed in black pants and a black jacket with a bright yellow blouse under it.

"Hi," Lopez said. "Mae, right?"

"Mae Brunnell," said the younger woman, smiling faintly. "Thank you so much, again, for your time. I'm a little nervous."

Lopez nodded toward the younger woman's bag: a weathered, heavy green messenger bag with a large yellow CAT label. "Now that's vintage hipster."

She smiled. "Guilty. Can I get you anything?"

"Just a coffee."

A waitress came over with a coffeepot. "Refill, honey?" she asked before frowning at the full mug. "Oh, you haven't touched it."

"It's fine. I'm just taking my time."

"I'll have a coffee for here and a veggie omelet with no cheese, no home fries, to go," Lopez said.

144

"I'm fine with coffee," Brunnell said.

"And a muffin," Lopez added.

The waitress walked away.

"They don't like it when you just order coffee," Lopez said. "Tell me how I can help. I have to be at Homicide soon."

"Well." Brunnell pushed her shoulder-length hair behind her ears with both hands. "I might be paranoid, but I don't think so." She shook a bit. Lopez wondered if she shouldn't have brought someone else with her. "You were so kind to me the other night, and I…I didn't know who to talk to."

"Are you going to disclose something I'm legally obligated to report?"

"I don't trust Eric Ross," the younger woman blurted out.

Lopez took her coffee from the waitress.

"Why?"

"You've seen Jessie. She's…edgy—and rude. I don't mind working with her," Brunnell hurried along. "She knows her stuff, and I'm learning a lot."

Lopez had given herself twenty minutes to meet with the forensics intern. She needed to hurry it along or she would be late for the team's meeting with Mikovich.

"Do you feel safe?"

"Yes."

"Has Ross done something to make you uncomfortable?"

"Maybe, but not to me."

Lopez pushed her back into the booth.

"See something you wish you hadn't?" the detective asked.

"Yes."

"Well what was it? You came to me, remember?"

"Jessie follows Ross around," Brunnell said quickly.

"On…crime scenes?"

"In his personal life."

"How do you know?"

"Because I saw her. And it was when I saw Ross too."

"What?"

"The other afternoon—Sunday," Brunnell said slowly, "I was walking my dog, and I saw her out running. She'd been really hard on me, and I thought maybe connecting outside of Forensics might help."

"So you followed her?"

"Yep. To Penn Treaty Park, not far from where we were. And I saw her suddenly stop and stare at something. So I did too. And what she was staring at—it was Detective Ross. He had been running too, I guess, and he had run into somebody—literally—at the park." She spoke without inhaling. "He got up and hobbled after the guy he hit. I didn't know it was him at the time," Mae Brunnell said, closing her eyes. "But I recognized him later at the crime scene in the cemetery."

"Okay. So did she help him up?"

Brunnell shook her head no. "It happened so fast. But she followed him, a little bit, walking away, as he was following the guy he hit."

"And you were following her?"

"I didn't want to anymore. I didn't want to disturb her, upset her. So I left."

"For where?"

"Home." She breathed heavily. "I live around here. But then I saw him later, up on Girard."

"Ross?"

"No, the guy he ran into. I stopped at the grocer's and on my way out, he was limping by me. I recognized his clothes." She shut her eyes tightly.

Lopez coaxed her along. "And Ross was behind him?"

"No, not anymore. I don't think. But I saw them both later." She looked like she was going to break.

"Where?"

"He was the dead guy. The guy in the cemetery. It was him, in costume, the guy Ross ran into and followed out of the park. And he was dead."

Lopez sat still.

"I wondered if Jessie recognized him, too, but she might not have because she was standing so far back, and I had seen him up close on Girard. He looked terrible. Like he was...was going to die. When we got the call later and I saw him there on the ground, I couldn't think straight."

"Didn't seem like Jessie recognized him."

She shook her head no.

"How about Ross?"

"I don't know. I couldn't tell." She shuddered.

The waitress came over. "Muffin wrapped too?"

Lopez nodded. She pulled twenty dollars from her pants pocket and put it on the table.

"Mae," she said gently. "You have to come forward with what you saw. It places Pedro Martinez before he died."

"I'm scared."

"Of Ross?"

She nodded.

"Do you think he killed him?"

"I think he knew who Pedro Martinez was. And he didn't say anything."

"Mae, you have to say something. Or I do."

"No, please. Give me till the end of the day."

"What's going to change?"

"I'll tell Jessie. I don't have anything to lose with her anyway."

147

Lopez looked at her watch. "I've got to go. Here's my number." She took a pen from the inside of her jacket and scribbled the number on a napkin. "You don't call me by five, I'm talking to Ross."

"Okay," the girl whispered.

Lopez slid out of her seat. "It will be okay."

The woman nodded as the detective rushed out of the diner without taking her food. Brunnell grabbed the leftovers and slipped them into her bag.

8:30 a.m.

CAPTAIN ANTONY MIKOVICH STOOD AT ONE END OF A large circular table that took up most of a conference room at Homicide. Photos of the four victims covered a movable white board next to him: Pedro Martinez, LeAnn DeVille, and the couple not yet identified from the previous night's killing.

Detective Eric Ross sat on one side of the table across from three of his colleagues, Homicide detectives Lydia Arabindan, Daniel McGee, and Oscar Marino. Lina Lopez slipped into a seat next to Eric Ross as soon as Mikovich began talking.

"Glad we could all make it this time," the captain said. "Let's start here." He threw the morning's *Daily News* on the table. The front page held a photograph of LeAnn DeVille and a headline reading, "Dead Social Worker Kept Them in Hell." The detectives had already read the story. In it, three young adults in their early twenties shared stories of LeAnn DeVille's incompetence as a foster caseworker. The woman, they said, ignored her clients' claims of abuse and allowed children of all ages to stay in homes where they were ill-treated and ill-fed.

"DeVille isn't the only social worker who ever overlooked abuse. What makes her the dead one?" Mikovich asked.

Detective Oscar Marino spoke up. "Checked her record with foster services," he said. "No outstanding complaints. Not sure if Pedro Martinez was in her care or not. Hard to track his background. Someone heading to Foster Services today?"

149

"We are," Ross said.

"How about the kids in the article?" Mikovich asked.

"Meeting them later today," Detective Lydia Arabindan said. "The girl is the only one without priors. The boys are cousins and both have records."

"Where are you meeting them?" Ross asked.

"Mantua—the new mural ceremony you learned about."

"Good. So why did DeVille leave Central High?" Ross asked.

"She was just a one-year substitute," Arabindan said. "Not much more there."

"Tell me about Grandma in Fishtown," Mikovich said to Ross.

"Doesn't want to cooperate or talk. Detail's been on the house since Monday."

"We need more connections," Mikovich said. "What connects these vics—same Wawa? Same dealer?"

"Not dealer," Marino said. "Forensics says the only substance inside the dead couple was arsenic. We'll see what a full autopsy pulls."

"Surveillance on Martinez?" Ross said.

"We can track him turning on Girard from Shackamaxon Street and walking toward Frankford," Marino said.

Mikovich noted Lopez staring at Ross.

"What have you two learned?"

"Spent some time at Penn Treaty Park," Ross said. "A couple of fishermen recognized Pedro. Said he didn't stand out much, but definitely a presence at the park. He seemed overly interested in the William Penn statue. Often alone, sometimes with a blond girl, sometimes with a heavyset black man his own age."

"No security cameras there?"

"Don't think so."

"I'll check on it," Marino said. "And on security cameras, we have plenty to pull for footage from last night's scene. Waiting to download from three businesses along the square—Fishtown Jewelers, Philly Bagels, and Grind coffee shop."

"DeVille's death just doesn't match the other three," Detective McGee said. "What are we thinking about a copycat? Tearing someone's throat out is so much more vicious than death by arsenic."

"Is it?" Mikovich asked. "Makes for a quick end. Arsenic is slower. And more painful."

"They happened in such close succession though," said Arabindan. "I don't know that a copycat would be ready to go so quickly. One night after? Person would have already needed a target, and props, and setting...this is premeditated."

"Or," countered McGee, "killer could have known what the first killer was going to do, had a victim and the props ready...just had to get the target to the scene."

"That's a big 'just,'" Arabindan argued.

The group sat quietly.

"McGee," said Ross, "Can you check on something with Narcotics?"

"Sure."

"The 26th is suspicious of increased activity of some sort in and around All Saints. See if anything new is on their radar."

"Okay." Mikovich paused. "Where's everyone heading?"

"Two of us need to hit Graterford," Ross said. "Inmate mural workshop today, and Lopez told them we were coming. We need to cross-check recent releases and re-offenders associated with City Murals, but Murals doesn't seem willing to cooperate."

"And if we're going that route," said Marino, "ex-cons could always have volunteered without identifying their pasts."

"Okay," said Mikovich. "Marino, McGee, can you take that? Ross, keep working Fishtown." He paused. "He showing you anything about the 26th you hadn't yet realized, Lopez?"

"Not yet," she quipped.

"Let's get to it then," the Captain said. "Ross, Lopez, hold back."

The others left.

"Still think the Fishtown kid told you everything?" Mikovich asked.

"Everything she knew to tell," Ross said.

Mikovich took a step toward Ross and lowered his voice. "Do we need to get her out of there?"

"Again. No." Ross locked eyes with the captain and was the first to look away. He moved toward the door, followed by Lopez.

Detective Oscar Marino was waiting across the hall.

"Ross, can I talk to you?" he asked.

"I'll meet you at Forensics," Ross told Lopez.

Marino waited for her to walk out of sight. "Listen, the footage of Pedro Martinez walking the night he was killed, the footage I grabbed based on your notes." He hesitated.

"Yes?"

"Someone interesting popped up on it. Not too far behind him. Just to Girard. Then the person turned and went in a different direction. I think."

"I did," Ross said. "Literally banged into the guy and followed him to see if he was okay. Turned off at Girard and saw him again as a corpse."

Marino nodded. "Sure." He stared at Ross. "Don't think anyone's ever going to question what you did or didn't see, Ross. Not after that Victor bullshit."

"What do you want to say, Marino?"

"Would have locked a killer up."

"For something he may not have done."

Marino rolled his eyes.

"You draw lines, too, Marino. This is mine. I don't know, I say I don't know. That made you look bad? That's on you."

Marino took a step closer to Ross and shook his head no. "Look bad? Me? I'm a team player. I came out of that a fucking hero. You're the asshole who let Victor walk on a technicality."

"On testimony."

"You know how many times I've defended you? Mikovich has defended you? People think you're a rat. They say you let him go. I say you weren't sure from the start. I say you are a man of your word. So don't gray area me, Ross. That's what you don't get!"

"What don't I get Marino?"

"Interpretation. I defend you because you're a good detective. I don't care what you say or don't say. What you see or don't see. I don't care. Victor. Was it him, was it not him? It was him. He facilitates deaths every day with that shit he pushes."

"What the hell does that even mean?"

Marino lowered his already quiet voice. "Some think it means you wanted him off, or someone else wanted him off and you did them a favor. I don't care, because you're a good detective. So I say that."

Ross looked away from Marino. "Okay."

"You're welcome."

9:20 a.m.

LINA LOPEZ MET ROSS OUTSIDE THE GLASS DOORS LEADING into Forensics. The hallways were lit with obnoxious fluorescent lights and during the day appeared brighter than the pristine labs that caught natural light on either side of the floor. Lopez noted team members at tables and stations inside each lab. Across from Jessie Wren's office, Lopez could see Mae Brunnell observing a male lab tech analyzing fluid samples. Wren studied paperwork alongside two other colleagues at a table in a different room. Ross tapped on the window and caught her attention. A minute later, she joined them in the hallway.

"Toxicologist agrees with arsenic as COD for Pedro Martinez," she said. "I had the lab fast-track Martinez's samples—we're reviewing them now. No traces of DNA outside of his own."

"Latent fingerprints?"

"No."

"Anything seem off?"

Wren frowned and shrugged. "That's what we're thinking about now."

"And nothing on the couple last night."

"I don't think we'll see anything different. Thought maybe we'd get a different fingerprint off the ice cream cone, if someone else did indeed supply it, but no."

"Marino's following up on security footage."

"Yep, he told me. We'll download and get working on it."

"And LeAnn DeVille?"

"Too early to tell. That's a lot of setup without any eye-witnesses."

"Different killer?"

"I don't know. Somehow involved with the other. The detail on those props gives me pause. Too early to know if DNA has popped up on those."

She hesitated.

"What?" Ross asked.

"We need more bodies to trace a pattern."

All three stood silently. "Dr. Brennard has his team of psychologists looking into the three murals of interest," Wren said. "They're meeting now."

"Finding a narrative thread?" Lopez asked.

"More interested in what the choice of three seemingly different murals from three very different neighborhoods could reveal about the killer. We'll see. I told him you'd be by," she said to Ross, who shook his head no.

"I'll wait to see what they say first."

"What I still want to know," Wren said, "is how someone smuggled a large bird's carcass into the cemetery during the day without anyone's noticing."

"I'll make another round of asks," Lopez said. "Maybe the press has shaken someone's memory."

"And what about arsenic?" Ross asked. "The killer could turn any household cleaner or insecticide into a deadly substance. Why arsenic?"

"Classic choice. Sends a message." Jessie Wren paused. "When we find that people have been poisoned, we don't normally think homicide, do we? We think suicide, because there is no overt trauma. Too clean. But what is throwing us off here are the props." She spoke slowly. "The props make us think homicide."

"And the knife in DeVille's throat," added Lopez.

Wren ignored her. "Let's say victims one, three, and four were victims of suicide. They poisoned themselves. What statement are they making by wearing these props? With the props, they are flipping the assumption. What we may have assumed was suicide by poisoning we now assume is a homicide."

"Is it pure arsenic?" Ross asked.

"Yep," said Wren. "No other substance in his system. But when would he have given it to himself? And why suffer to such an extreme? Intense, unbearable stomach pain would be immediate. Coroner says the poison was in his system for a while, perhaps hours before he arrived at Palmer Cemetery. How did he get himself there in a state of agony?"

"Maybe it was a type of dare," suggested Lopez, "some kind of sadomasochistic ritual or initiation."

Wren turned sharply toward her. "Maybe." She noticed Mae Brunnell standing in the lab's doorway. "What do you need?"

"Nothing. Just...done here." Brunnell walked away.

"Like you said," Ross told Wren, "We need to stop him, but we need more of a pattern to study him." He looked at Lopez. "I'll meet you at the car. Need to check on something."

Jessie Wren turned abruptly back toward her lab reports.

"Can I ask you something?" Lopez said, stopping her. Wren stood still as a way of saying yes. "Security footage. We review it here with you all, but who makes the ask, Homicide or Forensics?"

Lopez didn't need to ask the question, but she wanted to reverse any damage done by rebuffing the woman at the track.

"Usually Homicide asks, we download the footage, and detectives review on their own or with us," Wren answered, barely turning.

"Here? Or downstairs."

"Here. Our equipment's better."

"Okay."

"Need something else pulled?"

"No—" Lopez caught herself, remembering her lead from the Rodriguez library. "Actually, I might. I remember at the 26th, I would fill out a subpoena—"

Wren waved her hand in front of her face. "No need." She looked around the hallway. "Mae!" she barked.

The younger woman practically ran out of the lab one door away.

"Help the detective." Wren disappeared.

"Hi, again." Mae Brunnell smiled. "What can I get for you?"

Lopez was thrown both by Wren's brusqueness and Brunnell's bubbliness. "Security footage. Can you process something for me?"

"Sure?"

"The Ramonita Rodriguez library."

"Where's that?"

"Northern Liberties. Sixth and Girard."

"Okay—from when to when?"

"Last two weeks."

"No problem. Are you looking for a certain camera view?"

"Anything that captures the exit doors from inside the library. Both exit doors and the foyer in between."

"Done," Brunnell said. "Should I contact you directly?"

"Please. You have my cell."

"Got it."

"And about this morning," Lopez said. "I'm not forgetting. Just thinking."

She seemed to surprise the younger woman. Mae Brunnell looked confused and uncomfortable. "Okay. I'll see you later."

11:22 a.m.

Two corrections officers met Detectives Marino and McGee after they passed through security at Graterford. Located about thirty miles northwest of Philadelphia, the maximum-security prison should have closed two years before. Graterford State Correctional Institution dated from 1929 and held around 2,500 inmates. Officers had long complained about its security issues: the building held too many shadows and small pockets where a runaway prisoner could hide. And should a prisoner escape the building, his only outdoor barriers were a thirty-foot stone wall surrounding the property and a lookout tower. To remedy concerns, a new prison had been erected on the site. State Correctional Institution Phoenix would hold an additional 1,500 inmates in two male facilities, and include over thirty classrooms for vocational education, a gym, and a legal library. The $350 million project was the largest ever awarded by the Commonwealth of Pennsylvania, but the opening had been delayed due to lawsuits between the contractor and the state.

The detectives had been warned that the upcoming move had the prisoners on edge. Many were used to living in a single cell, and at Phoenix, most would have a cellmate. Upgraded security also meant a loss of privacy. Fencing, pressure sensors, and razor wire would upgrade outdoor security; indoors, safer conditions translated into better sight lines for corrections officers. Common rooms, including showers, would be located in the inner circle of cell blocks.

The guards led Marino and McGee down a dingy hallway with flickering fluorescent lights. They stopped at a large room, where another guard opened the door with a key fob. Bright colors instantly met the detectives. Across from the door, greens and yellows blended together on a parachute cloth hung from the wall. Several inmates held art supplies. They worked either on the cloth, in sketchbooks, or with pictures arranged on school desks. Marino started to circle but was cut off by a middle-aged civilian in an untucked plaid shirt, ripped jeans, and high-top Converse sneakers. Another guard standing at one end of the room stared straight ahead.

"Detectives, can we meet in the hallway please?" asked the man in plaid.

One of the guards explained. "This is Lonny Soto. He leads the workshop."

Before the introduction ended, Soto had left the room, leaving two guards stationed inside and two following the detectives.

Soto slunk against the wall. "This is a therapy class. The whole point is using art as therapy. Bringing an interrogation inside violates that contract."

"So you'd like to speak to us alone, here in the hall," McGee said with a steady tone. His confidence seemed to rattle Soto further.

"What is it, man?"

McGee observed the faces of the two guards who had escorted them. He thought he read disdain in them as Lonny Soto spoke.

"What?" Soto asked impatiently.

The officers didn't respond. Soto crossed his arms.

"You know why we're here," McGee said quietly. "The mural killings."

"Okay."

"Four people are dead," Marino said. "Sorry that interrupts your art class."

Soto bristled.

"How long have you been here?" McGee asked.

"About a year."

"Anybody not cooperate in about a year?"

"Nope. It's a voluntary program."

"Okay. Here's the thing," McGee said. "We're going to keep coming back, and we're going to have the right to talk to your students if we don't figure this thing out." He paused for effect. "Can you think of anyone who has had a particular interest in the murals chosen by the killer so far?"

"No," Soto said.

"Anyone who drew pictures of dead people?"

"Lots. It's therapy, remember?"

"Any in staged scenes like we've been seeing—"

"No," Soto said.

"Mr. Soto," McGee said, "we are in a prison, with offenders. I'm not sure why you're resisting us here."

"Look, these guys volunteer to work with art. To work their shit out. To better themselves. You know the recidivism rates of our students?"

"I'm sure they're impressive. But at least one of your students will reoffend. We want to know who you think that might be."

Soto shook his head no. "I just can't see my guys doing that."

"Reoffending?"

"Disrespecting the program."

Marino pulled out his notebook and started scribbling.

161

Soto ran his hands through his hair and shot a glance at the guards. "I'll think about it some more. But I really can't help you."

"Does an art therapist work with these men?" Marino asked.

"You're looking at him," Soto quipped.

"Okay," Marino said, pocketing the notebook. "You're done for now."

The guards held the door open. Marino started inside again, but McGee tapped his elbow.

"We're okay," he said to the guards. "We'll head back now."

———————•———————

"Guy sure as hell didn't like you," Detective McGee said as they walked into the parking lot. "You piss off a painter in a former life?"

"Not that I know of."

Both men turned as they heard heavy footsteps behind them. It was one of their escorts.

"Henry Crimmell," the guard said. "That's a name you want."

"Crimmell?" McGee spelled the name aloud as he wrote it down.

"Served seven years for aggravated assault. Odd bird. Released about a month ago."

"Didn't work well with the program?" Marino asked.

"Showed up but didn't communicate. Ever. Painted what he wanted. That guy had to come up with a project just for Crimmell."

"Do you remember what that was?"

"Some kind of sketching bullshit."

"Why is Soto so protective?"

"All these teachers are. Writing teachers, art teachers, Bible teachers…they all think their words and their paintbrushes are going to change the world. Anyone who disagrees isn't worth shit."

"Soto bother you?" McGee asked.

"'Course he does. He's an asshole. But he shows up. Every week. Hasn't missed one day. Same thing with the others. Can't stand them, but they show up."

11:30 a.m.

Ross and Lopez waited at the receptionist's desk in the Foster Services lobby. The room held many chairs and the smell of stale cigarette smoke. Yellowed pictures of flowers drawn by schoolchildren lined part of one wall. Parenting magazines were stacked on a large table in the center of the room.

Not acknowledging the detectives, the receptionist held a phone to her ear, discussing a schedule pulled up on her computer monitor. They didn't mind. As soon as they had arrived, Ross got a call: the couple from the night before had been identified. Clay Attle and Margot Step, both twenty-three. A few residents of the Emerald Street tent camp had seen the story on the morning news in the lobby of the free health clinic on Girard. The two had shown up a month or so before and were noticeable because Step was deaf. Lopez and Ross searched for their names on social media until a loud voice distracted them.

A weary middle-aged woman marched through the glass doors at the entrance and headed into the lobby. A sullen teenager wearing earbuds followed.

"Out of here. She is OUT OF HERE!" the woman yelled at nobody in particular. "Do you know what this little truant hussy stole? My mother's pearls. And pawned them. That's it. I'm done. Now."

She turned to the girl. "Sit the hell down and wait."

"What about my shit?" the girl said.

"Your shit is my shit. I should take those damn head-phones too."

"You can't do that."

"Sit your ass down."

The receptionist stood.

"Ms. Brady," she said calmly, "who is the caseworker?"

The woman charged her desk. "You know what? Been so long since I've seen her, I don't remember. But it doesn't matter. Goodbye." She stomped toward the door.

"You can't just leave her here," Lopez said.

"Can, will, am." She left the room.

"This is some bullshit," the girl said.

"Language," the receptionist said.

Another frantic middle-aged woman approached from a hallway. "What happened?"

The receptionist shook her head. She addressed the detectives. "Detectives Ross and Lopez?"

Lopez nodded.

"This is Fran Mason, our director. She'll see you now."

Fran Mason led the detectives into a cluttered office. The windows were closed, and the heater let off a dull sound and gassy smell. Stacks of file folders, papers, and binders cluttered bookshelves, cabinets, and Mason's desk. She cleared two chairs for the detectives by tossing stacks of folders onto the floor. Sitting at her desk, she took off her glasses and pinched her temple with her right hand.

"I know why you're here. I don't know what to say." She paused and leaned back in her chair. "The press stands ready to tear out our throats. Any chance of private funding is gone." She directed her comments to Ross.

"What do you need?"

"Any combination of connection between Pedro Martinez, Clay Attle, Margot Step, and LeAnn DeVille."

"Attle and Step?"

"Latest victims just identified."

"Well, I can speak to Pedro. Yes, he was with us, but he aged out. File's been closed for years."

"You do have a database of where they all lived and who with," Lopez said.

Mason closed her eyes. "I need a subpoena." She opened them at Ross. "And then we could check if the names are correctly spelled in the system and if the caseworkers correctly updated the records for every single move each kid made."

"That's a start," Ross said.

Mason smiled and opened her hands. "Look around here, officer." She lifted a stack of papers and dropped them back on her desk. "Our average kid is placed ten to fifteen times. Ten to fifteen. The average caseworker has fifteen cases at any given time. And makes less than $35,000 a year. I can't tell you how many people I've trained in the past six months. And I've been with the system for twenty years. *And* the mayor is making our lives a living hell right now."

"Three former foster kids and a social worker are dead," Lopez said. "Coincidence? Or just a pain in your ass?"

Mason groaned. "Yes. Former foster kids die all the time. Every day. Not in such spectacular fashion, but they die. The news gets some of the stories. You all, though, go after nastier perpetrators, and we pick up the pieces."

She and Lopez locked eyes.

"Why is the mayor a problem?" Ross asked.

"She's pulling money from all religious agencies discriminating against LGBTQIA+ foster parent applications," Mason said with exasperation. "So who gets those kids now that their caseworkers aren't gonna get paid?"

"What will happen?" Ross asked.

"Well," she said, putting her hands on her forehead. "Catholic Services is taking a line of credit to pay their workers until a judge decides whether to overturn the decision. Those kids are staying put. Others will be shoved here and there into homes already bursting at the seams. If they're old enough, group homes."

Lopez leaned toward Mason.

"So we should expect missing files and a lack of notes?"

"You should expect," said Mason testily, "that I'll do what I can. But it's nearly impossible to look back and find who lived with who for a few weeks and when."

She and Lopez glared at one another.

"What about personnel?" Ross asked.

"What do you mean?"

"If we wanted a record of former employees. Could we get that from payroll?"

Mason relaxed a bit. "Easier. Yes."

"How can we best reach you? Do you have a card?"

Mason smirked. "Yeah, it's around here somewhere." She put her glasses back on. "I'll be in touch, Detectives."

"By tomorrow," Lopez said. "And our colleagues will be stopping by with a subpoena for those files on DeVille's former clients."

Mason shook her head as her phone rang. "Subpoena all you want, but this will take time."

"Starting tomorrow," emphasized Lopez.

Mason answered the phone as the detectives left. "Hello? Nope, not busy at all."

Ross followed Lopez to the car. She slammed the door and stared out her window.

"I'm a product of this system, " Lopez said after a minute.

She lowered the window as Ross started the car. They didn't speak for a few minutes.

"In and out for years." Lopez spoke into the passenger window. "You live an adoption fantasy until middle school. Then you start realizing this is it."

"Ever live in a group home?" Ross asked.

"Once. Stayed with a family when I was a teenager that took in as many as they had beds for."

"How many?"

"Six."

"They rich?"

"No. Six hundred dollars per month per kid, but most of that goes to food. Or should." She was lost in her thoughts for a minute. "Anyway, told a teacher I needed to get out. She helped me find someone who basically let me sleep on a couch for my last two years of high school."

"Where'd you go?" Ross asked.

"Germantown."

"Closed now."

"I loved it. Got involved with Navy Junior ROTC. Was the best thing I could have done."

"Military then?"

"Yeah." She closed the window and he started the car. "But I always wanted to be a cop."

Ross drove past the church that hosted City Murals toward Girard.

"Group homes are a different animal though."

"I thought they were phasing out."

"They were. In the nineties, I think, Clinton pushed for adoption from foster families within a certain time period. So if you didn't get adopted by a certain age, you went to a group home. They're basically mental wards

168

for kids nobody can handle."

A construction truck put its flashers on a block away. Ross hit the gas pedal and the siren and steered down the middle of a two-way street until he reached Girard Avenue.

"What about you, Ross? You grow up on a farm somewhere?" Lopez grinned.

"Grew up with my dad in Jersey."

"Mom?"

"Died young." His tone didn't welcome questions. "Let's see how Ruby and Grandma are doing."

"Can you pull over at the Rodriguez Library first? I need to check on something."

2:15 p.m.

Lopez entered the library and greeted Ms. Jerry, the librarian.

"No detail today?" the detective joked, nodding toward the security station.

"Nope." The librarian smiled sadly. She looked around and lowered her voice. "Lucky bitch faking a headache no doubt."

Lopez smiled.

"Actually, Detective, you're right on time. We're getting ready to close early."

"Why?"

"Staff development."

Without meaning to, Lopez burst into a loud laugh. Ms. Jerry was pleased.

"I ain't shitting you."

"No, I…I'm sorry." Lopez noticed the same group of older homeless men reading newspapers at the table to her right.

"And don't worry—I'm going to pull that footage your Forensics friend asked for."

"Yes. Thank you. I just need to check one thing I saw on your posting board."

Lopez swung around the front desk and through the first exit door. The community board was overflowing with mostly the same flyers and index cards she had noted before. Flipping through pictures on her phone from her last visit, she stood still for a couple of minutes, comparing the past and present scenes.

"What am I looking for here?" she whispered to herself. "What were you looking for Pedro?"

Maybe just a job. Probably just a job. Again she took pictures, lifting and pushing aside flyers to make sure she had close-ups of the entire board. Block letters written in ink on a yellow index card caught her eye.

PENN TREATY PLAYERS
ACT 4 CALL
WEDNESDAY AT 9:30

"Ms. Jerry!" Lopez called.

"Yes?" She came through the door.

"Did you hear about the two deaths in Palmer Park last night?"

"No." She shook her head. "Heroin? Too many."

"Not heroin. Could you take a look at the victims? Tell me if you've seen them here before."

"Sure."

"The names are Margot and Clay. The only photos I have are from—"

"No." She inhaled. "A young couple? Skinny? She's deaf?"

"Yeah."

"I do remember them." The librarian's eyes watered.

"They hang out with Pedro?"

"I don't know about that."

"Why do you remember them?"

"They came by often, almost every day, even yesterday." She pointed straight ahead. "They looked at that board. Never looked at anything else. I thought they were dealing or getting here. Stuck Jane on them."

"The guard?"

171

"Yeah."

"She asked for their names. Clay and Margot. Said they just wanted work." She put her hand over her mouth and started to cry. "I feel bad for judging them so."

DETECTIVE LYDIA ARABINDAN WALKED DOWN A STREET of rundown two- and three-story rowhomes in the Mantua section of West Philadelphia, not too far from the campus of the University of Pennsylvania. Somewhat downtrodden, Mantua had pockets of revitalization where small murals decorated urban gardens. Arabindan headed in the direction of festive music, and a block later saw the makings of an afternoon block party inside a small neighborhood park.

She entered past a raffle table manned by two older women.

"Ten dollars for five tickets!" one said.

"Maybe on the way—ah!"

A boy had run into her, knocking them both to the ground. Pushing himself off, he took off laughing as others chased him in a game of tag. Balloons hung from a fence, and food trucks serviced small lines. Girl Scouts struggled to scoop water ice, and a local salon had set up a face-painting table with an arts and crafts station covered in paper and crayons.

Arabindan saw the new mural at one end of the lot. Called *Urban Horseman*, the work, a celebration of African American art, covered the side of a building. A young Hispanic man in an Eagles hat and T-shirt waved at her. She met him in the middle of the park.

"Sandro Gomez?" she asked. "Detective Lydia Arabindan. Thanks for meeting me here."

"Sure. My cuz Freddie's getting food. Mandi didn't come."

"She okay?"

"Article stirred some shit. My fault. When I saw that woman's face in the paper, I had to say something."

Freddie Lima, Sandro's cousin, approached, carrying a tray of sandwiches and fries.

"Hi, Detective," Freddie said. He was shorter than Sandro and overweight, his gut spilling over ill-fitting jean shorts.

"Thanks for coming, Freddie, although I have to say— shrimp salad served from a food truck?"

"If it's free, it's for me," he said, laughing. Sandro took food from him.

"So as I told Sandro on the phone," Arabindan said, "I learned about you all from the newspaper. How did the reporter find you all?"

Sandro raised his hand. "Messaged their tip line."

Arabindan nodded. "Article said you two have been out of the system for some years?"

Both nodded.

"How did you stay in touch with Mandi?"

"She was my foster sister," Sandro said, food spilling from his mouth. "I stay in touch with the good ones."

Children started shrieking from across the lot. Sandro turned as a spray ground system shot water in her direction.

"So like I said, I read the article. But tell me again why DeVille was so bad."

Freddie deferred to Sandro, Arabindan could see that.

"She didn't listen," the older cousin said.

"You both had her for a couple years?"

Both nodded.

"Freddie, the article says you told her a house parent tried to abuse you?"

174

Freddie glanced at Sandro, who nodded at him. "Lady said I didn't have proof. Said I made it up 'cause I didn't like it there."

"Shit happens like that all the time," Sandro said, finishing his fries and starting on Freddie's.

"Hey!"

"Get some more then."

Freddie obeyed.

"You know the system's broken, Detective," Sandro said. "I get it, you get it, but when a kid tells an adult that another adult wants to suck his cock, she should do something about it."

"Anywhere else for him to have gone?"

"His dad tried to get him back once, but the judge didn't listen."

"How come?"

"This reason, that reason. It don't matter. Point is, they find holes to stick kids in and leave them there until something happens that makes them look bad."

Arabindan nodded.

"Like now," Sandro said. "You watch. Three former foster kids and a social worker dead now. All of a sudden," he threw his hands in the air, "the mayor's going to start caring about poor kids again."

Arabindan watched the children laughing and shoving one another as they ran through sprinklers.

"What about you, Sandro," she asked gently. "You ever confront DeVille?"

"All the time!" he emphasized. "I'd tell her we didn't have enough food. Like, ever. House parents held allowances. Little kids in ripped clothes…" He licked his fingers and threw his trash on the ground. "Whatever. Nobody cared. You learn not to care."

175

"Try going over her head?"

He snorted. "Case manager is it. Nobody else is going to listen. They have other problems. Where's Freddie?"

"Over there," Arabindan said, pointing at a food truck without looking up from her notebook. "So these deaths—DeVille, and Martinez, Margot Step and Clay Attle—what do you think?"

"I know DeVille deserved it. Don't know about the others." His tone changed. "The Muralist is some bad-ass mother—."

"The Muralist?"

"Come on, Detective. What they're calling the murderer."

"Who?"

"Social media. People. You on Instagram?"

"No."

Sandro pulled up his feed and scrolled in front of her. It held posts shared from the same account named "The Muralist."

"Can I see that?" Arabindan asked. Grabbing the phone, she clicked on The Muralist's profile. It had only three videos on it, each a one-minute single camera view of the murals matched to the murders. The first, *Dream in Flight*, had been posted a week before Pedro died. *Ode to Life* had gone up the night of Pedro's death, around twenty-four hours before the discovery of DeVille's body. The third, *Summer Rendezvous* had been posted the evening before Attle and Step died, maybe before they even found LeAnn DeVille's body at the Central High track.

"Kind of eerie, isn't it?" Sandro said, watching her watch the videos. Just the still focus. Just the sound of the streets."

Detective Arabindan noted that the comments had been disabled. Each video had over one thousand shares.

176

"Notice anything else on here?" she asked.

"Did I look at the profiles of everyone who shared it?" Sandro asked. "Please.

"I noticed, before you got here," he continued, licking his greasy fingers, "most of these shares came through today." He took his phone back and smiled at her. "Set something up and follow me, Detective. @gummygo."

Arabindan smiled. "Be still my beating heart," she said sarcastically.

2:45 p.m.

"Something's up here," Lopez said to Ross back in the car after she left the library.

"Do you remember seeing my phone at Foster Services?" he asked.

"I...think so? Can't find it?"

"No."

"Want me to call anyone?"

"Foster Services. Maybe it's on a pile in that hot mess."

"Okay. But listen, this board—"

"Can you do it now?"

Lopez retracted her shoulders. She stared at the dashboard, slowly took out her phone, found the number, and handed it to Ross without looking at him. He gave it back to her a minute later.

"Reception will ask Mason."

"Listen, this board—"

"What board?"

"Announcement board at the exit."

"What?"

"Of the library!"

Lopez pulled up the photo of the Penn Treaty Players card.

"So librarians confirm that Pedro Martinez did hang out here, and he checked this board. Guess who else did? Clay Attle and Margot Step." Now she had his attention. Lopez skimmed through her photo roll. "Librarian says that each of the victims spent time looking at that board. That's why you were told Martinez had some kind of job here. He didn't. He just paid attention to the board."

178

"For what?"

"I don't know. But there's this card that announces the time for a Penn Treaty Players rehearsal. It says Act 4 will rehearse Wednesday at 9:30 p.m." Lopez realized as she said the information aloud how silly it sounded. "This card wasn't there yesterday when I first reviewed all of the flyers and announcements."

Ross was silent as he drove down Girard.

"It just doesn't fit," Lopez insisted, trying to validate what now seemed like a far-fetched idea. She entered "Penn Treaty Players" into Google. Nothing popped up. "I just don't think this is real."

"Could be a high school thing?"

"That relies on index cards to communicate? No way."

"So you think this is possibly a code of some sort? A communication encouraging the killer?"

"It's just odd information."

"It's a scribbling, right?"

"It could be an overlooked detail."

Ross pointed to movie posters shellacked to the side of a building. Someone had taken a can of blue spray paint and covered them with unintelligible graffiti.

"Do we interpret that graffiti? Analyze its meaning?" Ross's voice grew quieter, as if he were talking only to himself. "How do we know what are details and what's just bullshit leading us down a rabbit hole?" He shook his head. "You saw it. Your instinct. Follow it."

Lopez was quiet for a minute. "This feels off. Doesn't say what part of Act 4, what scenes, what the play is called, where they're supposed to meet. Pedro Martinez spent time at this board. He was looking for something. At Penn Treaty Park."

"Okay," Ross said sharply. "Something to consider. Call the local rec centers and see if they recognize the name Penn Treaty Players. Also try Temple's drama department, University of the Arts, schools that might have community outreach programs involving an older demographic."

Lopez was a little stunned that he was taking her idea seriously. She thought he'd handle it with silence, dismiss it as being too much of a long shot to absorb their time. In the validation of the moment, Lopez almost told him about asking Mae Brunnell to pull security footage from the library. Ross wasn't transparent about anything though, and this was the one action she had taken that she hadn't yet shared with him. He would no doubt ask for the footage any minute, but until he did, Lopez wanted to study it herself. She was more determined than ever to be the one to figure out why Pedro Martinez had ended up in that cemetery.

Traffic was stalled under the El bridge that crossed over Girard Avenue. Ross sighed and watched a man with an overgrown beard stand in the middle of the trolley tracks. He wore an oversized, filthy gray sweatshirt and baggy jeans and leaned into crutches. One hand held a cardboard sign scribbled with black marker reading, "Help a starving artist. God Bless." His right foot was wrapped in bandages, but he hobbled back and forth over the tracks, turning to one side of the avenue and then the other, intent on moving toward any driver who made eye contact with him. Nearby, on a cement platform between the trolley tracks, the man had a small pile of belongings: a dirty duffle bag, a take-out container of food, a box of granola bars.

Cars honked.

"You all right?" Lopez asked.

"Yeah, why?" Ross said, staring out the window.

180

"Because you've got a green light."

Ross broke from his reverie and hit the gas.

"When will you check in with Conor Mathew?" Lopez asked.

"Tomorrow. Unless we see him around before then."

"How long have you known him?"

"Years."

"He been using for years?"

"Not for a while."

Lopez whipped her head around. "That guy?"

"Did—that's what brought him here. But he kicked it a couple of years ago. May have fallen back, but I don't think so. I check in with him now and again."

"How does he stay clean and live on the street in this neighborhood?" Lopez murmured.

Ross shrugged. "People do it all the time, live in the houses where they used. His house is just outdoors."

Lopez rolled her eyes.

"The Penn Treaty homeless group is older—the old definition of homeless," he said. "Disabled veterans, alcohol abuse, mental illness. Conor lives among them. He's scrappy. He's got demons. But he chooses to be there."

They slowed down again. Ross noticed the stripper he had spoken with on Monday morning taking another smoke break outside of the strip club. He grinned when he remembered her quick wit. Lopez followed his gaze.

"She one of your favorites?"

Ross ignored the joke. "Ever deal with her?"

"A few times. She's an on-again, off-again informant for the 26th. You?"

"No. Just one encounter."

Lopez snapped her head toward him.

"Not that kind." They both smiled.

Several minutes later, Ross parked near the gates of Palmer Cemetery.

"What about Ruby?" Lopez asked. "Should we show her photos of Clay Attle and Margot Step? See if they look familiar?"

"Not yet." He stepped out of the car and scanned the neighborhood. "Where's detail?"

"Don't know. I'll walk around the block and make a call."

"Meet you inside the gates."

Lopez paused before they parted. "Hey, Ross?"

"Yep?"

"What would make you pull her? What would...have to happen?"

"No set formula. Instinct."

Lopez looked toward Ruby, who again sat near her sister's gravesite. "My instinct would have been to pull her as soon as we finished talking to her yesterday."

Ross's eyes also sought the girl by the grave. "It's still a little too loud around here," he said quietly. "Consider the facts while making as little noise as possible." Ross wondered if the man, Robert, was standing behind his screen door, shadowed by cats and his oxygen tank. His eyes searched the doors opposite the front gates. It appeared not.

"But Lopez," he added, "do find out where detail is."

Ted Morris, caretaker of the cemetery, gently raked the dead leaves that had gathered along the brick wall near the front of the gates. Across the cemetery, Ruby dodged between the hole in the oak tree and her sister's grave. She moved with the joyful enthusiasm of a child in fantasy play.

Morris smiled at Ross as the detective approached him. "You've been busy."

"Yes." Ross felt himself relaxing around the older man. He had been looking forward to returning to Palmer Cemetery all day. Morris seemed to read his mind.

"You like coming here, Detective." Straightening from his hunched position, the caretaker took a break. "I've noticed. Not just for the case, but to wander. He smiled again. "The place grows on you."

Ross noticed Ruby peering out at him from behind a grave marker.

"I wish more people did," Morris continued. "You know, in the nineteenth century, it was common to pack a picnic and take it to a family member's plot. Have a chat at the grave as you ate."

"No," Ross said. "No, I didn't know that."

"Child mortality rates were higher then. People included their dead little ones however they could." Morris tilted his head backward and steadied it again. "That's why I don't say anything when Ruby skips school now and again, hiding in that tree." He chuckled. "I tell neighbors that when they say the girl spends too much time here, talking to the dead." His expression sobered. "She's just doing what she's supposed to do. Not forgetting."

Good, Ross thought. The man may have spoken differently had he known the police had requested Ruby stay home from school for a bit. Detail was doing a good job staying out of the way.

"My partner and I are in the neighborhood following up on the Palmer Park deaths from last night."

Morris shuddered. "Awful. It must be connected to the death here."

Ross didn't answer. The caretaker picked up his rake.

"Just out of curiosity," Ross asked, "what happened to Ruby's sister?"

The man's eyes darkened. "It's a sad story."

"You mentioned a premature death the other day."

"Yep. At home."

"At home—here? Thompson's house?"

"Yes." Morris walked to a nearby bench and sat down. Ross stepped forward, facing Ruby.

"Who was there?" Ross asked.

"The night the baby died. Dorothy, her daughter Jane, who was Ruby's mother—is Ruby's mother—and of course, Ruby." Morris laid the rake across his lap and closed his eyes. "Neighbors called the police with all the screaming they heard. A woman's painful, childbirth screams. Then awful screams. Screams of sadness. Of death. Police came, an ambulance came. Jane refused to get into it. We heard later that she woke in the night in early labor, and Thompson helped deliver the baby. Died when…when the poor little thing had the cord wrapped around her neck." He slumped his shoulders.

"The police came before the ambulance?"

"Oh, I can't remember. Everything happened so quickly." Morris sighed. "Life is hard."

"What happened then?"

"Jane stayed at the house a day, maybe two, took off again. I don't know if she's been back. Baby was buried here, and Ruby, well, Dorothy had pretty much raised her to that point. Just kept on."

"Ruby—was she born at the house?"

"Not sure about that one. But I do know Thompson had no idea the father was black until she saw Ruby for the first time." He turned sideways and smiled. "She's still over there, isn't she?"

Ross nodded yes.

"I'm glad this place brings her happiness. I don't think Dorothy has ever known what to do with her." Morris stretched and yawned. "Anyway, it's been a day."

"What did Thompson do for work? Did her husband work?"

"Gordon died years ago. He had a factory job. They had a boy, too—not sure what happened to him. Left home after high school, haven't seen him in years. Dorothy though, yes. She's a retired librarian."

"Where?"

"Public library. Worked at the Fishtown branch for years. Retired right around the time Ruby started living here." Morris's face brightened. "Well, here's the sharp detective. Hello, ma'am!"

Lina Lopez stepped next to Ross. "Good to see you again, Mr. Morris. Nice tan."

The man laughed. "Just gardening." He yawned. "I'll get back to it then."

Lopez waited until Morris was out of earshot. "Northeast side of the park. Tinted windows, black Mitsubishi. They haven't seen anything but Ruby sneaking back and forth from the house. Thompson goes for walks to a corner store. Nothing else."

"Okay."

"Ross."

"Yeah?"

"We can't be seen talking to her again outdoors."

He glanced over at Ruby, still playing peekaboo from behind a headstone.

"Also, I checked in with Mikovich."

He turned sharply toward her.

"Didn't tell him about your phone. But did get an update from Marino and McGee. A guard gave them a lead on a name—some former con who didn't play nice with others."

"Where is he?"

"No way of knowing. They're on it."

Ross squinted at Ruby and turned around to leave. Lopez followed.

RUBY WATCHED THE DETECTIVES LEAVE THE CEMETERY.

"Well goodbye to you too, losers," she said out loud. Her shoulders slumped. She was bored. It had only been a day since they said she needed to stay inside and under police surveillance, and she felt trapped. Ruby didn't normally go anywhere besides school, the cemetery, the library, and sometimes a church youth group, but being told she had to stay in the house seemed like a punishment.

"I shouldn't have taken those eggshells, Junie. That's what got me into trouble. The old lady keeps saying so." Ruby stroked the dirt in front of June's headstone. "I just thought they could look like seashells. I knew they would make you happy."

Ruby smiled.

"I know. I'll get you some real ones one day."

She waited for a response.

"I don't know yet how I'm going to get there. I keep telling you, I can't just walk there."

Ruby giggled. She started imitating her grandmother. "Welllll, you got yourself...mmhmm...not anything I did. Hands to yourself..." She sobered suddenly. "She never looks at me when she talks to me. Only with her back to me, walking around the house like a crazy person."

Ruby's voice started shaking.

"I just sit there and say nothing. I hate her. I can't wait until I can leave…like Mama."

Tears welled in her eyes.

"No, Junie. I won't go far. I'll always come see you. You're my best friend."

Ruby wiped her face with the back of one hand.

"I don't know why she doesn't visit you," Ruby said quietly. "She doesn't visit me either. She just doesn't like coming here. She hates the old lady too, I bet. She remembers what she did to you."

Ruby shut her eyes tightly. "I know I do."

"You okay over there, Ruby?" a male voice called out.

"Yes, Mr. Morris!" she called back.

"I'm going to the farm lot later, Ruby," he said. "I'll bring back some flowers for you to plant. Still got your spade, don't you?"

"Yep. Thanks!"

4:00 p.m.

FROM HER PERCH BEHIND A LAB MICROSCOPE, MAE BRUN-
nell could see Jessie Wren packing up for the day. For the
past hour, the intern had been analyzing food samples for
bacteria strains and separating specimens into "clean" and
contaminated piles. It was a typical mini-lesson in forensic
epidemiology, and she had been surprised when Wren had
directed one of the techs to set it up for her. The exercise was
clearly connected to the recent victims of arsenic poisoning.
Somewhere in a different lab, Brunnell knew, pathologists
were doing a similar activity with Pedro Martinez's vomit
and the ice cream pulled from Clay Attle's limp hand.

LeAnn DeVille's death complicated things for the forensic psychologists whose meeting Brunnell had attended that
morning. Compared to the other staged bodies, DeVille's
corpse had been too easily categorized as a clean hit. The
murder weapon—most likely a dagger—had made one
point of entry into the victim's throat. The killer had to
have been tremendously strong and experienced to attack
her so accurately and quickly. Had the murderer then taken
precious getaway time to dress the body in costume? Had
an accomplice? Or had DeVille costumed herself? The
latter was unlikely. From what they had learned about the
woman, she had a loud voice that she wasn't afraid to use,
and nobody had heard her scream. She was either caught
unaware or frightened into silence.

Little personal information had turned up on Pedro
Martinez, who seemed to have lived off the grid, and the
search for details on Clay Attle and Margot Step was just

beginning. Martinez, Attle, and Step had died very different deaths from DeVille, with only costuming linking their ends. The couple seemed to have committed suicide, or at least gone along with their death sequence for some reason. As their cause of death mirrored Martinez's, the presumption was he had been in their same predicament. But while Attle and Step created a mural scene with their bodies, Martinez had to have had help.

Had DeVille's murder been a copycat crime committed in the wake of Pedro Martinez's death? Could Attle and Step have staged themselves in a separate copycat act?

Jessie Wren stuck her head in. "Okay?"

"Yep. I'll just do my best to break this down when I'm done?"

"Make sure a tech helps you."

"Of course."

Wren twitched, and Brunnell looked up.

"Everything okay?" Wren repeated.

"Yeah?"

"Just—your tone was different. This working out for you?"

"Yep." Brunnell smiled. "Just thinking about LeAnn DeVille, and how her killing does and doesn't match the others."

"Aren't we all." Wren stepped back from the door.

"Hey," Brunnell said, "I think I saw you running the other night. At Penn's Landing. Sunday?"

"Sounds about right. See you tomorrow."

Brunnell felt a wave of relief. She had downloaded the security footage from the Rodriguez library earlier in the afternoon and didn't want Wren to get pissed for not knowing about it. Detective Lina Lopez was clearly operating on a whim and seemed to be hiding the request from Ross.

Rest assured, Wren would go running right to him with any inkling of new information.

Mae Brunnell pulled out her phone and the card Lopez had given her earlier. "Hey!" she texted. "Footage in. Need to process, ready later. When can you meet?"

Jessie Wren waited on Ross's front steps in East Passyunk. The evening was warm and the humidity low. She leaned back against the top step, stretching her neck as she people watched. Groups of college-aged kids, probably art students, walked in packs toward Broad Street and its performing arts theaters. Wednesday nights were industry nights and students could go free.

Ross jogged down the steps. "Let's move," he said. "Stuck in a car too much today."

"Missing something?"

"What?"

She tossed him his phone.

"Where—?"

"Men's room. Top of the urinal. Marino found it."

She started running before he could ask her more.

The two jogged ten blocks to Penn's Landing. Crossing Delaware Avenue, they broke into a hard sprint for about a mile. Wren pushed the pace, harder and faster toward the pink lights outlining the Ben Franklin Bridge.

Ross stopped, feigning a calf muscle pill.

"You okay?" Jessie walked toward him.

Ross took off again. "Gotcha!" he yelled.

"Hey!" Jessie chased him, caught him, passed him. Reaching Penn Treaty Park, they doubled back and raced between traffic lights until they reached Penn's Landing again. Ross stopped first.

"Okay, okay," he said, gasping for air. "You've got this one. I'm soft."

"No, you're not." She was panting. "I'm just faster."

The harbor park drew fewer tourists on Wednesdays than on weekends. Carnival music played from the outdoor roller-skating rink. Children screamed as a small Ferris wheel lifted them into the air. Flickering lights outlined a floating bar tethered to the dock, and security guards wandered through hammocks strung from trees in a small riverside grove. A whiff of funnel cake caught Jessie Wren off guard and she coughed. The smell made her nauseous. The place made her nauseous.

"I miss you," she blurted out. "I miss talking to you. The Strangler always gave me a reason. I don't have one anymore."

Ross lowered his head. "Talking to me now, Jessie."

"We had our thing. For years. The Strangler was our constant. Then it ended. You got him, said nothing, and went away."

He straightened and looked at her.

"I can't give you what you want, Jessie."

"What do you think I want?"

"More than I can give you."

"But why did you cut me off—"

"I didn't cut you off. I did what I had to do. And it's like everything else. We move forward or we don't. There's no therapy. You worked on the Strangler. Lots of people did. Then he got caught. That's it."

"That's not it."

Ross paused, then changed the subject. "Arabindan says she told you about The Muralist on Instagram."

"Yep, but…that's a tough one."

"We can get the subpoena without a problem."

"I've told you this before. Subpoena for who? Account's

probably been created with made-up information. We're on it, and if we find a personal link, we'll need a warrant, but chances are unlikely. It's too easy to create an account with fake info. Takes a lot of time on our end running down a rabbit hole. But we're monitoring it, yes. If a new mural pops up on it, you'll be the first to know."

"When a new one pops."

"Maybe," Wren said.

"Are we tracking down security cameras around the murals at the time the videos were taken?"

"No way to know when they were taken. Could have been months ago and just uploaded within the last week. None of them was marked as a live feed."

"So when the next video posts, thousands of people will start looking for posed corpses."

"No. Thousands will see it, but they'll all watch for news headlines. The social media audience is in it for entertainment. Plus, none of the victims were found directly in front of the corresponding murals."

"I've got a headache," Ross said. He squeezed his temple with his right hand and started walking back toward home. She ran past him.

8:10 p.m.

Detective Lina Lopez was circling Penn Treaty Park on foot when she heard her phone buzzing. After visiting Palmer Cemetery, she had gone back with Ross to Homicide to debrief with the others.

McGee had a lead on Henry Crimmell, a now-homeless ex-con who had served time for aggravated assault. The team had briefly argued whether using resources to trace the guy was worth it. Marino thought it a desperate move. The prison guard, the detective said, could have just disliked the guy, or wanted to impress the detectives with a name, or just felt like screwing with them.

Lydia Arabindan had gotten further with her visit to the mural dedication. LeAnn DeVille's former clients hated her. She was a stereotypical figure in a broken system. But like Mikovich had asked, why her? Why was DeVille targeted as opposed to any other delinquent caseworker? And why was she killed at Central High School and the other three in Fishtown? The other victims had reason to be in the neighborhoods they had died in. They lived nearby. People had seen them before. Not DeVille. She lived in the suburbs and had no current clients in Olney.

The following day, Lopez was scheduled to accompany Lydia Arabindan to Central High School to interview the guidance department chair and the principal for any information they could provide on DeVille's short time with them. As McGee was going to spend the day reviewing security footage, Lopez volunteered to accompany Arabindan. Nobody seemed to care. She hoped Arabindan

194

would give her more perspective on what Mae Brunnell had shared earlier that morning. Her gut told her that Brunnell was right—Ross had seen Pedro Martinez and, for some reason, followed him. She wondered if Marino knew this after reviewing security footage and if that was why he had wanted to speak with Ross privately the day before. Lopez wasn't planning on telling Arabindan what Brunnell said. She just wanted the other woman's read on Eric Ross.

Before the meeting, Lopez had called the Fishtown, Port Richmond, and Northern Liberties recreation centers. Of the three, Northern Liberties had a weekly theater class, and the director was checking to see if the teacher knew anything about a small group that called themselves the Penn Treaty Players. Temple's drama department transferred her so many times that she hung up, and whoever answered the phone at the University of the Arts left her on hold.

Lina Lopez now hoped to find Conor Mathew or someone who could direct her to him. He would remember her from the night before, and she had a couple of twenties in her pocket. Ross clearly trusted the man, and if he lived here, he might have heard about the Penn Treaty Players. Maybe the group was an acting troupe that never set foot in the park. Or maybe it was a code that he could shed some light on.

Conor wasn't camped where she and Ross had met him. The pit bull was though. Lopez squinted. She could see a body wrapped in blankets next to the dog.

"Excuse me," she called out. "My name is Detective Lina Lopez. I was here with my partner last night."

The body moved.

"Could I speak with you, sir? Are you awake?"

A round of coughing answered her.

"Sir, I'm looking for Conor Mathew."

"Not him," the gravelly voice answered.

"Could I approach, sir?"

"No one's stopping you."

"Your dog is."

He said nothing.

"Sir, have you heard of a group called the Penn Treaty Players?"

"You gonna show me more pictures of dead people?"

"No."

She moved a few feet closer. "Could you hold on to your dog, please?"

"He won't hurt you."

The pit bull's guttural growl began.

"Now don't go getting my dog hauled away now."

"You answer my questions, you don't have to worry about that."

He cleared his throat. "What do you need?"

"Penn Treaty Players—have you heard of them? An acting group, or any group of some sort that might meet here under that name?"

"No."

"Anybody you can direct me to who might know?"

"Conor."

"Where is he?"

"Don't know. Told you that."

Lopez's phone buzzed with a text message. No cell number had registered.

"New phone," the message read. "Penn Treaty, meet you in parking lot at 9:00. New lead. Will wait for players."

"K," she responded. Ross must not have realized Marino had found his phone on the urinal earlier.

"Hey, any money in this for me?" the man asked.

"No, we don't work that way—"

"Your partner did the other night."

"Not sure about that. But thanks for talking to me."

9:05 p.m.

LOPEZ FIGURED ROSS WAS STANDING HER UP AGAIN. A FEW empty cars were scattered through the parking lot. She scanned the park and saw a flashlight beam moving around the perimeter.

"What the hell is he doing now?" she mumbled aloud.

Lopez paced around the statue of William Penn. She hated waiting for men. She noticed the beam paused around the spot where Conor Mathew had emerged the night before. She listened. Nothing but crickets. A few more minutes passed.

Screw you, Ross.

Lopez headed toward the beam. It moved farther back into the tree line.

The dog growled.

"Shit," she whispered. Hands shaking, she fumbled with her phone.

"Help me," she said. "At Penn Treaty. Now." She dropped her cell phone and her notebook and continued walking forward.

DETECTIVE ERIC ROSS JUMPED OVER THE CRIME SCENE tape and knelt next to the outline of a body. Inside the white spray painted lines, jumbo marshmallows specked with blood formed the shape of a smile in the outline of the head. Above the head, the letters "PO" had been sprayed into the grass.

"Hey!" yelled crime scene tech Mike Lee. "You can't be in here."

Jessie Wren stepped behind Ross. "Just let him."

"What are you talking about?" Lee said with disbelief. "We haven't processed this yet."

"I know. He's her partner."

"I know who he is. And he needs to get the hell out."

Wren put her hand on Ross's back. She helped him stagger under the tape.

A few minutes later, a female officer introduced herself.

"Detective Ross," she said, "I'm Officer Twyla Main, the responding."

Wren glanced at Ross. "Can you tell us how you found this?" she asked.

"Anonymous caller. Said a cop matching Lopez's description was attacked and lay bleeding here on the ground. Body was gone when we arrived on the scene. No witnesses in sight." Main paused. "We sent the blood to the lab of course—and we're trying to track any blood pattern from here out of the park. We haven't found anything."

Ross stared at the marshmallow smile. "The mural?"

"We think it's one at 22nd and Lehigh. Called *Heads to*

the Sky."

"Cop mural?" he asked.

"No. A bunch of headshots of people in different professions."

"Jessie, is it on—"

"Just went up on Instagram minutes ago," she said. "And Ross?"

"What?"

"Below the video of the mural is a close-up of Lopez's face. Propped. Her eyes are open in it."

Ross groaned. "Get a subpoena, warrant, whatever, and shut down the account!" he yelled. "I don't want her face out there."

"Fastest way is to lean on the FBI. We haven't had luck getting through."

"Just do it!"

"Can I…communicate anything for you back to the 26th?" Main asked. "I know you know she was one of us. We're going to do whatever—"

"What the fuck happened?" Officer Terrence Rivera yelled as he ran to Main. Two other officers approached him.

"Rivera," Main coaxed. "Let's go. No good standing here."

Rivera noticed Ross sitting on the ground.

"Ross."

The detective slightly moved his head.

"I swear to God, Ross, if this is about you…" The officer's body shook. "You're not even sad, you fuck. Or angry. She out of your hair now?"

"Get out!" Marino yelled.

"Let's go, Rivera." Main and two of her colleagues tried to ease him away from the scene. Rivera shoved each of them away.

200

"If this is about you, Ross, you're dead." Marino grabbed Rivera by both shoulders. He pushed him back to the parking lot and into a car.

"There's a guy with a pit bull around here," Ross said. "Probably hiding in the bushes. He might know. About all of this."

"Combing the riverbank right now for witnesses," Main said.

Inside the tape, Jessie Wren argued again with Mike Lee while other members of the forensics team and Mae Brunnell watched.

"I'm filing a report," he said. "You're encouraging contamination. And why?"

"I don't answer to you," Wren lashed out. "Now do your job."

"You do yours first."

"Get off the scene!" Wren snapped.

"Make me."

"You insubordinate prick."

"Will you two finish clearing the damn scene and give Ross five minutes?" Marino snapped. "Enough already." Wren glared at him.

"Ross," Marino said quietly, "what was Lopez doing here?"

Ross looked toward Columbus Boulevard, where cars slowed as they always did around police lights. Three days before, he had followed what now seemed like a ghost through this place, across that street. The image of Pedro Martinez limping forward with all of his might now seemed like a premonition. If only he had forced the man to face him, to talk to him. Would any of this been averted?

"At our briefing earlier," Marino said, "she had found out that Martinez, Step, and Attle were connected to an announcement board at a library. And she wanted to go with Arabindan to Central High tomorrow to ask about DeVille. Why was she here?"

"Rodriguez Library. She wanted to know more about that board," Ross answered.

Mae Brunnell sketched the crime scene on an iPad a few feet from where the detectives spoke. She strained to eavesdrop on their conversation. At the mention of Rodriguez Library, she stopped drawing and went to Jessie Wren.

"She found an index card on the board today," Ross continued. "Thought it was just put there."

"What was on it?"

"Rehearsal call for a group named the Penn Treaty Players. Said they would rehearse Act 4 at 9:30. That was it."

"9:30 p.m.? In the dark?"

"She must have thought so."

"Do you have a photo of this card?"

"On her phone."

"Phone isn't here."

Ross wiped his right fingers over his temple and closed his eyes. "It said Penn Treaty Players, Act 4 rehearsal, 9:30."

Marino checked his watch and ignored his buzzing phone. "She would have been killed before 9:30. But not by much."

"I told her to call the local recs, theater programs," Ross said. "Said to ask if they ever heard of such a group. I don't know what progress she made on that."

Jessie Wren approached with Mae Brunnell. Ross's phone started vibrating. He saw the name Mikovich on caller ID and tossed it to Marino.

"Tell them," she instructed her intern.

"Lopez asked me to pull security footage from the Rodriguez Library this morning. Seemed like she didn't want anyone else to know. So I did."

Marino narrowed his eyes. "She asked you how?"

"In person. When she and Ross came to talk to Jessie. After they talked to Jessie."

"You know about this?" Marino asked Ross. He shook his head no.

"I contacted Rodriguez and spoke to the security guard," Brunnell explained. "She said she didn't know how to pull it but would ask a librarian named Ms. Jerry. She sent it over, and I downloaded it on a computer for Lopez to borrow and review."

"Where is it now?"

"I don't know. I left the computer for her at our front desk and thought she picked it up."

"Okay," Marino said. "Anything else?"

"Just that the library called afterward and said they needed it back when we were done. They had somehow wiped out the content on their end after making the transfer."

Marino looked at Ross. "What do you want to do?"

"Ruby."

"I'll drive."

10:35 p.m.

Detective Oscar Marino parked across the cemetery from Dorothy Thompson's house. The five-minute ride from Penn Treaty was the most time alone he and Ross had spent together in months.

Arabindan and McGee could never understand why he wasn't more infuriated with Ross's mishandling of Victor Rafaella. Marino had spent more time than anyone else tracking the mind that had spun a jackass cousin's pharmacy into a major drug smuggling operation. Initially, Rafaella didn't deal drugs in Philadelphia; his business was in passing shipments from ports to other markets, a smart decision that kept him off the radar of competitors and authorities. Violence and philanthropy brought him exposure.

Young "Victor's" talent for small talk begged rivals to underestimate him. Those unfortunate enough to cross or disrespect him earned beatings that left them near death. Victor seemed to draw a line at murder, and his charitable contributions offered one reason why: he was a religious man who didn't want to play God. As far as Marino could tell, only churches benefited from Victor Rafaella's generosity. He gave to small congregations in need of operating funds and financed capital projects for historic churches needing preservation. Victor did so quietly but not anonymously. Upon hearing of a struggling congregation in the news or on the street, he would drop a traceable check in the mail, and if an online crowd-sourcing appeal reached him, he would finish the campaign and allow his name to run on the website. Occasionally, a church leader would balk when they investigated the source, but by then, monies had been deposited and bills paid.

Detective Marino, one of the chief liaisons between Homicide and Narcotics, didn't think Victor Rafaella put his hands on anybody—just like he shipped drugs without touching them, he ordered attacks without carrying them out himself. What Marino and Ross had witnessed in the warehouse several months before was clearly a scene carried out by one of Victor's henchmen. Ross's catching a glimpse in a shop window was a lucky break, until it wasn't.

That's why Marino accepted the strange timing of James Rosen's arrest. He didn't understand how the exact moment of the Strangler's capture could happen so close to Victor's trial. But he would accept it, just like he would accept Ross's vagueness over why he was caught on a security camera tracking Pedro Martinez just before he died.

As for the department's internal backlash against Eric Ross, it was unfortunate. The arrest of the Kensington Strangler should have been a good enough reason to let Victor off for the time being. Saving the lives of junkie prostitutes though had never been much of a departmental goal.

"Got something for you," he said to Ross, and pulled a bag holding a small memo notebook from his inside coat pocket. It was Lopez's. "Wren found it yards from the scene. She did a quick brush for prints—Lopez must have flung it before she fell. Wren's accounting for it but says we can have it overnight. She needs it back by 7 a.m." He handed it and gloves to Ross. "I'll check with detail on the kid." Leaving the keys in the ignition, Marino left the car.

Ross waited until Marino walked away to slip on the gloves and flip through the notebook. He winced at Lopez's chicken scrawl. He would have to concentrate to make

205

out words, much less phrases. On the last page, above the phrase "Penn Treaty Park Players," he read a short question hastily noted.

Wren followed Ross?

Ross felt a surge of acid in his gut. Through the front windshield, he watched Marino approach a squad car parked down the block from Ruby's house. He switched spots after a moment with the driver, a plainclothes officer who walked toward Thompson's house. Marino turned toward Ross and nodded. Ruby was okay.

Ross moved quickly into the driver's seat, started the car, and got the hell out of Fishtown.

Merging onto I-95 South, he exited on I-76, a four-lane highway that wrapped around Center City. Bordered by promontory rock on one side and the Schuylkill River on the other, the "Schuyl-KILL Expressway" connected Center City to its wealthy western suburbs and the Pennsylvania Turnpike. The site of mind-numbing traffic jams and accidents by day, I-76 was a daredevil's dream in the middle of the night. As the city slept, drivers cruised the empty highway's narrow curves with only their headlights illuminating stretches of darkness between the few streetlights.

Wren followed Ross? The question repeated itself in his head.

A mural of dancing ballerinas loomed large over the expressway as Ross merged onto it and whipped around the city.

Taking the exit for the Philadelphia Zoo, he circled the park grounds of the 1876 Centennial Exposition and blew a red light to West River Drive, a two-lane road that ran along the Schuykill River. Ross crossed the Falls Bridge and swung into Manayunk, another former industrial neighborhood

206

now brimming with craft breweries. He started a course that would take him through northwest Philadelphia, back down Girard, south on Broad through Center City, into Old City, and back through Fishtown: he made sure the route passed every mural patterned in the death scenes.

Ross drove the roads slowly. His eyes sought any mural at least partially illuminated by streetlight. He searched the pictures for easily imitable poses, figures, and aesthetics that might attract a killer. He saw Lopez's body in the position of each one. An angel. A dancer in ballet slippers. A clown, a rower, a cook, a ghost, an immigrant in a woolskin cap. A tall thin basketball player. An opera star.

By the time Ross circled back to Fishtown, the clock on the dashboard read 3:43 a.m. Outside of Penn Treaty Park, someone had tagged a large real estate sign with white spray paint and the letters "Jy." Ross followed Columbus Boulevard along the Delaware River. "Jy" appeared in at least one other place, as did "cleo," "#9," and other labels he wanted to track, words and symbols too innumerable to count or interpret or follow in blue and green and yellow and orange. His throat burned. His chest tightened. Sweat streamed down his forehead. Which were the ones? Which needed attention? Which had the one with a message as simple as "Penn Treaty Players. Act 4 rehearsal. 9:30" that got his young rookie attacked?

Pictures and text covered walls, billboards, flyers, signs. Ross drove slower and slower, coasting through lights and stop signs until he hit the gas, headed for a curb, slammed on the brakes, and skidded in a half circle. He opened the door and jumped out of the car. Rushing to the waterfront, he leaned into a rail, stiffened his body, and yelled through the burning.

207

THURSDAY

9 a.m.

Eric Ross woke up on his own couch. Marino sat in a chair with a folded up newspaper in front of him.

"Grab a shower. Mikovich moved briefing back to 10:00. Muralist videos on Instagram have over 100,000 shares. Was either leaked or savvy kids caught on." He threw the paper at Ross's chest. The front cover had a shot of The Muralist's latest post. The headline read, "'Muralist Stages, Takes Officer's Body in Latest Attack."

"I thought Wren was going to shut the account down."

"We could only get the last post pulled." He nodded to the paper. "Not before the press caught up. FBI is working on Instagram, but they are scared shitless of privacy concerns."

"Even though we don't know who this is."

"Last thing they want is distancing users who think cops are studying their selfies."

"How did you get in?" Ross asked.

"Pounded for fifteen minutes, then realized the damn door was unlocked."

Ross felt a sensation like static rush through his head.

"So was my car, jackass. Next time you steal my wheels, take care of them."

Ross stood up.

"Already took the notebook back to Wren. Hope you kept those gloves on." Outside, a baby wailed.

"Ruby's okay?"

"Obviously. No action there. Stayed there myself for an hour or two once you stranded me there."

"Witnesses turn up?"

"None. Guy with the pit bull came around. Said Lopez had spoken to him about some players group, and he told her to go the hell away. Seemed not to understand she was dead."

"I need to find Conor Mathew," Ross said.

"I can take that one."

"I need to talk to him."

"I'll try to stall Mikovich." Marino grabbed his keys and nodded toward Ross's phone on a coffee table. "It's charged. We stay in touch every hour." The detective paused on his way out the door. "It's time we moved the girl. She may have nothing to do with this. And we don't know who's watching."

Ross picked up his phone. Liam had called several times since seven. No voicemail. He assumed his brother had heard about Lopez. How, though, would he have known she was his partner? Had he seen them together? Conor Mathew had. And Michaela Alvarez.

"Okay?" he texted Liam.

The reply came swiftly.

"Now. Strip club under El."

Eric Ross just made it past the Marlborough Diner when someone shoved him into the wall next to it. He spun and grabbed his gun before realizing his attacker was Liam. His brother shoved him again, took two steps forward, and pushed him a third time. Ross stumbled in the middle of Front Street.

"What, Liam?"

Liam Ross pointed an index finger into his brother's face. "Conor's dead."

Ross bent over.

"How?"

"Heroin. They found him right fucking here this morning, on this block. You hear about it? No. Because he lives like a junkie, and nobody cares." His eyes moved with paranoia. "Unless streamers and glitter are coming out of dead assholes, nobody gives two shits."

Ross shrunk back. Within the righteous indignation of his younger brother's delivery, he saw their father. Liam had his right arm stretched stiffly behind him. If he would only roll his hand into a fist and swing it at his face.

"Let me ask you something, Detective. What the hell was Conor doing hanging around the GYM? He made it clear he wanted nothing to do with the place."

"When did you last see him?"

"Group yesterday. And lunch. I asked Michaela if he was back in the picture, and she said she didn't know. That he was probably doing your bidding."

"What?"

"She laughed when she said it, but it's true, isn't it?" Liam yelled.

"Liam, what are you talking about?"

Both panted as they stared at each other.

"Why would going to the GYM make him use?" Ross asked. "Did Conor run into someone there? "

"You are so clueless, Eric." He started running down Front Street.

"Liam!"

His brother ran faster.

The stripper with the black bob had appeared outside.

"What's your name?" Ross asked her.

"Doesn't matter," she answered.

She motioned for him to move toward her.

"Second floor," she said quietly. "GYM." Then she took a step backward. "Jack off, copper!" she yelled. A cook in a filthy white apron having a cigarette nearby chuckled.

Ross grabbed his phone and called Marino.

"Conor Mathew's dead."

He shut his eyes and sat on the curb.

"I don't know how I know."

"STILL DON'T KNOW WHY WE'RE HITTING IT DURING lunch," Detective Oscar Marino argued as the two detectives jogged up the front steps of All Saints. "Surprise factor aside, Michaela won't be here."

"Doesn't matter," Ross answered.

"Why are we here?"

"Got a tip to check the second floor."

"For what?"

"Don't know."

"Lopez?"

"Not sure."

Pastor Todd stood at the front of the sanctuary with his back to the front door. Marino waited in the foyer with his eye on the reverend while Ross entered a side stairwell and took two flights to a balcony box. Inside, three long pews stretched the full length of the sanctuary. Underneath each, bedding supplies were neatly rolled and stacked. Ross noticed a small stuffed parrot sticking out from a hymnal rack. He thought of the three children he had seen running around the sanctuary on Monday. The detective knew, as local authorities did, that All Saints operated a shelter off the books. He thought beds were only on the stage behind the curtain.

Ross noticed another door on the landing and tried the handle. A flimsy lock kept it from opening. Pulling a splinter of wood from the decaying doorframe, he used it to pry open the doorknob.

A room about half the size of the balcony led into another and another. Someone had at some point removed the interior doors that had once separated the spaces. Each space was empty and smelled like medical supplies. Ross walked across the squeaky floor. He texted Marino, who was still keeping a lookout on the foyer as Ross searched the second floor.

"GYM stage now. I'll take the back staircase. Go around the front."

Two minutes later, Ross saw Marino in quiet conversation with two security guards by the stage. In the middle of the gymnasium, four long cafeteria tables held dozens of adults sharing a family-style hot meal. Four older women with long white hair serviced the tables. In a far corner opposite the stage, a gated play area was full of toys but no children. Soft jazz music played from speakers by the back door. Ross paused by it to check the lists of those banned before heading toward Marino. Nobody involved in the meal seemed to notice or care about the bickering men by the stage.

"Just curious, that's all," Marino said.

"Private property, Detective," a guard said. "You want to search, you need a warrant."

"If nothing's wrong, I don't need a warrant."

The men stared at each other.

Michaela Alvarez stepped from behind the curtain. She smiled.

"Let the detectives come on back."

———————•———————

FOUR ROWS OF FOUR COTS LINED THE STAGE. EACH WAS covered in a white blanket and topped with a white pillow. At least five feet separated each bed from the others. The room held nothing else—no clothes, no bags, no smell of dirty bodies, or raggedy clothes.

"What is this, Michaela?" Marino asked.

"What do you think, gentlemen?" she said, chuckling. "So the secret that was never a secret is out. We let"—she paused for dramatic effect—"we let *poor people* stay here at night sometimes when they have nowhere else to go. Go ahead and write the citation. We won't read it, and we won't pay it." She chuckled some more.

"So why isn't anybody sleeping here now?"

Michaela motioned for the guards to move in front of the beds. "We do clean, thank you very much. And we're on a break right now until this Muralist mystery is solved. Don't want anyone we don't know staying over, and the easiest way is to keep everyone out for awhile." Her eyes settled on Ross.

"What happened to Lopez?"

"You're the police." She shook her head no. "I liked her," she said quietly. "Not good for anyone when a cop goes missing."

Marino smirked. "Conor Mathew the one who let you know?"

"I haven't talked to Conor in awhile."

"Wouldn't have thought so," Ross said, "as his name's on the prohibited list at the back door. But Liam tells me he was here yesterday for a meeting and a meal."

"Conor's name on that board?" Michaela asked. "That's the first I heard of it. Look into that, Mark. Or do you know?"

"I don't," said one of the two guards standing with her.

"If his name is on the list, how'd he get in the door?" Marino asked.

"Yes," Michaela said. "Look into that too, Mark. Or do you know?"

"I don't," the man repeated.

Ross quickly reached out and pulled a blanket from the bed. Underneath the cover, a sheet of sanitary paper ran down the length of the cot.

"This a hospital or a shelter?" Marino asked.

"Okay, detectives, we've answered your questions. We run a safe, clean operation that gets people off the streets. Now, with all due respect," the other guard accompanying Michaela said, "Fuck off."

A second black curtain lined the backstage. Ross turned to it now.

"We need to talk alone," he said to Michaela.

She nodded. Eyeing one another, the guards and Marino slowly stepped away.

Ross moved to the back curtain and searched for the opening.

"No need," Michaela said.

He stepped back, and she opened it for him. Crammed offstage were oxygen tanks, small cabinets of medical supplies, small refrigerators, and stacks of clean needles. Ross felt nauseous.

"Conor OD here?"

"People don't OD here. That's the damn point."

"What is this?"

"You know," she said, sighing. "You didn't use this tone when we got Liam clean. You trusted Conor to find him and bring him here. You trusted us to take care of him, get him clean, keep him that way, just as we did with Conor before him." Ross was frozen in disbelief.

"Some people aren't as strong as Liam." Her voice dropped. "They need a different kind of help. And I know you can trust us with that too."

"How long?" he asked with a dry mouth.

"Some time."

"You used the balcony."

"Yes. The need changed. So we adapted."

"This is why you needed Victor out of prison," Ross said. "He's your supplier." Dizzy, he hinged at the hips. A burning sensation in Ross's stomach rushed through his chest and caught in a ball at his throat. Michaela put her hand on his back.

"You knew this," she said soothingly. "You knew something about this."

"You set up a woman to be raped and killed," Ross said, wincing, "in order to thank me for letting Victor go."

"It was time. Time for James Rosen to get locked up. Time for his Strangler act to end. And yes, time to make you a hero and get the spotlight off Victor."

"Why wasn't James Rosen's time the moment you learned what he was? He hadn't attacked in awhile. You put him up to this—"

She groaned. "Ohhh, come on. He sure had. Just not on the news."

Michaela removed her hand and opened the curtain again. She pulled Ross's arm toward a table and motioned for him to sit.

"No," he said.

"Now listen…"

"No!" He pushed away her hand.

"A sicko raping women keeps assholes away!" she barked. "Makes those girls trapped in that life more vigilant."

Ross dry heaved above her feet. She didn't move.

"Safe injection sites on the mayor's agenda. She needs attention away from the Tracks mess. She needs junkies off the street. We want to help them. We're playing the same game—"

"The play area in the gym," Ross interrupted. "Preschool in the basement."

Michaela sighed.

"You running childcare for kids whose parents are shooting up here?"

"Wake up!" she snapped. "You either help, or you stay the hell away. Who's helping these parents? Who's keeping the kids out of foster care? Who's doing their part to clean up the shit and get people to a place where they can recover—"

"You're just God Almighty, Michaela."

"God watches," she said, quieting her voice again. "We act."

Ross swung off the bed, ignoring his vibrating phone.

"Two months ago," Michaela continued, "you were blind as a bat and worried for no good reason your brother was the Strangler. Now you see."

"Does Liam know?"

"On some level. He knows we helped him. He's thankful. He knows that unlike his paranoid older brother, we accept him for who he is and don't think the worst."

"Conor did. Conor knew. That's why he stopped coming around. That's why you put his name on the list."

"I don't know—"

"The hell you don't. You let your thugs kill him to teach me a lesson. I wasn't kissing your ass anymore, and Conor was punishment."

She sat down, smiled, and put her hands over her face.

"You had nothing to do with Conor's death?" Ross asked.

Pastor Todd emerged from the back curtain.

"What about you?" he asked the reverend.

"What?" he asked.

"Anything to do with Conor's death?"

No answer.

"You wanted to be alone," Michaela said. "Which means you're willing to keep this from your smug friend. Now is there an answer I can give you?"

"Lopez."

"No idea."

"What about you?" he asked Pastor Todd.

"From now on," Michaela said, "I answer for both of us."

"Haven't you always?"

"What do you want to know, Eric?"

"Who are the Penn Treaty Players?"

"Don't know."

"Then I'm done."

Pastor Todd stared at Ross. The detective didn't know if he read fear, confidence, or stupidity on the man.

"Penn Treaty Park," Michaela said. "Pedro Martinez spent time there—"

"I know that—"

"As did the couple who died in a similar manner."

"Yep," Ross said.

Michaela smiled. "Amateur actors. All of them. All three also connected to some house around Penn Treaty."

"How do you know?"

"Just do."

"What kind of house? They live together?"

"All we know is they were connected to some house by the park."

"Amateur actors—what do you mean by that?"

"I mean that's what we heard. That's all we know. Now we're done here."

In response, Ross took out his phone and snapped a picture of her.

"Tell him," Pastor Todd said in a quiet, authoritative voice.

"No," Michaela said quietly.

"Tell. Him." The reverend glared at Michaela.

Inhaling loudly, she walked to another area of the curtain and pulled it back. She motioned for Ross to come. He peaked through to the other side.

Lopez. She lay, limply, on a cot. An IV ran into her right hand. An ice pack covered half of her bruised face

"What?" Ross whispered.

"Not so evil we didn't save your partner's life—" Michaela retorted.

"What happened?" He didn't move.

Michaela softened. "Someone brought her here last night. Said she wasn't safe. From you or anyone. Wanted her off the grid for awhile."

Ross stared at Lopez.

"Who—"

"Our guys took her right away. Didn't pay attention to anything else. Didn't recog—"

"Who brought her?"

She pulled the curtain closed. "I don't know." She turned to face him. "They won't know either. And if you push it, she may not be so safe here." Michaela's voice took back its authoritative tone. "Whoever it is trusts us. And our people can take care of her."

"Her phone?" Ross asked.

"Not on her. No idea."

"All okay back there?" Marino called.

"Yep. Coming now," Michaela answered. She put her hand on Ross's back. He shuddered away as Pastor Todd stepped to the other side of him. Together they walked to the front of the stage. "Now I hope we won't have any of your colleagues snooping around here for awhile,"

Michaela continued. "Because if they do—" She smiled. "We'll make sure what bed they see."

2:15 p.m.

THREE COLUMNS MARKED THE WHITEBOARD STANDING AT
the foot of a table in the conference room next to Captain
Antony Mikovich's office. The first was a column of the
victims' pictures in order of their deaths: Pedro Martinez,
LeAnn DeVille, Clay Attle, and Margot Step. Lopez's name
was in parentheses at the bottom. The face of DeVille, the
only confirmed stabbing victim, was circled. The second
column read "Murals" and had, in corresponding order,
photos of the murals patterned in the killings. The third
column was blank.

Mikovich stood by the board in front of a full table
of detectives. Arabindan and McGee sat to the captain's
right, Marino and Ross to his left, and another team from
Homicide—four detectives and a captain—on either side.
Opposite Mikovich, two federal agents leaned over yellow
notepads. Normally, the FBI stepped in as soon as Homicide whispered the words "serial killer." The arsenic deaths,
though, could too easily be explained away as suicides: the
victims were poor and without noisy parents posting reward
ads, so the feds didn't feel pressure like they could have. But
"The Muralist" had quite a social media following, one that
created a different kind of urgency. Fake Instagram accounts
appropriating the Muralist's name had photos and videos
of murals from every corner of the city. Some had staged
bodies in poses. There hadn't been any reports of these
bodies being actual corpses like the Muralist's victims. Yet.

Now with an officer down, and her potential manner
of death so closely echoing one just three nights before, the

appearance of the FBI indicated an impending takeover of the case. This case had moved more quickly for Mikovich than any in his career.

"We know there is tremendous cause to believe the arsenic deaths were suicides," Mikovich began by saying. "As we believe they are connected to the knife attack and whatever happened to Lopez, our working theory is that there is a mastermind behind each of these—he pointed to the faces on the whiteboard—"and I'll be referring to them as homicide victims for that reason until we know more." He paused and made eye contact with the agents in front of him, then with Ross. "So. Common threads." Mikovich stepped farther away from the board. "What do we see?"

Ross recognized his moment. If he began by sharing all he knew, his team would be less likely to demand how he knew what he knew. They wouldn't allow themselves to look anything less than unified in front of their colleagues and the feds.

"Martinez, Attle, and Step all died in Fishtown," Ross stated. "Lopez disappeared there."

Mikovich wrote "Fishtown" in the third column with a red marker and drew arrows from it to the three names.

"We know the couple staged themselves in position before they died." Ross paused as Mikovich made more notes on the board. "They and Martinez also showed signs of intense gastrointestinal pain prior to their deaths."

"How do you know this about Martinez?" someone asked.

"Caught on security camera," Marino answered.

"No vomiting at Lopez's scene?" a fed asked. "No diarrhea?"

"No," Marino said. "Just the blood inside of the body sketch. We'll know for sure soon, but we're assuming it's hers based on the anonymous caller and the presence of her notebook about fifty yards away from the sketch. No other forensic evidence yet."

"And nobody's heard—" the same agent started to ask.

"No. Nobody's heard from her," Ross interrupted. "Then there's foster care." Mikovich switched to a black marker. "DeVille was a caseworker. Former clients hated her. Lopez grew up in the system. Didn't know DeVille or the others. We've asked Foster Care to identify whether Martinez, Attle, Step were in the city's system." He looked at Arabindan and she nodded to confirm. "We haven't gotten an answer."

"They're disorganized, they have no interest in cooperating, and to be frank, the topic is a rabbit hole," Arabindan said with frustration. "If these victims were in foster care, they could have been in private care, care in another state. But we'll keep applying pressure and sending subpoenas their way."

"No family members have stepped forward on behalf of Martinez or the couple," Marino said. "We know each lived in meager circumstances, so the foster care thread is all we have right now." He looked directly at the federal agents. "The press has picked up on the phrase 'former foster kids.' We're waiting for more people to recognize these faces and names."

The federal agents at the end of the table stared and said nothing.

"There's something else," Ross said. "I recently learned that Martinez, Attle, and Step were connected to the same house near Penn Treaty Park." Ross continued. "Not sure how, or exactly where, just that they were connected."

Mikovich paused for a second before drawing a house on the board next to Fishtown and connecting it to the appropriate faces with another set of arrows.

"How do we know this?" the captain asked.

"Source said so today."

Captain Wayne Lassoner, head of the other Homicide team, spoke up. "Foster care in the news again with the mayor's cutting funds to agencies that discriminate against gay foster parents."

"Would that be enough to motivate this though?" Arabindan countered. "Someone's pissed off at City Council? For punishing a conservative policy?"

"Cutting funds cuts homes for kids who need foster parents," Lassoner reasoned. "I could see someone getting violent over that. Especially a former foster kid screwed by the system. Don't discount it."

"Attle and Step, Martinez—they chose to endure incredible pain," Arabindan said. She stared at the board and leaned back in her chair. "I mean, they either killed themselves or were complicit in their own deaths. To call attention to foster care?" Arabindan shrugged. "Maybe. But there's a larger message somewhere."

"So let's say they knew each other as former foster kids. And they stayed in touch. Their shared agenda is calling attention to problems in the system. What else?" Mikovich asked. "Exploitation of kids? Authorities punishing kids for political reasons?"

"If that's the case," Arabindan added, "whoever attacked Lopez, and whoever got those kids ice cream cones…is probably another foster connection."

"Marino," Lassoner asked, "anything from Narcotics on heroin or fentanyl laced with arsenic on the street?"

"Not that I've heard," Marino said.

"Forensics doesn't think drugs were a factor, but they're still waiting on pathology," Ross said. He leaned forward and nodded at the agents at the end of the table. "Maybe we can get some help having those reports expedited."

"Okay," Mikovich said. "Anything else?" He glanced at Ross, whom he expected to jet out of the room.

"Penn Treaty Players," Ross said quietly.

"What?" someone asked.

Mikovich wrote it on the board. "The last thing we know Detective Lina Lopez was pursuing. Martinez, Attle, and Step were known to congregate at the Ramonita de Rodriguez Library in Northern Liberties. It's a popular spot between the two methadone clinics on Girard. And a hangout for the homeless like every other library in town."

"There's an announcement board between the two exit doors that Martinez, Attle, and Step consulted often," Ross said. "Lopez found a card on it yesterday announcing the Act 4 rehearsal of a group called Penn Treaty Players at 9:30."

"What exactly did it say?" Lassoner asked.

"Penn Treaty Players, Act 4 rehearsal, 9:30," Ross repeated.

"We don't know what it means, but she felt it carried a message," Marino added. "That's why she was at the park last night we believe—to see if it was some kind of code for people meeting at 9:30."

"And apparently it was," McGee said. "So a group of former foster kids meet, stay in touch, maybe live together, into acting…they call themselves the Penn Treaty Players. They communicate off-line, on a bulletin board at a library. Why?"

Nobody had a quick answer.

225

"It's a game," Detective Lydia Arabindan said with a shrug.

Marino nodded in agreement. "Traditional, old-fashioned communication…and Lopez figured it out. Then she showed up for rehearsal, and she was attacked. Why didn't they leave her body? Why take it with them?"

"And if Acts 1, 2, and 3 were the first staged scenes, how could the killer be sure Lopez would be in the right place at the right time to become Act 4? If that's a connection?" Arabindan asked.

Mikovich looked at the federal agents. "We appreciate any help with text for the press."

"Not yet," one said.

"Huh?" Marino asked.

"No press. Not yet."

"What are you scared of?" Ross asked.

No response.

Mikovich grunted and turned to Lassoner and his team. "Hassle City Murals more for us. Are there any connections they see between the chosen murals? What memories do instructors have about overly curious or frustrated volunteers? This is an often court-ordered program. There have to be stories we don't know."

"Got it," Lassoner said. "What else?"

"We still haven't figured out where the tropical bird in Pedro Martinez's death scene came from," Ross said. "Lopez checked for missing large preserved birds in pet stores and zoos from here to Cape May and Delaware. She also asked for leads on private collectors. Nothing came of it."

"There's also the matter of the knife that killed DeVille," Marino mentioned. "Flesh wounds consistent with those of a close-combat weapon, a push or thrust knife, probably military grade or an antique."

"Okay," Lassoner said. "My team, our room."

The other detectives left, followed by the FBI agents.

"We'll be in touch," one said to Mikovich on their way out.

"We're heading to Fishtown now," Detective Oscar Marino said, standing up. "We'll ask questions around the park. McGee and Arabindan, can you start at Girard and head east toward us? Let's divvy up the neighborhood between Girard and Columbus Boulevard once one of us gets that far."

"I'm still planning on hitting Central High to ask around about DeVille at four," Arabindan said. "Then I'll be there."

"Can you function on your own McGee?" Mikovich asked.

"Not sure. Maybe I'll ask the feds for backup."

Marino laughed.

"Don't worry about them," Mikovich said. "They're mine." He pointed to the board. "Take a picture of this. The answer is here somewhere. What message lies in these murders?" He paused and stared at the board. "I'm working to get a bigger fire lit under Foster Services' ass," Mikovich said. "But Ross, I want a tour of the neighborhood around Palmer Cemetery. Show me where Pedro Martinez died. Introduce me to the neighbors."

ROSS WENT DIRECTLY TO PALMER CEMETERY FOLLOWING
the briefing. He wasn't planning on introducing Mikovich
to Ruby or Dorothy Thompson no matter when or if the
captain came asking. Should Mikovich show up at their
door, however, Ross wanted to make sure they already
knew what had happened to Lopez. Ruby had clung to her
the day she visited and would no doubt take the news hard.
Ross had wanted to be the one to tell her that morning, but
Conor Mathew's death had kept him away.

Oscar Marino agreed that if Ruby were in danger, detail
would have noticed someone loitering by Palmer Cemetery
by now. Clay Attle's and Margot Step's deaths had eased
Mikovich's concern over protective custody; most likely,
the team reasoned, the couple's circumstances echoed that
of Martinez, which meant he most likely had the poison in
his system before arriving at the cemetery and staging his
own scene. If this scenario were indeed the case, then Ruby
was not a loose end on a killer's agenda.

Ross and Jessie Wren didn't think that Pedro Martinez
had staged his scene alone though. His props were arranged
more carefully than those of the others, evidence of another
person's handiwork. That was what Ross and Lopez sensed
that Ruby knew more about, even if she didn't realize it.

Eric Ross entered the cemetery. Before talking to Dorothy Thompson and Ruby, he wanted to think about the case
summary shared at Homicide, and the death of the woman
who had walked these grounds with him the day before.
Ross was annoyed that Lopez's name was only mentioned

as it fit into a list of victims. Someone could have suggested a moment of silence, or even made sure the chair she had last sat in remained empty. He knew everyone wanted to nab the killer as fast as possible, but he should have said something about her. He just couldn't.

Just as he checked the children's section to see if Ruby was playing peekaboo behind a grave marker again, Jessie Wren called.

"Yep," he answered.

"You find where Lopez put that laptop with the Rodriguez footage?"

"No idea."

"Well, I checked with the librarians, and they say they can get it to us again."

"Didn't your intern say—"

"They don't seem to have much of a clue over there. But at any rate, it opens again at ten. I can swing by, download the footage, and send you a link for streaming."

"Thanks, Jessie."

"You okay?"

"Talk to you soon."

Ross ended the call and inhaled deeply. He didn't see Ted Morris the caretaker, but the shed was open and small piles of sticks dotted the grounds. Ross grabbed a black trash bag and a rake and started clearing the twigs. Morris had been right. Something other than Ruby was drawing him to the place. He moved slowly, noticing the names on the graves: Benedict Oreland, Amelia Ann Ramer, Absalom Ender…

He had lived near his mother's grave as a boy but only visited it once a year. Her stone was in a small, nondescript cemetery behind a small Baptist church a couple of neighborhoods away from his South Jersey house. Carol Linden Ross had been interred when he was eight, and every year after that, her two sisters would take him and Liam to the gravesite on their mother's birthday. She had died from labor complications after giving birth to her third son. Next to Carol's stone was that of the baby, a little boy named Edward, who had passed a day after his mother.

At the cemetery, the ladies would recite Psalm 23 and try to coax the boys to sing something like "Jesus Loves Me." Ross had stopped visiting when he joined the military at nineteen. It seemed Liam kept up his visits.

Ross filled one bag with sticks, tied it up, and strolled over to June's grave. He brushed aside a dead leaf stuck against it and wondered where Ruby had been that day. Glancing at Dorothy Thompson's house, he noticed the woman entering the front door with plastic bags full of groceries.

Exiting the cemetery gates, Ross found himself staring at the man across the street, Robert, who again leaned into his screen door and gazed at him with dead eyes. The detective held his breath and approached.

"Mr. Robert. Are you okay?"

The man nodded yes. His eyes appeared more jaundiced than they had on Monday morning.

"Have you thought of anything, sir, that you may have seen on Sunday night?"

He shook his head no.

Ross reached for his notebook and a pencil. He gently opened the door and placed both in the man's hand.

"Anything you can write down for me?"

With thin and faint penmanship, Robert wrote the

number 972 and let the pencil drop to the ground.

"Okay, 972," Ross said. "That's Dorothy Thompson's house number."

The man stared at him.

"Do you think that Dorothy Thompson knows something she isn't telling me?"

His chin wavered up and down.

"Can you tell me what it is?"

Robert stared at Ross.

The detective pulled the picture of Michaela Alvarez up on his phone. "Does this woman look familiar to you?" he asked.

Robert shook his head no.

"Does Thompson get any visitors?"

He shook his head no again.

———————•———————

DOROTHY THOMPSON ANSWERED BEFORE ROSS HAD TO knock twice.

"Yeah?"

"New development. I need to talk to you."

She grunted and moved away from the door. "Welllll…" she warbled on her way into the kitchen. "Putting groceries away." Her words faded into an awkward silence.

"Where do you shop?"

"Garrison's, around the corner."

"Isn't that an auto shop?"

"Garrison's has a corner store too." She handed him a bag of canned food to unload. "Put it there. Cabinet closest to the door."

Ross opened the cabinet and saw one empty shelf and another half-full of macaroni and cheese boxes.

"Eh, I'll do it. Your hands are too pretty," she said, chuckling nervously. Ross took a step back.

"So why you here?" Thompson asked.

"Where's Ruby?"

"Where else? In her room, looking at the damn graveyard. Or on the roof looking at the graveyard...or maybe in the graveyard." She threw up her hands. "Here somewhere."

"If necessary, could you take Ruby somewhere out of town?"

"No."

"I'll pay for you to stay somewhere—"

"I can pay," she said. "Just nowhere to go." She considered the idea for a moment. "Where? Where would we go? We're here." She turned on the sink as if to wash the stack of dirty dishes, then changed her mind and walked into the living room.

"You already got a car on us," Thompson mumbled. "Leaving would make it worse. We can stay here."

"You and Ruby may need to leave for a while. We just don't know enough."

Thompson rocked in her chair. "Think about the girl. What would she do away from that graveyard? It's her life. She don't care—"

"She doesn't care about what?" Ross interrupted. "Her safety? She doesn't have a say, Mrs. Thompson. She isn't her own caregiver."

Thompson stood. "Gotta make a call upstairs. Be right back."

Ross lowered his head and pressed his thumbs into his eyes. He heard her speaking upstairs in low tones. A couple of minutes later, Ruby followed her grandmother down.

"What did you all decide?"

"About what?" Ruby asked.

"About my asking your grandmother to take you out of town."

"Why?"

"For your safety, Ruby." Irritated, Ross glanced at Thompson.

"I said I had a call to make, and I did!"

"Who'd you call?" Ross asked.

"Nobody," Ruby said. "She just doesn't want to be alone with you."

"Ruby!" The old woman shook.

"Can't you just stay with us?" Ruby asked. "What about Detective Lopez?"

She hadn't heard. Ross wasn't sure how she would have, cloistered in this house and probably uninterested in the news. Thompson didn't seem surprised.

"Do you know, Mrs. Thompson?"

"Just heard down at Garrison's."

"What?" Ruby demanded. "Did something happen to her?"

Ross waited for Thompson to say something.

"Yes, Ruby," he finally said. "Someone attacked her at Penn Treaty Park last night. We think it's someone connected to the death here in the cemetery."

Ruby groaned and sat on the bottom step. She began to cry.

"Is she dead?"

"We don't know," Ross answered quietly.

"Come on now," Thompson said.

"I'm not going anywhere!" Ruby yelled. "I have to stay here and protect June."

"Protect her from what?" Thompson said with exasperation. "She's dead."

"Yeah," Ruby choked. "Dead. Dead because she had no one to protect her! *And why's that?!*" she screamed.

Ross couldn't be sure, but Dorothy Thompson seemed to gasp. Ruby seemed shocked by her own words. Now sobbing, she stomped upstairs.

"I'll stay here tonight," Ross said to Thompson. "And tomorrow night. The couch is fine."

He suddenly hated to leave Ruby alone with the woman. She bent back into her rocking chair and closed her eyes.

"I'll let myself out," Ross said. "And be back later tonight."

6:20 p.m.

Ross tried to focus on Dorothy Thompson as he
walked from Palmer Cemetery to Penn Treaty Park. Was
she more than an odd bird taking care of a grandkid she
didn't understand? Did her neighbor Robert have it out
for her because of an old grudge, or was he aware of some
key information that he wouldn't state directly? The frail
old man was too easy to dismiss as someone in need of
attention. Ted Morris, the most engaging of the local old
timers, seemed to think the woman was fine. But he did say
Thompson had a key to the cemetery. Had she opened the
gates for Pedro Martinez that night and helped him with
the props? Why would she?

Baby June's death was certainly suspicious in Ruby's
mind. The story that Morris told Ross—that Ruby's
mom went into early labor and the baby died before
the ambulance could come—was plausible. But could
Thompson have been responsible for the death of her
own grandchild?

By now, Ross expected that Mikovich, Marino, Arabindan, and McGee were fanning through the Penn Treaty
neighborhood and asking whether anyone had seen the
young arsenic victims together in a nearby residence. Based
on an earlier text from Marino, people recognized different
combinations of the victims' faces, but nobody so far had
any idea where they had lived.

Ross checked his phone for messages. Call missed from
McGee.

"Hey," Ross followed up promptly. He ducked into the

storefront of an Indian café so he could concentrate away from the street noise.

"Pick me up on your way," he said. "I'm walking on Girard now."

HENRY CRIMMELL GASPED WHEN HE AWOKE TO THE SUN
setting through azalea bush shrubbery. It was the first night
he had passed in his favorite spot since getting out of jail
the month before.

Crimmell, fifty-six, was sentenced to Graterford for
seven years following a botched armed assault. He had
taken a heavier sentence instead of disclosing the location of his partner in crime, a fellow unemployed drug
user whom he had once worked with at a piping plant in
northeast Philadelphia. Crimmell saw himself as the one
who got away though. Prison had forced him to sober up,
while his friend now haunted the north Kensington streets.

The homeless scene had changed during his seven
years behind bars: gone were the angry war vets who had
traditionally camped in the azalea garden behind the Art
Museum. Young white kids with zombie eyes had replaced
them. They refused to fight over turf, preferring to take a
punch over moving a muscle when they didn't feel like
it. Crimmell had to wait a few days, but they eventually
migrated away, and today he had made camp under the
large bush, sleeping next to the items gathered by his head:
a trash bag of clothes, a half-eaten Tastykake, a pocket New
Testament, and a small notebook.

Breathing in the fragrance of azalea buds, he sat up. A
few hundred yards away, two middle-school boys kicked
a soccer ball on the grass. A third filmed his friends with
his phone. Crimmell leaned on one side and grabbed his
notebook. A pencil fell out, and he started using it to sketch

stick figures of the kids. The notebook was filled with similar cartoon-like drawings that lacked captions.

"Crimmell!" a voice yelled behind him. He froze. "Step out of the bushes."

Henry Crimmell put down his notebook.

"Why?" he barked.

"You need to answer some questions."

"Who's talking?"

"Police. Now get out."

"I don't want to!" he yelled. He noticed in his peripheral vision a figure partially blocked by a sycamore tree. It seemed unaccompanied. Crimmell squinted through the setting sun's glare off the Schuylkill River.

"Answer questions about what?" he asked more calmly.

"A murder."

"Don't know nothing about any murder—hey!"

An arm reached through the top of the bush and yanked him forward by the neck.

"No. No!" Crimmell yelled. Ross dragged him onto the grass.

Crimmell bit his leg.

"Hey!" screamed Ross. He jumped on the man's stomach and punched him in the face.

"Ross!" Detective McGee wrapped his arms around Ross's stomach and pulled him off Crimmell.

"I didn't do nothing!" the homeless man cried.

"Anything," Ross said. "You didn't do anything."

"You're coming with us, Crimmell."

"Why?"

"Just get in the damn car," McGee said in a quiet, low tone.

Ross walked over to the bush and started sifting through Crimmell's belonging.

238

"Leave my shit alone!" the man yelled. The three soccer players stood still, mouths agape. "Hey, kids!" he called. "They can't do this! Can't do it. Leave my bag!"

Crimmell kicked his heels into the ground as officers forced him away. A sob caught in his throat. "My bag!"

Ross emptied his bag onto the ground and sorted through the items. A picture of a man holding a baby. A few Snickers bars wrapped in Bible verses. He flipped through the notebooks. Scenes filled each, ranging from stick figures to detailed sketches of landscapes.

THE SMALLEST INTERROGATION ROOM AT HOMICIDE STUNK of stale coffee and cigarettes. Crimmell slouched across the table from Ross and Captain Mikovich. An oversized coat covered his hearty figure. Under an old Penn baseball cap, thin greasy hair fell to his shoulders. Crimmell kept his eyes closed, occasionally hummed, and alternated between quivering and acting like a tough guy.

Since learning the man's name from the prison guard on Tuesday, Detective McGee had contacted homeless shelters throughout the city asking about Henry Crimmell. Earlier that evening, he had gotten a call from the minister of St. Stephen's Episcopal Church in Center City. A few nights before, "Hank" Crimmell had signed into a dormitory the church ran for homeless men, but he had been kicked out that morning after getting into an argument with a roommate and putting his hands on the man. The fight had put the ex-con's name in the mind of the reverend, who had just learned of a detective looking for that very last name. On his way out, Crimmell said he would rather sleep outside than in any church dump. The roommate remembered him saying he liked the garden behind the Art Museum.

"WHY DID YOU FIGHT US?" MIKOVICH ASKED.

"Attorney."

"Why did you resist arrest?"

Crimmell opened his eyes. He stared at Mikovich. "A-ttor-neyyyyy," he said in a singsong voice.

"You guilty, Crimmell?" Mikovich asked nonchalantly. "You take out that social worker?"

"What?"

"You like knives, right?"

"Lawyer."

"Need an attorney to save your smelly ass?"

Crimmell smiled. He pointed at Ross. "He's the one who smells bad."

"Funny," Mikovich said.

"Caught a whiff when he pulled me by the neck and humiliated me in front of kids."

Neither Mikovich nor Ross spoke.

"You-got-nothing." The singsong voice returned.

"You resisted a detective, Crimmell. Then you bit him."

"Self-defense. Lawyer."

"On his way."

"I want a girl lawyer."

"You don't get to make that call." Mikovich smiled. "But maybe we can make that happen."

Crimmell leaned back in his chair, balancing it on two legs. He started humming. Ross couldn't place the tune, but it sounded like something from a carousel.

"What do you draw pictures of, Henry?" Ross asked.

"Things I see," he retorted. "Drawing one of you in my mind right now. Naked." He pointed to Mikovich. "That guy is behind you in it. He's naked too."

Mikovich laughed.

"We got all day," Ross said.

"No, you don't." Crimmell grinned.

"Why didn't you play with the others in your prison mural class?" Ross asked.

Crimmell twitched. "I did what they said."

"Don't you like to color?" baited Ross.

"Why do you care?"

Ross stretched his arms and walked around the table to a corner behind Crimmell. Mikovich leaned in.

"We care, Henry," Mikovich said coolly, "because a psychopath is arranging dead bodies into mural scenes. You like to draw. You worked on murals. You made our lucky list."

"A list of what?" he asked.

"Of psychopaths," Ross said from the corner. Crimmell twitched again.

"You know, Detective, you're on *my* list," Crimmell said.

Ross waited.

"A list of cops who rough up men like me and hope they don't have a voice."

Mikovich stood up. "Break time. We're not getting anywhere."

Crimmell laughed. "Oh, we obviously are."

Someone knocked on the door. Mikovich opened it a crack and spoke in low murmurs.

"Ross. Let's go."

———————•———————

ROSS FOLLOWED THE CAPTAIN FROM INTERROGATION into his office. Mikovich shut the door and walked to his desk. He tapped the knuckles of his fists on the front page of the *Philadelphia Daily News*. It looked almost identical to the *Philadelphia Inquirer* front page that Marino had shown him earlier. Smack in the middle of the cover was an enlarged shot of Lopez's face, stuffed with marshmallows and covered in blood. The headline read, "The Muralist Leaves Another Portrait, Takes Detective's Body."

"You're a liability, Ross."

"I kept it together in there."

Mikovich typed something into his computer. He stood back and frowned. "Mr. Big Shot kept it together. Where are those gold stars?"

"What is it, Mikovich?"

"Roughing up a homeless guy in front of kids isn't going to help find Lopez." The captain pointed to his monitor.

On *Philly.com*, Ross saw a picture of himself on top of Crimmell and under a headline reading, "Police Terrorize Homeless Man."

"Shit," he whispered. Mikovich scrolled down and clicked on a video link. Ross saw himself pressing Crimmell's body into the ground. The soccer player had filmed it all.

"Didn't know you were on camera?"

Ross didn't answer.

"Superintendent called while we were in there."

Ross walked to the door and pressed his body weight against it.

"What do you want me to do?"

Mikovich raised his voice. "I want you to thank me for getting ready to tell her that you had reason, and that the ten-year-old is a fucking editing wizard."

Ross put his hand on the doorknob.

"You've got one day. Then you're off the case. Maybe the force."

"Fine," Ross whispered.

Mikovich waited a minute.

"Penn Treaty Players—anything new there?"

Ross relaxed his shoulders. "No. But I'm going to spend the next couple of nights on detail inside of Dorothy Thompson's home. I think there's more to look at there."

"You pulling the car?"

"I'd rather not. Still not sure who might be watching."

"You know some people are watching," Mikovich said methodically. "City Hall. The commissioner. But you don't give two shits about them. So who aren't you sure about?"

Ross stared straight ahead, maintaining eye contact with Mikovich.

"Victor?" Mikovich asked. "Because you know you saw him. And he knows you saw him. And he doesn't leave loose ends."

"You think Victor had something to do with this?"

"No."

"Then why bring him up?"

"I think you're scared. Which means you're distracted."

"I'm scared we won't find Lopez. I'm scared she might be dead. But I'm not scared of Victor." Ross turned to leave. "And I can only think of one reason why you'd mention his name now."

Mikovich said nothing.

"You're scared." Ross opened the door. "And I don't know why."

9:20 p.m.

Mayor Glynda Green pushed her chair away from the conference table and opened her eyes with a sigh. She had never been one for power napping but had hoped for a little shut-eye before getting behind the wheel to drive home. Swiveling in her desk chair, she gazed out at the city's lights through the floor-to-ceiling window that formed one wall of the room. Increasingly, tall office buildings blocked what used to be a clear view of the Art Museum.

Green had only dreamed of being Philadelphia's first female mayor—and a black one at that—for two years before assuming office. She had grown up, as her mother and father before her, in East Germantown, where she had participated in the East Germantown Civic Association most of her life. At fifty-one, she spun her favorable reputation as the association's president into a successful run for district committeewoman. In that role, she had led a fight against the Housing Authority when it announced a plan to implode a public housing unit that had sheltered generations of low-income families. Green challenged HUD officials in open hearings with long, impassioned speeches, and a local reporter had taken note. News stories strengthened Glynda Green's status, and a year after she brokered the deal, she rode a wave of public service popularity into the mayor's office.

Her platform was housing: more of it for low-income families, and subsidies for health clinics and shelters. She wanted people to pay less to live in safer spaces, and she found the funding for her initiatives in a soda tax. The seventeen-member City Council allowed the tax because it wasn't really her idea—they had debated it for years. All the council seemed to want to do now was force her into an ultra-liberal agenda that would redirect voters toward a more establishment-friendly candidate in two years.

Repeatedly, council meetings had become consumed with two progressive topics: an ordinance for safe-injection sites that would presumably decrease the city's skyrocketing number of heroin overdoses, and a proposal to deny funding to religious foster care services that discriminated against LGBTQIA+ parent applications. If she would back the plans, the council president hinted repeatedly, her housing initiatives would have an easier go. So she agreed to play along. Immediately, the Archdiocese of Philadelphia filed a lawsuit against the city in district court, and she distanced herself from single moms, one of her biggest constituent bases.

When Green moved to allot the first of the soda tax levies to support plans for new low-income housing, City Council balked. The monies were better spent on public schools, they said.

To defy them all, Glynda Green called an unannounced press conference and stated that since City Council had no interest in furthering her housing platform, she was tabling it until the next election, when she would hopefully have a more humanist group to work with. The second half of her first term, she said, would work on promoting and enforcing safe streets. If only Homicide had kept Victor in custody, she would have had the narrative she needed to secure reelection.

Glynda Green walked around the room to wake herself up. She turned the lights back on and looked at her watch.

The commissioner had five more minutes to call her back, or she would draft a statement calling for Detective Eric Ross's resignation; the detective who had essentially freed Victor had been caught on camera that evening roughing up a homeless man. The front page of *Philly.com* read "Glynda's Goons" over a picture of Ross riding a bum. It was an allusion to her new tough streets a. To save any kind of face, she needed that asshole gone.

Green tidied her workspace and searched her large handbag for her car keys. The mayor rifled through the various compartments, and coming up empty, dumped out the contents. No keys. She shuffled around the table, lifted stacks of papers, scanned the floor, and sifted through the trash. They couldn't still be in the ignition—she remembered unlocking her own office door that morning as her lazy secretary hadn't yet shown.

It was late. She was exhausted. Green hit the security button on her office phone.

"Hi, I can't find my keys. Has anybody—no, no, I know I had them." She paused. "Can I get an escort out of the building? I'll just get a cab home and bring a spare tomorrow."

FRIDAY

10:45 a.m.

DETECTIVE ERIC ROSS SAT ON THE COUCH NEXT TO ELEVEN-
year-old Ruby Thompson. Legs stretched on a coffee table,
Ross held his laptop on his lap. Ruby flipped through the
channels on a small television sitting on a rickety wooden
bench.

"I don't even know why we have a TV. She never lets
me watch it."

"Watching it now, aren't you?"

Ross clicked the link Jessie Wren had just sent him and
began surfing through security footage of the goings-on at
the Rodriguez Library over the past two weeks.

"What am I supposed to call you?" Ruby asked.

"Detective Ross."

"No. How about Ross?"

"Okay."

"Does this bother you?"

"Your talking?"

"No, I know *that* bothers you. I mean flipping channels."

"Nope."

Ruby channel surfed for about fifteen minutes, then
tossed the remote.

"What are you doing?" she asked.

No answer.

"Aren't you supposed to look at people when they talk
to you?"

"You talking to me?"

"Who else?"

Ross closed his laptop. "Fine. I'm looking." He widened his eyes in mock obedience, and Ruby giggled.

"You going to work all damn day?" she asked.

"Darn day. And yes, that's my job."

"Let me help you."

"Your grandma wouldn't like that."

"She's sleeping. And I'm stuck inside because of you."

Ross grunted. "How long does she usually sleep?"

Ruby shrugged. "She naps a lot."

Ross opened the screen and played with the fast forward functions.

"You don't talk much," Ruby said.

"So I've been told."

"By a woman?"

He smiled. "Yeah."

"Your wife?"

"No wife."

"Mom?"

"She's dead."

"June's dead, but I talk to her all the time."

Ross nodded.

"How'd she die?" Ruby asked.

"Childbirth."

"June died right when my mom had her."

"I'm sorry."

"She barely lived."

"See your mom much?"

"No. You an only child?"

"I have a brother."

"You hang out a lot?"

"No."

"That's sad. If June were here, we'd hang out all the time."

"You're a good sister."

Ruby smiled at the computer. "So you can keep talking or let me help you."

Ross grinned. "All right. But once I hear her coming down the stairs, the TV is back on, got it?"

She scooted toward him.

"This is security footage from the library. We're looking to see if anybody lingers by the announcement board."

"Why?"

"Not telling."

They concentrated on the screen for several minutes, watching people enter and exit through the lens of a camera mounted high on a wall across from the checkout counter. Ross sped forward between lulls, occasionally hitting pause or rewind.

"How long we doing this for?" Ruby asked.

"This is the job."

Suddenly the angle shifted.

"Come on…" Ross said. He isolated the transition and moved forward in slow motion. A kid's face popped into view as he jumped up to smile into the camera. The guard grabbed him and pushed him out the door, then the kid ran back and knocked the camera out of focus. Ruby laughed. She and Ross could now only see the lower half of bodies that came and went.

"Unbelievable," said Ross.

"Hey, go back!" Ruby said. "That's my friend Maggie's bag." A CAT bag passed through the frame backward. "She says I can have it when she graduates college. She goes to community college now."

Isolating the bag, he increased its size on the screen. Moving forward for a minute, he saw that the carrier didn't linger long but had stopped at the board.

"She works for the police, kind of. Hey, you might know her!"

"Tell me about her."

"She works for real life CSI."

Ross sat up. Dorothy Thompson started descending the stairs.

"Where did you meet her Ruby?"

She noticed his serious tone. Tears filled her eyes.

"Did you meet her here? In the cemetery?" Ross asked.

"Yeah," Ruby said. "She visits her sister there too."

Ross let the footage begin again and squinted at the images on the screen. Again he could make out the lingering bag.

"Ruby, did Maggie talk to you the night of the killing?"

Ruby shook her head no.

"What does she look like?" he asked.

"What does who look like?" Thompson moved too quickly and slid down the last few stairs.

"She...she has had different colors of hair, and she's about the same size as Detective Lopez. And she's white."

"Her name's Maggie?"

"Who's Maggie?" Thompson demanded.

"Does she have any other name, Ruby?"

The girl shook her head no. "Like what?"

"Was she in the cemetery the night of the murder?"

Ruby burst into tears and shook her head yes.

"*Who?*" Thompson yelled. Ross ignored her.

"Where did you see her in the cemetery that night Ruby? Was she—was she by the angel's body?"

"Ye-ye–yes," the girl said, borderline hysterical. "But she was, was working."

"Does she go by the name Mae?"

"No!" Ruby wailed.

"Did you see her before or after the man died?"

"After, I said!"

"Did she tell you which grave belonged to her sister?"

"Yes. One that didn't have a stone yet. She said she was saving up her money until she could afford a real nice one." Ruby started crying harder. Thompson moved past the back of the couch and tapped Ruby's back with her hand.

"Ruby," Ross said. "I'm sorry about this. I am so sorry about all of this. But I need you to tell me everything Maggie told you."

Ruby turned toward the back of the couch, got up on her knees, and buried her face in her grandmother's clothes.

Ross picked up his phone. A few seconds later, he had Jessie Wren.

"Jessie. It's your intern. Mae." He paused. "No, she'll run. She there?" He waited. "Get back to me."

MAE BRUNNELL POKED HER HEAD INSIDE JESSIE WREN'S workstation at Forensics. Crime scene technicians Adam Vance and Mike Lee worked on opposite sides of a large table in the center of the room, sifting through boxes full of papers and photos under fluorescent lights.

"Hey guys, seen Jessie?" she asked. "I need her to sign off on something."

Both paused from their work at the sound of her voice. She smiled and leaned a shoulder against the doorway.

"Bet you do," Vance said.

Brunnell cocked her head. "Whaddya mean?"

"Gunning for Mike's position?" the other asked.

"Nnnnooooo?" she said, moving toward the table. "Wouldn't get it. Still in school."

"You don't need a degree for that," Mike Lee said. "Plus, you're enrolled in a program. They always take that into account." He looked up at her and smiled. "Wren just called HR for your file."

Mae Brunnell took a step backward and turned toward the doorway.

"Don't worry, fellas," she called over her shoulder as she walked out into the hallway. "Not asking anyone for favors."

"Favors?" Vance called out. "I'm uncomfortable. Don't harass me in the workplace."

"You're an asshole," Lee murmured. "She's out of your league."

"But is she out of Wren's?"

Both men laughed.

Strolling down the hall, Mae pulled off her white lab coat and threw it into a trash can. She turned into a stairwell.

Dorothy Thompson followed Ross and her granddaughter across the street to the cemetery. Ruby sobbed, brushing snot from her nose with one wrist and rubbing her eyes with the other. The threesome stopped in front of June's grave. Ruby choked on her tears and fell to her knees. She hugged June's gravestone.

"Junie. Junie."

"Come on now," Thompson mumbled. Stumbling, she reached out to the gravestone to steady herself.

"No!" Ruby yelled. "You don't get to touch her!"

Thompson recoiled.

"Ruby," Ross said gently, kneeling next to her, "Ruby, I need you to be strong."

Ruby pushed herself away from the grave marker and stumbled to a small rosebush a few plot-lengths away.

"I met her here. She said when she could afford it, she wanted to get a stone for her sister and put it here, by the roses. She said her sister was as old as June."

Ruby sat on the ground.

Ross turned to Thompson. "You ever see this woman here?"

"No."

"You know Ruby was talking to a stranger here?"

"She wasn't a stranger!" Ruby yelled.

The older woman shook her head no. Removing her glasses, she wiped her eyes and sighed aloud. "Ruby talks to lots of people here. She knows everyone. They know her."

"But did the regulars know Maggie?" Ross asked. "Ruby, did she ever talk to anyone else?"

255

Ruby shrugged her shoulders and collapsed back onto June's gravesite. "How should I know? She was just here." She put her forehead against the stone. "I miss you, Junie," she cried. "I want to see you."

Ross looked at Thompson, who stared down at the rosebush.

"Ruby," he knelt again, "does Maggie know that you saw her take pictures here that night?"

Ruby shrugged again. "No. I saw her from the window."

"How long has she been talking to you, Ruby?"

"A while."

"When did she first approach you?"

"I just started talking to her one day," she said, sniffling. "It was time to go home, and she said she was sad the cemetery closed at night because she couldn't see her sister after her work, so I…"

She started crying harder again. "I told her my grandma had a key and I could lend it to her if she didn't tell anybody."

"Oh," Thompson softly wailed. "Oh no. Oh no."

"Am I a murderer?" Ruby wailed.

"No, Ruby," Ross said gently. "No, sweetie. Not at all." He looked up at Thompson. "Take her inside. Lock the door. An officer from the car will take my place inside."

"Let's go, Ruby," Thompson muttered.

"Ruby," Ross paused as he pulled out his phone. "Ruby, do you know if she had any other jobs?"

"The casino."

"Which casino?"

"The one by the big park."

"Penn Treaty?"

"Yeah."

SugarHouse.

1:00 p.m.

MAE BRUNNELL STOOD OVER A KITCHEN SINK FULL OF warm, sudsy water. She washed a few dishes, slowly running a sponge over each before plunging her hands to the bottom of the sink and staring into the water. Above the sink, a plant sat on a shelf. She reached into it and pulled out a small razor blade. She pricked her left forearm and lifted it to watch the blood move slowly down her wrist, her hand, her fingertips, then drip into the sink.

A banging on the door distracted her. The second gained her full attention. She walked across the suite reserved for VIPs at SugarHouse Casino, moving from the kitchenette through a living room. Sidestepping a large brown package on the ground, she pulled a gun from a small desk near the door.

1:05 p.m.

Detective Oscar Marino met Ross at the entrance to SugarHouse Casino and walked with him to the security desk just inside the entrance. Ross showed his badge as Marino threw a file folder in front of the guard and spread out photos of Pedro Martinez, Clay Attle, Margot Step, and Lina Lopez.

"Recognize any of these?"

The guard took a step back. He pointed at Martinez, Attle, and Step. "Seen them before."

"Call your boss over. And your coworkers."

Ten minutes later, several security guards and a manager stood around the photos. Most recognized different combinations of the faces.

"That one," a manager said, pointing to Pedro Martinez, "wasn't he a friend of Hal's?"

"Yeah! Yeah," another guard said.

"Who's Hal?" Marino asked.

"One of us. Works as a bouncer mostly back there at the club." The manager pointed a long finger toward a door at the back of the room. A sign outlined the words "Sugar Babies" with fluorescent lights.

"Hal a larger black guy?" Ross asked.

"Yeah."

"Is there anything else any of you can tell us about these people?" Marino asked. "We think one person instigated each of their deaths."

"Well," said a nervous-looking redhead with a face covered in large freckles. "This girl," he pointed to Margot Step, "hung out on the back patio sometimes with another girl."

"What did she look like?"

"I don't know, hot, I guess. Blond hair one day, brunette the next."

Ross pulled up the picture of Mae Brunnell that Wren had scanned from her personnel file and emailed to him.

"Yeah, that's her."

"Wait," another guard said. "Margaret?"

"Her name's Margaret, you think?" Marino asked.

"Her name *is* Margaret. Margaret Brunnell," the manager said. "She works weekends in guest services as a VIP concierge."

"Ever hear what the women would talk about?" Ross asked the redhead.

"No. Always seemed serious though. Most girls laugh—not them."

"Is Hal here now?" Ross asked.

"No," someone answered. "Off."

"And Margaret Brunnell?"

"Haven't seen her. We can check," the manager said.

"We need his address. And hers."

"Sure," the manager said. "Ricky, get it for him." The redhead nodded and practically skipped away. "Detectives, can I have a word?"

Marino and Ross followed him to a large display case just outside the casino floor.

"Hal—Hal LaMour is his name. We've actually been preparing to question him about items missing from two exhibits."

Entitled "Pack Iron," the display in front of them featured weapons prominent during the Old West: among the rifles, shotguns, daggers, and derringers, Ross noticed a set of four T-knives in various sizes.

"Let me guess," he said. "One of these push knives was taken?"

"Yes, or what we call a push dagger. A favorite of river-boat gamblers around New Orleans. Easy to hide, easy to use as long as you weren't afraid of it."

"When did you realize it was missing?" Ross asked.

"About a week ago. The private collector who owns these is a regular, and he noticed. We checked the initial inventory, and it was definitely on the list, but I don't think it ever made it behind the glass."

"What made you suspect Hal?"

"He stood guard when we installed the exhibit in case someone low on his luck felt like swiping one. This crowd will pawn anything."

"Did someone see him?"

"Only about twenty security cameras. It's not very obvious, but if you know what to look for, you can see him quickly reach a hand toward the case and step away. It was our best guess until now anyway."

"What was the other item?"

"Two others. Stuffed birds."

Ross and Marino glanced at each other.

"We had an exhibit to coincide with a Native American festival in Penn Treaty a few months ago," the redhead explained. "Birds, trees, William Penn dummy, all of it. The Franklin Institute lent us some items, including two large colorful stuffed birds, but they disappeared from the case one night. Security cameras had been down, but when we connected Hal to the knife...connected him to this too."

Ross pulled up a picture of Pedro Martinez's death scene inside the cemetery.

"This one of the birds?"

260

"I don't know. Same color. Same size, I guess," the red-head said. A few people passed the phone around and shrugged.

Marino turned back to the weapons exhibit. "Would an attacker have had to sharpen the stolen knife before using it?" He squinted at the blades to see if they were dull.

"Depends on how strong the user is—probably, but if the attacker were Hal, I'm sure even a dull blade would be lethal. Especially in a surprise attack."

Captain Antony Mikovich pounded on the dilapi-dated door between two crumbling brownstones in South Kensington, a few blocks north of Girard Avenue and just east of Fishtown.

"Police, open up!" he yelled.

Two dogs started barking in the house next door. Mikovich gave the signal, and Marino kicked in the door and entered, followed closely by the captain and Ross, all with guns raised. An alley led to a small cabin that could have served as a guesthouse for one of the properties now separated from it by metal fencing.

Marino knocked and tried the door. It opened. A figure stood several feet in front of him.

"Hands up!" the detective yelled. "Now!"

Ross and Mikovich filed in behind him.

A tall, broad-shouldered twentysomething black man with a shaved head stood in front of them. He wore a white flowing robe, a cheap-looking gold crown, and fake eye-lashes. Smiling, he held up his hands.

"Get against the wall!" Ross yelled.

The man obeyed and chuckled as Ross handcuffed him.

"Who are you?" Mikovich asked.

"Hal."

"Prince Hal? We have some questions for you."

"I want a lawyer."

"We'll call one from Homicide, your majesty," said a voice from the front door. Detectives McGee and Arabindan had arrived. The partners read Hal his rights and escorted him out, leaving the others to search the small home.

They stood in the middle of a living area connected to a kitchenette and a small hallway that led to a bedroom and bathroom. Mural illustrations and photographs had been shellacked to the walls and overlapped in a collage. Under a shabby couch were a few rolled sleeping bags, and across from it, a small coffee table that held a television.

Ross crossed into the kitchen, where magnets affixed a yellow index card listing grocery items on the refrigerator. They also held photos of the victims, of other young people, and of Mae Brunnell and Hal LaMour. Ross took a step back, opening the cabinets and refrigerator as fast as he could, as if he were expecting to see a bomb. Nothing was out of sorts. He noted a bag of jet-puffed marshmallows twisted and tied on the counter.

"Come here," Mikovich called.

Ross tossed Marino his vibrating phone. "It's Jessie. See where Brunnell lives."

Ross and Marino moved slowly through the living room and scanned the apartment from ceiling to floor. The tiny bedroom was crammed with three single beds and various storage boxes. Along a wall was a large mirror covered with photos of the murals patterned in the deaths, and above the photos, yellow sticky notes with names written on them.

"What are these names?" Mikovich asked. He pointed to the first photo on the left. A sticky note reading, "Maggie" stuck to a picture of the mural that inspired Pedro Martinez's crime scene.

Mikovich moved his hand above the others. "DeVille's mural is labeled 'H & M' on the note. Step and Attle's as 'Hal.'" He quieted. "Lopez's says Hal as well."

A blank sticky note was stuck to a picture of another mural, one the killer had not used yet. It was a painting of a girl looking upward as she sat at a desk with an opened book in front of her. Rainbow-colored beams of light reached from the book to the sky above her.

"What's this?" Mikovich asked.

"Ruby," Ross whispered. He stepped out of the room with his phone.

"Fishtown kid." Mikovich grimaced. "Maybe," he said out loud to himself. "Or could be for Lopez."

Marino entered holding an envelope. "Wren confirmed Brunnell's legal name is Margaret, her address is this location, and she worked part-time at SugarHouse. Didn't think she was still employed there. Says she doesn't understand how she had the time." He waved the envelope. "And this is a paycheck for a Hal LaMour. It's from SugarHouse as well."

"Our bird man," Mikovich said.

"Our bird man," Marino repeated. He rifled through the drawers in a small bureau.

"Okay," Mikovich said, returning to the sticky notes. "So Birdman supplies the exotic bird and is maybe responsible for Pedro Martinez's staging. The other names…are those the ones responsible for the stagings? Hal for DeVille's props—and probably her murder—and the ice cream for Attle and Step."

Ross re-entered.

"The girl okay?" Mikovich asked.

"No action. I'll still head over tonight."

1:05 p.m.

MAE STOOD IN FRONT OF THE DOOR, HER RIGHT INDEX finger on the trigger. The doorbell started ringing in rapid succession.

"Just a minute!" she yelled.

"UPS!"

Mae opened the door with her left hand, shielding the gun behind her back.

"Someone from this suite requested a pickup?" asked a middle-aged delivery man in the trademark brown uniform.

"Yep." Mae smiled. "You alone? It's heavy."

The man nodded. "Stronger than I look, sweetheart."

"Well, come on in then."

He entered Suite 6, one of ten on the top floor of Sugar-House Casino. He walked toward the package. Putting his clipboard under an armpit, he squatted to lift it up. Mae put a gun to his head.

WEARING A SHORT BLACK WIG AND A BASEBALL CAP PULLED low over her forehead, Mae Brunnell walked through the casino gaming area on her way from the elevator to the front door. She wouldn't miss the smell of stale smoke, the veiny old people who deposited coin after coin into monotone machines, the bright fucking lights, and the twittery cocktail waitresses who traded out plastic cups of stale Pepsi and warm Budweiser.

The UPS uniform did not fit her well, and she paused a couple of times to keep from tripping over the long khaki pants. She had hoped the delivery person would wear shorts that she could simply cinch with a belt.

Brunnell climbed into the UPS truck, buckled herself in and took a deep breath. The keys hadn't been on the man's body, so she had hoped he was dumb enough to leave them in the ignition. He was. She steered the truck off the curb.

"Proud of me now, Phil?" she said out loud.

Mae Brunnell had lived with Phil, the closest thing to a father-figure she ever had, during a transitional period in middle school. A mailman in West Philadelphia, Phil and his sister took foster kids into their Kensington home to supplement their income, and because they did, kind of, care about helping homeless kids. Every night, he would tell Mae and a table of two or three other youths about the day's adventures—stories full of dogs, pepper spray, lonely old people, and nasty smells.

Phil encouraged all of his mentees to get a job with the postal service, praising the merits of a government pension

266

and the ability to work outside "with no one fuckin' bothering you." She had liked him well enough but couldn't stand the sister, who forced her foster daughters to do all of the household chores. Particularly fed up with dirty dishes after school one day, Brunnell replaced the dishwasher soap with dish soap and flooded the floor. Hal, a large but slow kid at the house, squealed with joy when he saw the mess, and when Phil's sister came home, she found the two in giggles and told them to pack their bags.

Neither Phil nor his sister could get ahold of their caseworker, a woman named LeAnn DeVille who had just quit social services for a long-term substitute position as a guidance counselor at Central High School in Olney. The next morning, Phil dropped fourteen-year-old Mae and thirteen-year-old Hal at the front door of the high school with their bags. Feeling responsible for a foster brother she had known for six months, Mae Brunnell navigated the high school hallways with Hal and their bags until she found an adult who made eye contact with her.

DeVille refused to come out of her office and told a secretary to call the police. The foster siblings were put in a group home back in Kensington, the district where they were registered. For the next four years, under the care of a rotating shift of social workers, the two lived in a house with between ten and twelve other displaced teens.

The food was awful, the walls thin, and the hot water was never hot, but the two came to love the group home: it was there that they met their family. Within the first of their four years there, they connected with several other young teenagers placed temporarily in the shelter. Others came and went, but because Mae's group had learned the rules of the game—keep mouths shut, complaints few, and hands to yourself—they somewhat easily flew under the radar.

Early in their time together, Mae and her friends hung out at a recreation center that ran free drama workshops. The acting exercises fostered a group dynamic that bonded the teenagers. They chose a name for themselves based on one of their favorite hangouts: the Penn Treaty Players. Soon, the group was pooling resources from part-time jobs and babysitting gigs to get clothes from better thrift stores, better food, and used phones.

The drama workshop leader had encouraged them to go online to find scenes they could practice together, and when she learned they didn't have a computer at the home, recommended they visit a local library and ask for help identifying classic scenes with multiple parts. She gave them a list of playwrights to look for: Shakespeare, Ibsen, Checkhov, Beckett, Miller.

A local part-time librarian named Dorothy Thompson assisted them. She knew almost nothing about the theater, but she could Google "Scenes for Student Actors" and hit print several times. Even after she retired, she would make copies of scenes she found online, put them in a manila folder, and thumbtack it to the library's announcement board.

Gradually, the teenagers started writing their own scenes and monologues, pieces that gave them a place to creatively share and relive their own stories of abandonment, abuse, and neglect. One piece, written by Mae Brunnell, was about a group of foster kids who set out to attack those who had wronged them. Over the years, they remembered it, entertaining and tweaking the increasingly dark and disturbing plot until, at Mae's gentle prompting, the plot became a plan. If they wanted to teach the system the ultimate lesson, she repeated, they would need to make the ultimate sacrifice.

The oldest among them, Mae Brunnell was the first to leave. She found a job as a live-in babysitter for two small children, and on a walk along a side street one day, noticed a small cabin plopped between two fenced-in back lots of rowhomes. After a little investigation, she learned a rickety door between two adjacent rental properties led into an alley that functioned as a private entrance to the cabin. From the looks of it, nobody lived inside. She checked city records to find out who owned it, but according to the city, the place didn't exist. As it was between house number 1442 and number 1444, she painted a 1442 ½ on the rickety door and affixed a mailbox to it. The adjacent properties, apartment conversions, had such high turnovers that nobody paid much attention to the rickety door with the odd house number.

Mae Brunnell made a right on Columbus Boulevard and pulled the UPS truck into the parking lot of Penn Treaty Park. She rested for several minutes, smiled, and said goodbye.

"So who are you?" Mikovich asked. Hal LaMour increasingly looked less like a mental patient and more like a tired kid. His fingernails, bitten to tiny slivers, were either caked in dirt or painted black. Ross couldn't tell.

Hal uttered an odd bestial sound in an attempt to laugh. His eyes, Ross noticed, still looked arrogant.

"Who are you?" Ross echoed.

"The Prince of Wales," Hal said with a smile. The public defender sitting next to him almost rolled his eyes.

Ross pushed back from the table and walked behind Hal. "So Mae didn't warn you to clear out when she knew we were coming?" he asked.

"She didn't." Hal paused. "She didn't?" He stared intently at Mikovich, whose posture slightly stiffened.

"How do you know her, Hal?" Ross asked.

"She's my sister."

"You meet her in foster care?" Ross ventured.

"Yes."

"That where she met all her victims?" Mikovich asked.

Hal sobered. "Her family."

"Why did Mae choose to kill your family?" Ross pushed with a stronger tone. "Why is she going to kill you?"

"They chose to die."

"You choosing to die?" Mikovich asked.

"Yes." The young man smiled.

Mikovich leaned forward. "Why LeAnn DeVille? She your caseworker?"

Hal sat still.

270

"Mommy figure?" Mikovich asked. He spoke slowly. "Mommy who didn't listen? Didn't care?"

Hal leaned forward. "No," he whispered.

"She was another killer," said Ross.

Hal turned sharply to face him. "Yep!"

"Who'd she kill?" Mikovich asked.

Hal snapped around toward him. "Us."

"How'd she do it?" the captain asked.

"Ignored us."

Without making a sound, Ross stepped behind Hal.

"What about Lopez?" he whispered directly into his ear.

"Oooh!" the suspect taunted.

"Lopez," Ross said.

Hal shook his head no.

"Why Lopez? Why the costumes? Why poison?" peppered Mikovich.

"What video would you have posted next, Hal?" Ross tried to throw him off.

Hal jerked his head and smiled.

"You posted those videos, didn't you? Had to build the drama, huh? Set the stage?"

"Yes!"

"What's the next mural, Hal? Who's the next victim?" Ross pushed. "SugarHouse knows about the birds," Ross said. "And the knife. Is the other bird coming up in a new stage scene, Prince Hal?"

Hal's eyes widened.

"Why Lopez?" Ross asked.

Hal smiled.

"The yellow index cards," Ross said. "She figured them out. Knew that was how Mae summoned her family to kill." Ross sat back in front of Hal.

"Where's Mae, Hal?" Mikovich asked.

"Maggie Mae!" Hal countered. His eyes seemed to widen. Ross wondered if he could have gotten high in the car.

Mikovich opened a folder. He read from a single piece of paper. "Margaret Brunnell. Entered the foster system at age five when Foster Services took her from her junkie mother. Seven foster placements in nine years, then a group home." He looked up. "That's rough, Hal. You get around too?"

Hal laughed. "Oh. Yes." He sighed, then doubled over, clutching his stomach without warning.

Ross jumped up.

"What did you take, Hal?"

Mikovich jerked his head toward Ross, then looked at Hal.

"Mr. LaMour," the lawyer said, "What—"

"Damn it, Hal, what did you take?" Ross rushed to him, yanked him from his chair and pushed him into the wall. "Where's Lopez?"

Mikovich opened the door. "Get a doc. Now!" he yelled into the hall.

Ross stared at Hal, who was murmuring a pattern of words.

"Rubies, fairies, favor, rubies, fairies, favor—"

Ross dropped his hold and pushed past Mikovich.

"Ruby!"

Hal vomited and started convulsing. His lawyer moved to a corner of the room near the door. Mikovich grasped Hal's shirt with his fists and shook him.

"Where's Ruby? Where's Lopez?"

Tears falling from his eyes, Hal shook his head no.

"Save her. Save this kid. You're dead. She's not."

Hal groaned and grabbed his stomach. He pushed his face into the floor and cradled in the fetal position. His lawyer left the room.

"He dies—" Hal tried to spit.

Two nurses ran into the room. Mikovich ran after Ross.

Two squad cars blocked the street in front of Thompson's house when Ross arrived. He rushed from his car through the front door. Officers stood by another lying face up on the floor. Ross's replacement had been shot in the forehead.

"Ruby," Ross said.

"Suspect took her," someone said.

Ross ran upstairs. Another officer sat next to Dorothy Thompson on the bed in Ruby's room. She rocked back and forth, clutching an old stuffed rabbit. Tears marked her face, but she didn't sob. Her voice sounded watery and broken, a painful series of sounds.

Ross stood in front of her.

"It was a UPS worker," Thompson uttered, squeezing her eyes closed. "Where—where is she?"

Ross shook his head. "We just found out. I don't know. We're going to look—I'm going to look—until I find her." His phone buzzed with a call from Jessie Wren.

"You'll be back, and she'll be dead," Thompson said. The officer next to her breathed in sharply.

"It's my fault," Thompson rambled. She looked aside. "It's your fault," she mumbled. Ross stood still.

"She shouldn't have been here. Ever." Her volume lowered as she spoke.

"Like June, you mean?" Ross asked. "That why you were so attentive to that baby?"

She looked directly into Ross's eyes, but only for a moment. They were rimmed with red. "It don't matter."

"It does."

"No, it don't." She hardened.

"You did know Mae Brunnell before this started, didn't you?"

"No!" she said, with enough force for Ross to push his hunch. She rubbed her eyes.

"You did." He waited for her to return his gaze. "Were you waiting for her tonight?"

The woman's shoulders slumped. "Go away." She lay back on Ruby's bed. Ross indicated to the officer that she wasn't to go anywhere.

"I'm going to find her, Ms. Thompson."

"I know," she murmured. Ross hesitated before leaving the room.

*But she'll be dead...*he could almost hear her say.

AT 19TH AND WINTER STREETS, A FEW BLOCKS FROM FOSTER Services, a brick wall bordered a small parking lot in the museum district. Ross stepped into the glare of police headlights shining on a mural along the wall. In the picture, a smiling young girl with a long ponytail sat behind a desk, holding a pencil to paper as colors burst from the page. It was the last mural picture taped to the wall at the Penn Treaty house.

Detectives McGee and Arabindan met Ross, Marino, and Mikovich in the lot. Jessie Wren scrolled through her iPad.

"Instagram frozen, no updates. But listen to this," she motioned for them to gather around the iPad.

"First look at the line on the mural," Wren said. Ross stepped forward and squinted. A painted line spilling from the pages of the book read, "And Now I Will Unclasp a Secret Book."

"Okay," Ross said.

"It's Shakespeare," Wren said. "Googled it. *King Henry IV Part 1*. Guess what the King's name was when he was younger?" She paused. "Prince Hal."

Ross felt frozen. Nobody else spoke.

"Mikovich told me about Hal and his crown and that 'rubies fairies favors' line. Googled that too. Also Shakespeare. *A Midsummer Night's Dream*."

"What's the Prince Hal play about?" Marino asked.

"A group of rebels who try to overthrow a king," she said. "Mae isn't following the plot though. In the play, the character Hal turns on the rebel leader before they kill the king. That's changed here. This rebel leader is rewriting the end."

"The common thread in all of this—?" Mikovich asked.

"—is foster care," finished Ross.

"King of foster care?" McGee asked.

"Who is the head of it?" Wren asked aloud. She locked eyes with Ross. "It's the mayor. She's in charge of the city. She's threatening the system."

"A queen, not a king?" Ross asked.

"I don't know," Mikovich said. "That's a stretch. But I'll call the commissioner and get the mayor secured." He pulled out his phone. The others spread out and gazed at the mural, looking for any other clues.

"The girl is Ruby," Ross said.

"I know," Jessie answered.

"Hey!" Mikovich barked from one hundred yards away. "Mayor didn't show today. Secretary couldn't get ahold of her. Security said she lost her keys at the office last night and took a cab home."

"East Falls," Marino said.

"Meet us there," Mikovich said. "Ross, you're with me. McGee and Arabindan, have backup ready."

"Can I come?" Jessie Wren asked.

"Don't care. Call radio now!" he ordered Marino.

"I'll call," Ross answered. Mikovich paused and answered his phone while Ross and Jessie jogged to the captain's car. Wren sat in the back, and Ross called dispatch from the passenger's seat.

"This is Captain Antony Mikovich," Ross announced. Send SWAT to 30th Street Station. Muralist sighting. Repeat. SWAT team to 30th Street Station for a sighting of the Muralist."

"What are you doing?" Wren asked.

"The whole force can't show up at the mayor's house. I need time."

277

"You're not going to fool him for that long."

Mikovich walked toward the car.

"SWAT team to 30th Street Station for sighting of the Muralist," the operator responded.

Mikovich jumped inside and turned on his siren.

"Repeat," radio said. "SWAT team to 30th Street Station for—"

"Aughhhhh!" Wren screamed at the top of her lungs, attempting to distract Mikovich over the dispatcher.

"What?" the captain yelled.

"I'm, I'm sorry," she stuttered. "I thought you were going to hit that car."

An ambulance and fire engine came from behind them, blocking the circle in front of the Philadelphia Museum of Art. Four lanes of traffic started cramming into two. Mikovich steered the car onto and over an island, then sped up as he navigated around the circle the opposite way.

"What was that?" Mikovich asked. "SWAT at 30th?"

He hopped the car onto and over another two islands before reaching a side street running parallel to the Parkway.

"Captain Lassoner called," Ross answered. "Said someone saw the Muralist at 30th."

"Why would they say the 'The Muralist' over radio? Every nut in the city is going to show."

Ross held his breath, wondering if the captain was going to switch course and direct them there. "Mayor okay?"

"Security at City Hall says she lost her keys at the office last night. They tried her cell but no answer." Mikovich clipped a mailbox and a bike rack. He turned onto another street only to find it shut due to construction.

"Shit!" he yelled.

7:30 p.m.

NESTLED UP A HILL OPPOSITE THE SCHUYLKILL RIVER, THE
East Falls neighborhood connected Center City with what
remained of the Wissahickon woods in northwest Philadelphia. East Falls, with its generous urban yards and close
proximity to City Hall, attracted numerous politicians,
including Mayor Glynda Green.

Captain Mikovich turned off his headlights and drove
past the single homes on Green's upscale block. Trees tow-
ered over each plot.

"What are you thinking?" Mikovich asked Ross.

"How do we know she is the mastermind?" mused Ross.
"If this ends tonight, how do we know she is the center of
this, and not Hal or someone else? If she isn't calling the
shots, who else is?"

Ross noted an SUV parked in her driveway.

"Where is everyone hiding?" Mikovich asked. "They get
the wrong...?"

He turned sharply toward Ross.

"Let me out a few doors up," said the detective, taking off
his seatbelt. "You park a block away and meet me back here."

Mikovich stopped the car suddenly. Ross lurched forward and hit the dashboard. He turned to Mikovich.

"One more day, Captain."

Wren looked from man to man. "What the hell does
that mean?"

Detective Ross crept toward the side of Mayor Green's
house. The neighborhood was silent. Falling to his knees,
then to his stomach in an army crawl, he moved slowly

until he could see the backyard. He heard soft crying but saw nothing. Ross realized someone—Ruby or the mayor maybe—was on a back porch. He turned onto his back and shimmied a few feet farther, until he could see Ruby's profile. She sat behind a desk that had been staged on a well-lit patio. Near her, the mayor was tied and gagged.

"Well, if it isn't our favorite detective," said a low, calm female voice. Ross rolled back onto his stomach. The voice came from above. She was in a tree.

"Out, out, I see you," sang Brunnell. She shined a red laser in Ross's eyes.

"Hands up," she ordered. "Put your gun down and walk to face Ruby."

Ross obeyed. He went to Ruby and stood a yard away from her. Brunnell had positioned her in the scene from the mural he had just left.

Another tropical bird carcass hung from an awning over the desk. Ruby sat behind an open book. Her right hand, clasping a pencil, shook. But the crying he had heard had been the mayor's.

"Ruby," Ross said softly. "Ruby, look at me."

She refused.

"I'm here with you," he said quietly. Turning his back to her, he looked up to find Mae Brunnell in the trees.

"That's right, Ruby," Brunnell said from her perch. "Keep smiling and I won't shoot him." A thud hit the ground in the dark. Ross jumped. Holding a gun in her outstretched left arm, Brunnell moved from behind a tree to face him. They stood twenty feet away from one another.

"Don't pretend you care. You need her for redemption," Brunnell said.

"And you need her for revenge," Ross responded. He took

steps to his left. Brunnell mirrored his movements.

"Stop moving," she demanded.

He kept up the slow movements, gradually rotating so that he faced Ruby and Brunnell's back was to the porch. Ross took a step closer to her.

You want me to move," he said, maintaining eye contact. "You need me to unclasp your secret book. Right?"

Brunnell smiled. "Detective Shakespeare. And how is Hal?"

"Dead," Ross retorted. Mayor Green groaned. Ruby cried.

"You've made your point, Mae," Ross said. "Why Ruby? Tell the mayor what point you are using her to prove."

"Nope," she said.

"Why hurt Ruby?"

"I may not hurt her."

"You already have."

"No, you have," she said. "She would have been fine if you had just left her alone. But you had to keep sniffing around." Brunnell fired a bullet to the right of Ross. He jumped. The mayor shrieked.

"You've won, Mae!" Ross said. "You did it. You've called attention to foster care. To what a broken, mean, abusive system it can be. The mayor's seen that."

Brunnell's gun stayed on Ross.

"She won't do anything," Brunnell said. "She may wait a year to cut funding, but she won't do shit to change anything."

"So why do this?"

"Because of the story," she said, smiling. "People will remember the story. They will shake every time they see a mural in this city. Every time they see a lonely kid on the streets." Her voice seemed to catch. "They'll get it. And public pressure will force dirty little secrets to come out."

281

"So what is Ruby here to illustrate?" pushed Ross.

"Maybe rubies," Brunnell said, shrugging. "Hal couldn't believe the girl's name was Ruby. He's been obsessed with that fairy play forever." She took a deep breath.

"Was Hal the mastermind, then?"

"Oh, no no." Mae smiled. "Took your friends longer than I thought to get here. They just pulled up, so you know."

"This is all anger, Mae."

"You don't know me."

"I know you were taken from your mom—" started Ross.

"Junkie named Sharon," Brunnell interrupted.

"I should have been taken from an abusive father," Ross said.

"Stop it," she chuckled. "We aren't the same."

"Abandonment, abuse," Ross said. He saw Mikovich deftly move from one side of the house toward Ruby.

"I didn't abandon anybody," she said. "You did."

"No. No, I didn't."

"You did, asshole. You let a murderer walk because you got scared. Then you let a rookie detective off on her own, and she disappeared." She smiled and looked into Ross's eyes. "Maybe you are right about me." She cocked her head to one side. "Maybe you do know me."

"How long have you been in Michaela's pocket, Mae?"

Her smile faded.

"Tell Captain America to put his gun on the desk," she snapped. "Or the bullet after this one blows off your knee-cap." She fired to the left of Ross.

The captain stepped forward with his hands in the air. After placing the gun in front of Ruby, he gently pulled the girl from her seat. Ruby's hands clasped the book from the desk as Mikovich led her from the porch.

"Michaela is the only reason you would say that I let a murderer walk," Ross continued. "No other way you would know."

"I work in Forensics," she groaned. "Everybody whispers about the great and powerful Ross."

"Then how did Lopez end up where she ended up?"

"Don't know what you're talking about."

"Hal is—was—stronger than you. He carried her to All Saints. Knew she'd be okay under the eye of the woman who nurtured you along."

Mae shook her head no with a smile.

"What do you want, Mae?"

"Maybe nothing."

"Sure you do. All of this—the props, the poses, the deaths—what is it?"

From the other side of the house, Marino and McGee moved toward the porch. Lydia Arabindan lay on the ground in sniper position and aimed a gun at Mae Brunnell. Brunnell sensed the men but not Arabindan.

"Guns on the desk," she directed.

"Do it," Ross said. Marino took both weapons and followed instructions. Instead of walking back off the porch, he crouched behind the mayor's seat.

"Why did you kill your friends? Your family?" Ross asked.

"They chose to die." She smiled. "What do you choose, Ross? Are you going to die?" She paused for a second, then twirled around to shoot Glynda Green in the neck.

Ross rushed toward Mae Brunnell. She pivoted toward him, fired, shrieked, and dropped her gun. Arabindan had shot her in the arm. Brunnell grabbed her gun with her opposite hand and moved closer to Ross. He knelt in a hunched position, applying pressure to the bullet wound in his right shoulder.

Mae Brunnell aimed at Ross's head.

"Gun on the porch, bitch who shot me!"

Detective Arabindan tossed her weapon near the desk. Police sirens approached.

Brunnell took a deep breath. "The mayor's dead, isn't she?" she asked.

"Yes," Marino answered.

"Move her."

Detectives McGee and Marino lifted Glynda Green's body and placed it on the grass. The sirens grew closer. As soon as the porch was cleared, Mae Brunnell sprinted onto it. Ruby saw the mayor's corpse and started crying louder.

"Ruby!" Brunnell called out. "Ruby, I wouldn't hurt you."

"Liar! You lied!" Ruby screamed. She ran to Ross and fell beside him. Mikovich followed her. Arabindan crouched on one side of the porch. McGee and Marino waited on the other. Gesturing with their hands, the three planned how they might overpower Brunnell.

"You stole me!" Ruby screamed.

"I asked your grandma for help, Ruby. When I was a girl. She ignored me too."

"I hate you!"

"You can save this little girl," Mikovich said in a stern voice. "Right now."

"I've got a scene to finish first." Sitting behind the desk, Mae Brunnell put the gun to her temple.

Mikovich grabbed Ruby and buried her head in his chest. He watched Brunnell pull the trigger. She fell to one side. Ruby screamed hysterically at the sound of the final bullet.

"Arabindan!" Mikovich cried. The detective ran to Ruby. Wearing latex gloves, she held the book Ruby had dropped.

"Check this out Captain." She handed it and another pair of gloves to Mikovich. He put them on and started flipping through the pages.

"Ruby," Detective Lydia Arabindan said quietly, trying to calm the screaming girl. "Ruby. I'm right here. It's over." She pulled the girl up from the ground and led her away.

Blood covered Ross's upper torso. He kept applying pressure to his shoulder. Mikovich crouched next to the detective with the book. It was a play, a copy of *King Henry IV, Part One*. Mikovich held it open to Act 1, Scene 3, where a red colored pencil had highlighted a passage.

> Peace, cousin, say no more:
> And now I will unclasp a secret book,
> And to your quick-conceiving discontent
> I'll read you matter deep and dangerous

But it was three words at the top of the page that captured Ross's attention. In thick, black marker, someone had written, "VICTOR SAYS HI."

Ross moved quickly to his feet and looked at Mikovich. The captain's face dissolved into a blur.

THREE SATURDAYS LATER

4:00 p.m.

Holding a spade, Detective Lina Lopez sat on the ground next to Ruby, helping her plant flowers around June's gravesite.

"So then, Mr. Stevens told me I had to move my seat because I was talking too much, but I wasn't talking too much! I wasn't talking at all. He just thought I was and couldn't catch me. I was making Colleen laugh so hard she couldn't breathe, but I wasn't talking while I was doing it," she babbled. "But then I started laughing—just in my mouth—and I was shaking, and I knew if he called on me, I would start laughing so hard that he would throw me out. So I just sat there shaking with tears in my eyes, and he didn't tell me to move my seat until the end of class. Whatever."

Smiling, she grabbed Lopez's spade. Lopez grinned and played with a handful of dirt.

"Haven't you ever planted anything before?" Ruby asked.

"No."

Ruby laughed.

Dorothy Thompson called from her door. "Ruby! Come inside."

"My grandmother still doesn't like you," Ruby said. "She blames you."

Lopez exchanged waves with Ted Morris. It was cleanup day at Palmer Cemetery.

"She killed Junie you know," Ruby said softly. Her voice hardened. "I remember."

Lopez stared at the grass. "We don't know everything we think we know."

"Why'd she do it?" she whispered, stroking the headstone.

"Ruby, we'll never know what happened," Lopez said gently. "You can come up with all kinds of ideas, but you'll never know. And you have to figure out how to live with that."

"You feel like it's right I stay here with her?"

"Where else would you go?"

"Somewhere else."

"Do you feel safe here?" she asked.

"Yes!" she said, her attitude having returned. "Do you?"

Lopez grunted. "I don't think I've ever really felt safe."

Ruby looked at her. "Why didn't they kill you?"

"They just needed to use me," Lopez said. "They had somebody tell them to use me but not to hurt me." The two sat quietly for a minute.

"Who's that somebody?" Ruby asked. "Is he in jail now?"

"No," Lopez said. "She isn't. She probably never will be."

"That scares me," Ruby whispered.

"Don't be scared," Lopez said forcefully, grabbing Ruby's hand. "Ross and I know that person, and we know that she doesn't want to hurt you at all. She wanted to hurt the mayor, and to try to make things better in a very...difficult way."

"Are you going to keep an eye on me forever?" Ruby asked.

Lopez smiled. "Is that okay?"

Ruby shrugged. "Sure. But I have a lot of other people watching me."

"Your teachers?"

"No. People *here*. My friends in the graveyard. They watch out for me, and I watch out for them." She started gathering her tools.

"Is Ross coming soon?"

"I hope so. One day soon."

"Is he going to keep being a cop?"

"I don't know."

"He could always drive a UPS truck, you know."

Lopez smiled. "You've got a crazy sense of humor, you know that?"

"Ruby!" Thompson called.

"That's your grandmother," Lopez said.

"Wow," Ruby teased. "You're a really good detective."

Dusk

Ross watched Ruby and Lopez leave the graveyard, laughing and talking together. The wind picked up. He pulled his Phillies cap a little tighter with his good hand and winced. The shoulder cast that stretched across his chest restricted his breathing. Ted Morris caught his eye and nodded. The caretaker meandered along the central cemetery path as he always did before locking the gates.

Ross thought about the first night he had entered the cemetery, the moment Ruby's figure rushed through the graveyard and over the wall. She would be okay. But for her to be okay, he would have to ignore whatever role Dorothy Thompson had played in June's death and in Mae Brunnell's life. Lopez insisted on it. And he had come to agree. Any investigation into Thompson's past could send Ruby from the only house she had known into the foster care system.

Ross looked toward Robert's house. The door was open, and he was fairly confident the old man was there, barely alive, leaning against the screen door with an oxygen tank and a roomful of cats. The law wouldn't convict Dorothy Thompson, but every day she would be judged: through the jaundiced eyes of a dying old man, the life of a child she would never understand, and the presence, day after day, night after night, year after year, of that child's friends.

Thompson and he both knew there was a higher authority watching over Fishtown, over Philadelphia, keeping its vices in check. As much as he hated it, Ross recognized that he was merely one of her pawns. She operated under a system that she defined a little differently every day, one that used cops and drug dealers, troubled kids and needles, interchangeably to draw attention where she wanted it. She had reigned from her perch in a church for decades. But she wasn't an outlier anymore. Her reach had extended itself in recent circumstances, and Ross suspected her reign was coming to a disastrous end. Time would only tell if he was right.

And he thought that time would be sooner rather than later.

AUTHOR'S NOTE

THIS STORY STARTED WITH A VISION. SOMETIME BEFORE the summer of 2011, when I still worked as a high school teacher, a mural caught my attention during a commute home in Philadelphia rush hour traffic. I had driven past the illustration for years, but in the boredom of this particular moment, its explosion of color grabbed my eye. The image celebrated the worlds that children find inside of books.

It made me think, "What if a killer staged bodies in mural scenes?"

The question struck me as so cinematic that I decided to explore it in a screenplay. It would take years to write. At the time I spotted the mural, I was beginning a career as a nonfiction writer, an effort soon marked by the publication of my true crime book *we is got him*. After its release in 2011, I took a leave from teaching and picked up a copy of *The Complete Idiot's Guide to Screenwriting*. I worked through its exercises on and off for a few years as I entered the full-time hustle of a freelancing career.

The story's plot became informed by the people, paths, buildings, and landmarks that I encountered every day on walks with my baby girl, and then a few years later, with her and my baby boy. As a girl the age of my daughter now, I visited the city on Sunday mornings when my father had gigs as a lay preacher. I loved entering those stately old church buildings. I loved their smell, their dusty stained-glass windows, their creaks, their heavy doors. I imagined their innumerable hiding places held portals to other worlds. They invoked a reverence within me, and an appreciation for places of meditation within the chaotic city. It is for this reason that I wander local cemeteries when I can. The one I visit most is Fishtown's Palmer Cemetery, where my niece Molly is buried. Time spent there inspired large sections of this book.

The story's structure became realized on a beach vacation. After seeing a flyer for an evening screenwriting workshop at the Nature Center of Cape May, I took my loose outline to a Stockton University professor named Robert Steele, an excellent teacher. Once I had a draft, a producer acquaintance paired me with scriptwriting mentor Magnus Monroe, whose connections recommended I turn the story into prose.

To expand the plot, I relied on my skills as a journalist. I researched mural teaching programs and foster care services, talked to muralists and foster care parents and social workers, and interviewed prison guards and addiction counselors. The 26th Philadelphia Police Precinct granted me a ride-along, during which I learned quite a bit about the minutiae of police work, the process of crisis response, procedure when a medical examiner is unavailable, and how different officers cope with stressors of the job. My law enforcement knowledge was also furthered by former FBI profiler Bill Fleisher, who again guided my questions.

One of the best decisions of my professional life was to contact Peggy Hageman, the acquiring editor for my first book, who had since moved to Scotland to pursue life and love. After encouraging me to write more than the few chapters I first sent her, she served as the book's editor. Sadly, she died of cancer in 2020.

I became aware of Luminare Press, a hybrid publisher out of Eugene, Oregon, when I worked on a memoir as a ghostwriter and connected my client to them. Thank you to Patricia Marshall for your vision, to Kim Harper-Kennedy, Melissa Thomas, and Sallie Vandagrift for your patience, and to Jenny Wierschem, the best copyeditor on both sides of the Mississippi. And thanks to my local team! Elliott Woolworth is a master graphic designer whose cover design immediately captured the book's aesthetic. I am grateful also for his website design, and for Lukas Huber's photos. Michelle Townsend's wit and knowledge of digital marketing make her a treasure on any team. Thank you also to my mom, Dianne Alexander, and to my Aunt Denise, both of whose lifelong reading recommendations led me from Nancy Drew to Agatha Christie to Elizabeth George, Ann Cleeves, and Louise Penny.

The last words are to my children. This city has taken a violent toll on our family this past year. On dark days, your energy reminds me of where I want to focus my center. I love walking outside with you on foggy Saturday mornings, when the streets are quiet and the air smells fresh, and we find small "treasures" in the park—a gold stone, a purple flower, a coin dropped by a pirate from outer space. Hard things frame life around us. But they don't erase the glimpses of beauty we find when we look, and see, and think about our place in this world.

Made in United States
North Haven, CT
27 October 2022

25982922R00178